GEOSTORM: The Pulse

The Geostorm Series
Book Two

A novel by

Bobby Akart

Copyright Information

PRAISE FOR AUTHOR BOBBY AKART
and *THE GEOSTORM SERIES*

"With his 40th novel, Bobby Akart turns the world upside down again!"

"The Geostorm series comes out of the gate at full pace and action to let the reader know that this book will be filled with things that you can't unsee and leaves you with that *look over your shoulder* feeling."

"Polar shifts, GPS navigation issues, strange animal behaviors and even stranger weather, and scientists unwilling to move off the popular narrative all combined and masterfully crafted in Mr. Akart's engaging storytelling style."

"Wow, I didn't see this coming! The type of book an adrenaline junkie loves!"

Other Works by Amazon Top 40 Author, Bobby Akart

The Geostorm Series
The Shift
The Pulse
The Collapse
The Flood
The Tempest
The Pioneers

The Asteroid Series
Discovery
Diversion
Destruction

The Doomsday Series
Apocalypse
Haven
Anarchy
Minutemen
Civil War

The Yellowstone Series
Hellfire
Inferno
Fallout
Survival

The Lone Star Series
Axis of Evil
Beyond Borders
Lines in the Sand
Texas Strong
Fifth Column
Suicide Six

DEDICATIONS

I published my first novel, The Loyal Nine, in June of 2015. Geostorm The Pulse is my fortieth. I'm proud to say that I've accomplished this in just over four years and my passion for writing has never waned. Throughout times of adversity and hardship, the love of my life has encouraged me and had my back as I continue to tell stories that folks seem to enjoy reading. This novel is dedicated to my wife, Dani. I love you so much. I look forward to writing the next forty with you by my side.

For many years, I have lived by the following premise:

Because you never know when the day before is the day before, prepare for tomorrow.

My friends, I study and write about the threats we face, not only to both entertain and inform you, but because I am constantly learning how to prepare for the benefit of my family as well. There is nothing more important on this planet than my darling wife, Dani, and our two girls, Bullie and Boom. One day the apocalypse will be upon us, and I'll be damned if I'm gonna let it stand in the way of our life together.

The Geostorm series is dedicated to the love and support of my family. I will always protect you from anything that threatens us.

ACKNOWLEDGEMENTS

Creating a novel that is both informative and entertaining requires a tremendous team effort. Writing is the easy part. For their efforts in making the Geostorm series a reality, I would like to thank Hristo Argirov Kovatliev for his incredible cover art, Pauline Nolet for her editorial prowess, Stef Mcdaid for making this manuscript decipherable in so many formats, Chris Abernathy for his memorable performance in narrating this novel, and the Team—Denise, Joe, Jim, Shirley, Kenda, Karl, Anthony, and Aunt Sissy whose advice, friendship and attention to detail is priceless.

I'll never forget when I reached out to the folks at NASA's Jet Propulsion Laboratory in Pasadena, California. I knew I wanted to tell the story of the Yellowstone Caldera, and through my conversations with the geologists at the USGS, I discovered that the JPL would be a tremendous resource as well. That trip to California has led to three hard science fiction, technothriller series, so far.

In the Yellowstone series, this led me to the concept of using a method similar to fracking to not only cool down the caldera, but to extract clean energy from it as well. Dr. Brian Cox warned of the catastrophic consequences of this method, and a plausible fiction story was born.

But several scientists had other opinions as to the threats we face. Some pointed to space and said the real planet killers reside in the sky—near-Earth objects. As a result, I wrote the Asteroid series.

Even more scientists warned that under our feet, deep down in Earth's core, lies the key to another catastrophic event in the making. As you will read in my author's introduction and interspersed throughout this story, the flow of liquid iron that generates electric currents, which in turn produce the magnetic fields that protect our planet from the Sun's harmful rays, is subject to change. When these changes occur, our poles could move, with potentially dire consequences, as you will see.

I would like to thank the following for providing me in-depth studies on this phenomenon. Once again, as I immersed myself in the science, source material and research flooded my inbox from scientists, climatologists, and geologists from around the world. I am so very thankful to everyone who not only took the time to discuss this material with me, but also gave me suggestions for future novels. Without their efforts, this story could not be told.

From the farthest point on the globe, thank you to Professor Andrew Roberts from the Research School of Earth Sciences at the Australian National University College of Science. Professor Roberts opened my eyes to the impact a magnetic field reversal has on our magnetosphere, and the corresponding threat from our Sun. As he put it, "a field reversal would have much more of an effect than the solar storm that hit Earth in 1859 (the Carrington Event)." That got my attention.

Closer to home, Dr. Arnaud Chulliat, with the NOAA's National Centers for Environmental Information located at the University of Colorado at Boulder, is a geomagnetist who developed field models, including the World Magnetic Model. His research raised awareness about the possibility of a fast pole shift. Plus, as a Frenchman, he inspired me to take the story to Paris, an incredibly beautiful place.

Speaking of NOAA and the NCEI, I've been amazed at how folks have bent over backwards to answer my questions and indulge me when some were considered off the wall (climate change related). They respected that this was a learning process for me early on, and their patience was remarkable. Special thanks to the research assistants in the Geophysics Information division at NCEI. The geophysical data as well as climate model data helped me create an alternative explanation to the rising temperatures and melting ice caps. Thank you for indulging me!

Finally, as always, a special thank you to Dr. Tamitha Skov, the Space Weather Woman. She assisted me over three years ago as I researched the Blackout series. It was during this time that she planted the seed in my mind of how devastating a weakened magnetic field would be for our planet. At the time, I didn't get into the specifics of magnetic field reversals and pole shifts, but it was Dr. Skov who told me that when the magnetic field is weak, we're exposed to the Sun's deadly effects. As she put it, a *relatively benign solar event could suddenly destroy life as we know it.*

This is why I wrote the Geostorm series.

Finally, unrelated to the research, but of equal importance to me, as I write these acknowledgements, it is the tenth birthday of the princesses of the palace, Bullie and Boom. Dani and I love them dearly.

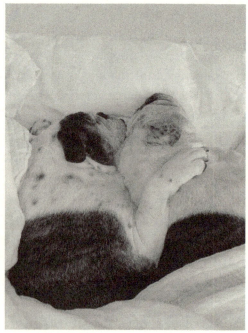

These girls are our life, and I wanted to honor two people who've taken extraordinary care of them throughout their lives—Dr. Kristi Lively (the girls' godmother) of the Village Veterinary Medical Center in Farragut, Tennessee, and Dr. Thomas McNair of Wilkes County Veterinary Services in Washington, Georgia. You'll meet the fictional characters Kristi and Tommy in the story, who in no way resemble the actual Kristi and Thomas, our favorite vets. Their named characters will be a constant reminder to us of how they've loved our princesses as much as we have.

And finally, Dani and I have been proud to support Operation Gratitude in its efforts to forge bonds between Americans and our military personnel and first responders who serve and protect our great nation. Recently, we put out a call to action to our readers to purchase items on Amazon to be included in Operation Gratitude care packages sent to these real American heroes and their families. I want to take a moment to personally thank Annie Bo, Cherye Elliot, Cindi Grayer, Jon & Cindy Judd, Denise Keef, Nancy Parkinson, Sheila Rambeck, Angela M. Reardon, Frank Springer, Linda Tesenair, and Debbie Williams for answering the call to duty!

Thank you all!
Choose Freedom!

ABOUT THE AUTHOR

Bobby Akart

Author Bobby Akart has been ranked by Amazon as #35 on the Amazon Charts list of most popular, bestselling authors. He has achieved recognition as the #1 bestselling Horror Author, #1 bestselling Science Fiction Author, #5 bestselling Action & Adventure Author, #7 bestselling Historical Author and #10 bestselling Thriller Author.

He has written over forty international bestsellers, in nearly fifty fiction and nonfiction genres, including the chart-busting Yellowstone series, the pulse-racing Asteroid series, the thought-provoking Doomsday series, the reader-favorite Lone Star series, the critically acclaimed Boston Brahmin series, the bestselling Blackout series, the frighteningly realistic Pandemic series, his highly cited nonfiction Prepping for Tomorrow series, and his latest project—the Geostorm series, a scientific thriller that will remind us all that life on Earth is subject to change when we least expect it.

His novel *Yellowstone: Hellfire* reached the Top 25 on the Amazon bestsellers list and earned him two Kindle All-Star awards for most pages read in a month and most pages read as an author. The Yellowstone series vaulted him to the #35 bestselling author on Amazon, and the #1 bestselling science fiction author.

Bobby has provided his readers a diverse range of topics that are both informative and entertaining. His attention to detail and impeccable research have allowed him to capture the imagination of his readers through his fictional works and bring them valuable knowledge through his nonfiction books.

SIGN UP for Bobby Akart's mailing list to receive special offers, bonus content, and you'll be the first to receive news about new releases in the Geostorm series:

Visit Bobby Akart's website for informative blog entries on preparedness, writing, and a behind-the-scenes look into his novels.

BobbyAkart.com

VISIT Amazon.com/BobbyAkart, a dedicated feature page created by Amazon for his work, to view more information on his thriller fiction novels and post-apocalyptic book series, as well as his nonfiction Prepping for Tomorrow series.

Author's Introduction to the Geostorm Series

September 1, 2019

Our planet is alive.

Deep beneath her skin is our planet's lifeblood, rivers of molten iron pulsing around a core—her beating heart. This moving, fluid iron generates the magnetic field maintaining the delicate balance of life on Earth.

Until she has a change of heart.

Are we on the verge of a natural disaster brought about by the Earth itself?

Earth's magnetic field surrounds our planet like an invisible force field—protecting life from harmful solar radiation by deflecting charged particles away. Far from being constant, this field is continuously changing. Indeed, our planet's history includes at least several hundred global magnetic reversals, where north and south magnetic poles shift and swap places.

When is the next reversal going to take place? There's evidence that a pole shift is underway now. The simple fact that we are overdue for a full reversal and the fact that the Earth's magnetic field is currently decreasing has led to suggestions that the field may be in the early stages of flipping.

During a reversal, the Earth's magnetic field won't be zero, but will assume a weaker and more complex form. It may fall to ten percent of the present-day strength and have magnetic poles at the equator or even the simultaneous existence of multiple "north" and "south" magnetic poles.

Full geomagnetic reversals have occurred many times throughout the planet's history, and they will again. There can also be temporary and incomplete reversals, known as *events* and *excursions*, in which the magnetic poles move away from the geographic poles—perhaps even crossing the equator—before returning to their original locations.

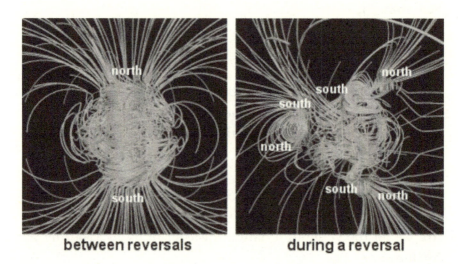

between reversals   **during a reversal**

The alteration in the magnetic field during a reversal will weaken its shielding effect, allowing heightened levels of radiation on and above the Earth's surface. Were this to happen today, the increase in charged particles reaching the Earth would result in increased risks for satellites, aviation, and ground-based electrical infrastructure. Geomagnetic storms, or geostorms for short, driven by the interaction of large eruptions of solar energy with our magnetic field, give us a taste of what we can expect with a weakened magnetic shield.

In 2003, the so-called Halloween storm caused localized blackouts and grid failures in Sweden, required the rerouting of flights to avoid communication failures and radiation risk to passengers, and disrupted satellites and global positioning systems. But this event was minor in comparison with another geostorm of the recent past, the

1859 Carrington Event, which caused aurorae as far south as the Caribbean and telegraph lines to catch on fire.

In terms of the direct impact a pole shift will have on living species, scientists cannot definitively predict what will happen, as modern humans did not exist at the time of the last full reversal. Several studies, including one by Harvard scientists published in *Nature* magazine, have linked past reversals with mass extinctions—suggesting some reversals and episodes of extended volcanism could be driven by these sudden pole shifts.

In addition, a study published in *Current Biology* magazine confirmed that many animal species have some form of *magnetoreception*, enabling them to sense the Earth's magnetic field. They use this to assist in long-distance navigation during migration. The study also showed that the weakening of the magnetic field, or shifts in the poles, also impacted animal and human brain waves.

These magnetic pole shifts also affect our planet's weather patterns. NASA has discovered a weakening in the Earth's magnetic field that seems to be altering both wind and atmospheric pressure norms. One study claims the reversal has given rise to the recent superstorms around the world and the disastrous floods in Australia, Pakistan and the Philippines. NOAA records also indicate wide temperature *extremes* are the most pronounced in hundreds of years.

Based upon the research, the most likely harm to humans when the poles reverse again would be the ways in which a geostorm impacts the Earth's electromagnetic field. An ordinary, relatively benign solar event could cause exponential damage because of the weakened magnetic field.

Aviation would probably need to be halted in order to take into account the pole shift, our satellites would need to be redesigned and repositioned, and the planet's power grids could collapse under the weight of the solar particles that are ordinarily deflected, but allowed to pass through the weakened magnetic field.

That being said, while scientists are unwilling to predict exactly when the next full reversal will occur, most don't think it could lead to a mass extinction event unless humans have evolved to the point where they, literally, can't live without their electronic devices.

And we're not there yet ... right?

Right?

Thank you for reading the Geostorm series.

REAL-WORLD NEWS EXCERPTS

Which Way to the North Pole?
The north magnetic pole is moving eastward at an accelerating pace.
~ The New York Times Editorial Board, February 7, 2019

The part that feeds their doomsday scenarios is the possibility that the poles are preparing for another polarity reversal, which would cause a compass to point south instead of north. The quirk is normal — over the past 20 million years, it has occurred, on average, every 200,000 to 300,000 years. The last one was about 780,000 years ago, so another may be overdue.

That could lead to a temporary weakening of the magnetic field that protects Earth from cosmic radiation.

"It's time to wake up to the dangers and start preparing," evoking a world in which a devastating stream of malevolent cosmic radiation would wreak havoc on lives and power grids…

Solar Storms Can Devastate Entire Civilizations
~ Irina Slav, Contributor to Real Clear Energy, October 12, 2019

Climate has inarguably become a hot topic of discussion in developed economies over the last decade, and it is getting hotter by the day as study after study warn we are close to doomed if we don't change our ways urgently.

Yet climate on Earth is not the only problem that humankind faces. There is another climate we need to pay attention to, and there is nothing we can do to change that.

A geostorm, whose more scientific name is coronal mass ejections or geomagnetic storm, occur a lot more frequently than people think…

"Take a moment and think about how you would function for weeks or months without electrical power, GPS, or air travel."

PG&E's Big Blackout Is Only the Beginning
~ Wall Street Journal, October 12, 2019

PG&E Corp.'s decision to shut off power to more than two million Californians this week represents a new reality: It now plans to pull the plug as a desperation measure whenever its equipment threatens to spark destructive and potentially deadly wildfires.

The Wall Street Journal detailed in April how PG&E intended to use the outages, known as public safety power shut-offs, to reduce wildfire risk, a strategy that carries consequences for medically vulnerable populations who rely on electric devices to survive, and businesses that could lose customers and inventory.

California officials say man using oxygen tank died within minutes of PG&E power shutoff
~ The Hill, October 12, 2019

The deceased was one of 2 million residents across central and northern California left without electricity after PG&E shut power off in anticipation of high dry winds that create perfect environments for wildfires.

The move has been highly controversial in the state.

Denver hit 83 degrees on Wednesday afternoon. Eight hours later, it was snowing.
~ The Washington Post, October 10, 2019

"That's our largest one-day temperature change on record," said Russell

Danielson, a meteorologist at the National Weather Service in Boulder. "We've told people around here to dress in layers because sometimes you get summer and winter in the same day."

That chalks up to a 54-degree temperature drop within one day. It also marks a 40-degree plummet in four hours, the mercury diving from 81 degrees to 41 between 4 and 8 p.m. As the winds switched around from the north, gusts up to 55 miles per hour heralded the bone-chilling change.

Terrifying scene plays out as 300 Birds ram into NASCAR Hall of Fame
~ *The Charlotte Observer, October 16, 2019*

In a bizarre scene straight out of a horror movie, hundreds of birds flew into the NASCAR Hall of Fame in Charlotte and crashed to the sidewalk.

A video by an eyewitness shows the birds striking windows and doors near the main entrance. The videographer reported that this went on for more than an hour.

"Don't let them hit you. There's something wrong with them," someone says in the video. "It's a whole flock. That's odd."

The scene got stranger still, she reported, when some birds got up and tried "killing themselves again … running into different buildings."

"It's unusual for Chimney Swifts to collide with windows. Audubon volunteers have documented this a few times in North Carolina cities, but only one bird at a time – not a large-scale event like this one," said a statement issued by Kim Brand, senior network manager at Audubon North Carolina.

"It's also odd that these swifts were out last night after 9 p.m. Normally, even during migration, Chimney Swifts go to roost in a chimney for the night around dusk. Yesterday, the sun set around 7 p.m."

Magnetic pole shock: Radiation warning as scientists make worrying discovery

~ The Sean Martin, Science Reporter, UK Express Online, October 4, 2019

In recent years, scientists have been gearing up for a potential flip in the magnetic field – a natural phenomena which had thought to occur every 200,000 to 300,000 years when the north and south poles switch. The poles attempted to swap 40,000 years ago but the process failed. As a result, the last time the poles switched place was 780,000 years ago, meaning we are long overdue a flip in the magnetic field. However, by analyzing a three-million-year period around 500 million years ago, researchers discovered there were 78 pole shifts, according to the research published in Earth and Planetary Science Letters.

Yves Gallet, of France's Institut de Physique du Globe de Paris and study lead, told National Geographic:

"We expected a very high magnetic reversal frequency, but of course not with such a high value. However, all the effects we currently see during strong solar/geomagnetic storms would likely increase and occur during moderate solar activity."

EPIGRAPH

"When the switch happens, we will be exposed to solar winds
capable of punching holes into the ozone layer. It's likely to render
some areas of the planet uninhabitable by knocking out power grids."
~ Daniel Baker, Director, Laboratory for Atmospheric and Space
Physics at the University of Colorado in Boulder
*****

"This is serious business. Imagine for a moment your electrical power
supply knocked out. No lights. No computers. No cell phones. Even
flushing a toilet would be impossible. And that's just for starters."
~ Richard Holme, Professor of Earth, Ocean, and Ecological
Sciences at Liverpool University
*****

"We have blithely built our civilization's critical infrastructure during
a time when the planet's magnetic field was relatively strong, not
accounting for the field's bent for anarchy."
~ Alanna Mitchell, Author, The Spinning Magnet
*****

"…this will be preceded by a solar eclipse more obscure and more
dark…than any since the creation of the world except that after the
death and passion of Jesus Christ."
~ Nostradamus, The Epistle to Henry II, verse 87
*****

"Things will fall apart; the center cannot hold; mere anarchy is loosed
upon the world. The blood-dimmed tide is loosed and everywhere
the ceremony of innocence is drowned. The best lack all conviction
while the worst are full of passionate intensity."
~ William Butler Yeats, Irish Poet, 1929

GEOSTORM: The Pulse

The Geostorm Series
Book Two

Prologue

July 2020
World Futurists Conference
Washington Hilton Hotel
Washington, DC

"At a time when people are fearful, and many dystopian scenarios lurk ahead, it's up to us to collectively imagine and build the future we want. Humans are the only species on the planet that need not just accept or adapt to changing circumstances—we have the capacity to consciously evolve and engineer our surroundings. We have the ability to imagine, the drive to discover, and the power to come together to turn our greatest challenges into opportunities. A brighter future is possible for all of humanity!"

Kimbal Brandt stood back from the podium and accepted the raucous applause of the attendees of the World Futurists Conference in Washington, DC, during the hot summer of 2020. The nation's capital was experiencing a record heat wave, generated naturally in part due to shifting weather patterns, and politically, as the country was bitterly divided over an acrimonious presidential campaign coupled with impeachment proceedings of a sitting president, which were tearing America apart.

Throughout his keynote address to his fellow futurists, Brandt initially tried to remain upbeat about the planet's prospects for the future. But then, it was if a sense of reality swept over him, so he decided to remain true to his principles.

"This week, our speakers have laid out a vision of the future that promised everything from driverless cars to eerily humanlike robots. The scientists among us have described a gradual transition from the internet to a *brain-net*, a network in which human thoughts, emotions, feelings, and even memories might be transmitted instantly around the globe.

"By 2035, three-dimensional printers will print clothing at such a low cost that labor will no longer have to be exploited in developing nations. Shopping will reach a whole new level, as consumers will be able to download their clothing in the comfort of their home and print it on these magnificent new machines.

"Artificial intelligence will become as smart as or, most likely, smarter than humans. AI will be embedded in every part of our lives, from homes to hospitals, vehicles to robots. Robo-surgeons will flawlessly perform complex surgeries, and robo-docs will even deliver babies. Predictive medicine will take place via a cell phone app, and payment for such services will be made digitally using digital currency like bitcoin.

"To many, it sounds like exciting times ahead, and I don't disagree."

Brandt paused and rubbed his temples. He had been chosen as the keynote speaker for a reason. He was highly respected for his work at Tesla and SpaceX. His visions from decades past had come to fruition. And he wasn't considered too extreme in his prescience.

Yet this group, no, the entire world needed to open their eyes. Brandt had a foresight, a clairvoyance, that he couldn't explain, but one that had proved itself over and over again. It was time to shock his audience, mainly because they needed it.

"Ladies and gentlemen, where one period in the history of humanity ends, another must begin unless, of course, we face extinction. Sixty-five million years ago marks the base of the Palaeocene period. Many of you know it as the *K-T Boundary*. This was a time characterized by a mass extinction of many forms of life on this planet, including the dinosaurs. The K-T extinction event was most likely caused by the massive asteroid that crashed into Earth at Chicxulub, which is now buried underneath the Yucatan Peninsula in Mexico.

"To some, this may seem off topic, but I bring it up for a reason.

It's fun for us to gather and discuss the extraordinary technological advances that will change daily life as we know it. On the other hand, it's difficult to accept the reality that our days on this planet are numbered. Now, to be sure, there is disagreement as to when and how the next extinction of life on Earth will occur, but make no mistake, it is coming, and I believe it may be sooner than we all want to acknowledge."

Brandt paused and allowed the murmur of the futurists conversing with one another to roll through the conference hall. He'd put a damper on their evening, as his keynote speech of hope and excitement was turning to an apocalyptic view of humanity's fate.

"The K-T extinction was a geological epoch that lasted nearly ten million years, an unfathomable length of time when it is compared to our days on Earth. But as I said a few moments ago, when one period ends, another must begin. And it did. Some argue that the catastrophic events that followed the Chicxulub asteroid impact gave rise to life as we know it today. A new epoch, one that has produced the most technologically advanced species in the history of the world.

"Will this new epoch end? My friends, the answer is yes. Throughout Earth's four and a half billion years, extinction-level events have occurred that destroyed virtually all living organisms, only to replace them with others. To think it won't happen again is naïve.

"I stand before you today to say that we are entering the early stages of another epoch. Some refer to it as the Anthropocene, or *new man*, epoch. They maintain that recent human impacts, from environmental pollution to habitat destruction, has resulted in animal and plant extinctions so great that it's changing the geological makeup of Earth.

"My research goes beyond blaming man and the industrial revolution for the woes on Earth. To be sure, these advances over the last two centuries have had a profound impact on our environment. However, I'm referring to a greater threat, one that doesn't have anything to do with what mankind inflicts upon the planet. I'm talking about a natural phenomenon that has the ability to destroy life as we know it, and change the face of the planet. I'm referring to a full reversal of the Earth's magnetic field."

If Brandt hadn't stirred them up with his earlier statements, then this certainly did. Several of the attendees voiced their displeasure with his statements. The concept of the wandering poles was accepted by all in the futurist and scientific community, but most adhered to the premise that the reversal of the magnetic field would take thousands of years to occur, allowing man to adjust accordingly. In the minds of the futurist community, a pole shift was hardly a scientific theory that would result in an extinction-level event.

"Please, my friends, hear me out. The prospect of a pole shift is very plausible and entails more than the needle on a compass pointing in a direction different from the norm. It's what happens during the magnetic field reversal that should concern everyone in this conference hall. We rely upon electronics and our glorious technological advances, yet we underestimate the natural phenomena that could erase two hundred years of scientific breakthroughs."

A member of the audience shouted, "An epoch doesn't occur overnight!"

"In most cases, that's true, and we should be grateful for that. Other than the big ones, like eruptions of supervolcanos or massive impact events, an epoch is usually gradual. There are exceptions. The geologic record reflects that the planet's magnetic field has wandered and reversed in the course of a human lifetime. Think of this for a moment, over the past several days, we have excitedly laid out our vision of future technologies in the years 2035, 2050, and beyond through the end of this century. Fifteen, thirty, or even fifty years from now, the pole shift could occur, resulting in a complete reversal of the magnetic field that protects us from the Sun.

"Without that protective shield, all of our grand technologies will be rendered worthless, and moreover, what was once frozen will melt, and what was once barren will flood. It will be an environmental disaster of epic proportions, and we are wholly unprepared to accept this premise, much less adjust our visions of the future based upon this eventuality."

Brandt had thrown down the gauntlet, and he backed away from the podium, fully expecting that these would be his final words for the evening.

Kimbal Brandt was right in two respects.

First, they were his last words spoken at the World Futurists Conference on that occasion, as well as any other.

Second, a pole shift and the resulting reversal of the planet's magnetic field would occur within their lifetime, with catastrophic consequences.

CHAPTER 1

Brookfield Zoo
Chicago, Illinois

In the blink of an eye—life can change. Scientists have studied the phenomena associated with how quickly the human brain can process information. Imagine seeing dozens of pictures flashing by in a fraction of a second. The brain can see these images, analyze them, reorder them, and even imagine scenarios in which they interact.

This ability of rapid-fire processing helps direct the eyes, quickly shifting their gaze as much as three times per second to their next target of interest and then back again. The eyes' job is simple—get information to the human brain, which must think rapidly enough to know what it should do next.

"Tooommmyyy!"

Tommy Bannon's eyes responded to Kristi Boone's voice before she'd finished screaming his name. His brain acted reflexively, sensing the fear and foreboding in her voice, calibrating his eyes so they moved around as quickly as possible, searching his surroundings for danger.

He whipped his head to the right. His vision locked on an unexpected movement. It was imperceptible, fluid, and stealthy. The rustling of the tall grasses, the sound of gentle crunching on the ground, and the brief glimpses of white fur intermixed with the light green and tan hues of the landscape grabbed his undivided attention.

His brain processed the shape, color, orientation, and sounds. Instinctively, a fight-or-flight response to a perceived threat to his survival was initiated. In animals, the reaction varied from escape to fight when cornered by an attacker. In humans, the consensus was that men were wired to fight while women tended to flee. It was simply human nature.

Tommy was familiar with snow leopards. He'd extensively studied Taza, the ten-year-old snow leopard, while at the Lincoln Park Zoo. Until the cat was transferred to the Potter Park Zoo in Lansing, Michigan, Tommy was a frequent visitor to Taza's habitat. The two had bonded somewhat, or at least as much as any zoologist could with a wild and deadly animal.

Taza had been a rescue from the Rafah Zoo in Gaza, the Palestinian territory on the eastern coast of the Mediterranean Sea that had been the center of Arab-Israeli strife for centuries. When Taza was only fourteen months old, zoo workers at Rafah had held a bag over the cat's head and removed his claws so that children and visitors to the zoo could play with him.

It was a barbaric, vicious procedure that caused long-lasting damage to Taza. He was prevented from most natural behaviors, such as grabbing food or climbing rock formations. When he began to suffer from bouts of infection following the operation, international rescue workers petitioned the United States to intervene. Taza was brought to Lincoln Park, and he became one of the first animals that Tommy cared for.

His brain immediately recognized the stalking movements of the white leopard approaching him. Its large thickly furred paws, which acted like built-in snowshoes in the wild, gave him away as he moved surreptitiously through the grasses. Tommy was being hunted by the big cat, which, unlike Taza, had not been declawed.

Snow leopards, contrary to their lion counterparts, cannot roar. Their method of attack was far more stealth-like. Ordinarily, they were not aggressive toward humans, and to Tommy's knowledge, there had never been a verified snow leopard attack on a human being.

But his brain, processing the threat at the speed of a supercomputer, reminded him that animals' behavior at the moment was anything but ordinary, and *there's a first time for everything.*

Fight or flight?

His brain responded before his conscious thought could finish the question.

You cannot outrun a snow leopard. If you do, you'll only die exhausted.

Being charged by a big cat was frightening, and it was difficult for Tommy to keep his composure. If he ran, it was more likely to prompt an attack. He stood his ground and raised his arms high in the air to make himself look bigger, not unlike what a person would do when confronted by a bear.

"Goooo!" he shouted at the snow leopard as the creature revealed itself from the tall grasses. Tommy began to clap his hands, using a cupping gesture to make the sound louder. He followed this action with waving his arms over his head.

Ordinarily, snow leopards would turn and walk away. Perhaps they might perform mock charges toward their target in an effort to force their prey into a mistake.

Kristi was coming toward him and he quickly held his left arm out toward her, instructing her to stop. Fortunately, the cat didn't see her advance. Tommy glanced over his shoulder at an arched bridge that crossed the watery moat that was supposed to prevent the big cats from escaping their habitat. Clearly, that security measure hadn't worked.

"Kristi! Stop! Go back and get the cart. Meet me on the bridge!"

"But!" she shouted back.

"Trust me!"

She had the presence of mind not to make any sudden moves that might startle the snow leopard. She, like Tommy, began to slowly retreat toward the walkway where the maintenance cart was parked. This enabled Tommy to focus on the task at hand.

As the snow leopard crept forward, his rigid tail indicating his intent to hunt, Tommy slowly retreated. He continued to alternate between clapping his hands and waving his arms high overhead. His shouts at the snow leopard went largely ignored, except by the lions below, which continued to feast on the zookeeper and periodically glanced upward at the commotion.

The sound of the maintenance cart caught the cat's attention, providing Tommy a welcome distraction. He retreated several paces in just a few seconds, putting a little more distance between him and his attacker.

In a flash, the snow leopard rushed toward Tommy, only to skid to a stop twenty feet away.

A mock charge.

Tommy stood his ground and shouted at the cat, a deep, sincere, from-the-belly plea to leave him alone.

It lunged at him again, closer this time. Tommy instinctively flinched and backed up several paces, but his shoulders remained squarely facing the snow leopard.

"I'm here!" Kristi shouted.

It took only a second. Tommy looked briefly behind him to confirm her position. He didn't need to, but his memory reflexes caused it to happen.

In that second, the snow leopard closed the fifteen-foot distance between them and lunged for Tommy's throat.

CHAPTER 2

Brookfield Zoo
Chicago, Illinois

Tommy had never experienced fear like this before. The air sucked a guttural scream out of his throat like a long hemp rope. Yet, despite the adrenaline surging through his body, he held his ground like a half-wit heavyweight boxer willing to be pummeled into submission to earn his share of the prize money.

Attacking like his cousin the lion, the snow leopard was airborne, open mouth bearing deadly fangs, heading straight for Tommy's face and throat. Tommy defended himself the only way he knew how. He pulled his right arm back and levied a powerful punch toward the nose of the agile cat.

He caught the animal squarely in the nose with a solid right, but the big cat's sharp teeth cut a gash between his index and middle fingers. The momentum of the snow leopard's leap caused it to crash into Tommy's chest, knocking them both to the ground.

Tommy scrambled to his knees, cupping his hand to his jawline, blood dripping between his fingers, which had been sliced open by the snow leopard's sharp claws.

The lions noticed the scrum and were oddly howling and roaring in an inharmonious cheer for their cousin. The cat responded to the encouraging roars and lunged at Tommy again, biting at his face and forearm that Tommy used for protection. Tommy was able to force the animal off him and down a slight embankment.

Tommy's instincts kicked in. He had no choice but to fight back. He grabbed two softball-sized rocks and threw them at the snow leopard as it made another lunge. One of the rocks caught the creature on the side of the head and bounced back toward Tommy.

He quickly picked it up and used it to pound the animal's side as it attacked again.

The counterattack surprised the snow leopard, but it refused to give up. It came at Tommy again, so he prepared a one-two counterpunch. As the leopard raced toward him, Tommy threw the rock as a distraction and prepared to kick the animal in the jaw.

His timing was perfect, although the animal's fangs pierced the laced-up part of his boot. The snow leopard fell hard on its side, and Tommy became the aggressor. He jumped on the cat's back and grabbed it around the throat, using his powerful arms to squeeze the snow leopard's throat.

The animal thrashed about, angrily trying to claw at Tommy and twist its head to gnaw at the man's arms. However, the zoologist was undeterred. Crazed, in fact.

Tommy let out a low growl and then he began to scream at the top of his lungs. The primal yell quietened the lions, who had been cheering their fellow cat along. Tommy continued to squeeze, and despite the fact that the seventy-pound animal had succumbed to his death grip, he continued until his arms finally relented.

Finally, Tommy let go of the cat, and his emotions. He fell back on his butt and raised his knees to his chest in a fetal position. Then he cried. Deep sobs of despair as the man who'd devoted his life to caring for magnificent animals like this one had just done the unthinkable—he intentionally killed one of them. His favorite. A snow leopard.

"Tommy! Are you okay?"

Kristi raced from the bridge to where he was curled up next to the dead animal. Tommy wiped the blood, sweat and tears off his face and remained on the ground, staring at the dead creature.

When she reached his side, he mumbled, "They were always my favorite."

Kristi didn't respond and focused her attention on his wounds. While she looked at the cuts and scrapes he'd received, she glanced around their surroundings to make sure none of the other ferocious cats had escaped the habitat.

The superficial wounds he'd endured would heal, but his soul might not. Kristi sat next to him and put her arm around his shoulders in an effort to comfort the man she'd only recently met. Neither said a word, opting instead to watch the sun begin to drop over the horizon. Had it not been for the circumstances, the two could be any couple sitting on a rock outcropping overlooking the grasslands in Botswana, admiring the giraffes meandering across the landscape, or the African fish eagles diving for a meal.

In a way, perhaps they were. A couple, that is, whose minds temporarily took them away from the chaos unfolding at the Brookfield Zoo and transported them into the middle of sub-Saharan Africa.

Ten minutes later, Kristi whispered to Tommy, "Hey, we need to get you checked out at the hospital. Can you stand?"

He nodded his head and pushed off the ground after giving the dead snow leopard a final look. Tommy winced as he gave himself a quick medical evaluation. His clothes were bloodied and torn. His right hand was beginning to swell from the trauma when his fist had smashed into the face of his attacker.

"I'll be all right," he mumbled. He stretched his back and then rolled his head around his shoulders to relieve some stress. The soft lighting that illuminated the pathways through this area of the zoo began to come on as the last vestiges of daylight gave in to the night. "Kristi, where is everybody? You'd think that someone would've come by during all of this."

Kristi led him to the cart and helped him stay upright as he stumbled over a rock. She quickly assessed his body to see if he was losing blood from another wound she hadn't previously discovered. Apparently, his inability to walk was from both physical and mental fatigue.

"I don't understand it. Nobody came looking for the zookeepers or us. I don't like the feel of this."

"Same here. Should we go to the administration building?"

Kristi gently pulled at his shirt. The blood was beginning to dry and was clinging to his skin. "I think we should get you to a hospital first, don't you think?"

"Nah, I'll be fine. Let me get to my locker. I've got a change of clothes in my backpack. I can wash up in the restroom."

"Listen, Tommy, please don't make me pull rank. You need to dress these wounds properly so you don't get an infection."

After a brief back-and-forth argument, she drove the maintenance cart toward Tommy's office. The lights were off inside the small, block building. Apparently, none of the other zoologists had bothered to stick around that evening.

The two of them cautiously entered the building until Tommy could find the light switches. Nothing appeared out of the ordinary, so he cleaned up while Kristi searched the kitchen area for a first aid kit.

Fifteen minutes later, Tommy lied and proclaimed himself *good as new*. His wounds would eventually heal, but psychologically, he never would.

And this was just the beginning of their nightmare.

CHAPTER 3

Northwest Ontario
Canada

All our fears are darkest before sunrise.

The Hudson Bay Lowlands were considered one of the largest continuous wetlands in the world. One of the flattest parts of Canada, the lowlands were created millions of years ago when Ice Age glaciers retreated toward the North Pole, leaving flat land exposed that eventually began to dry. Because its altitude was near sea level, the lowlands didn't drain properly, and they remained marshy, especially in the spring and summer months. The snow melt from the Canadian Shield's interior plains flooded the lowlands, leaving them in a condition not unlike Florida's Everglades, without the snakes and alligators.

Over eighty percent of the region was made up of peat or muskeg, a swamp-like bog of water and dying vegetation. This swampy forest was a challenge for the native species that inhabited the area, which included woodland caribou, moose, the arctic fox, and as winter approached, the Hudson Bay wolf.

On the Hudson Bay Lowlands, which stretched along the southern shores of the world's second largest bay, which connected Northern Canada with the Atlantic Ocean, you could slog through the wetlands for days without seeing another living soul. If you were lucky, you wouldn't find trouble there and trouble wouldn't find you.

Levi Boone, however, had already found trouble.

It was late August and the passengers of the puddle jumper to the hunting camp at Smoky Falls shouldn't have been in the midst of blizzard-like conditions, yet they were. It had all happened so fast.

Their pilot, a seasoned veteran of shuttle flights throughout Canada, had been guiding their aircraft toward what should have been a routine water landing at Smoky Falls.

Rather than dropping the float plane gently on the water, his wings clipped the tops of several one-hundred-foot-tall red pines and then collided with the white birch trees that were abundant in the lowlands. The airplane broke apart, throwing gear and passengers in all directions. Within seconds after the right wing snapped in half, the aircraft flipped over and rolled through the fresh snow until it abruptly stopped against a snowdrift.

Levi remained strapped into his seat harnesses in the back half of the airplane, which had been separated upon impact with the ground. The fuselage of the tail section and rear seat had wedged between two trees, which continued to shake from the impact, sending globs of snow on top of Levi's head.

For a moment, he experienced an out-of-body rush. Blood hammered through his ears, and his heart raced. His scalp began to tingle and his eyes darted in all directions. Then, like the flip of a light switch, his thoughts became crystalline. He was suddenly keenly aware of his surroundings.

He instinctively wiped the cold moisture off his face and then checked himself to confirm all of his body parts were intact. Remarkably, nothing was broken, and except for his face being scratched by the red pine's branches, he'd survived unharmed.

Levi took a deep breath and allowed himself a moment to gather his wits. He slowly wiped his face off again, this time squeezing his forehead and cheeks as if to pinch himself awake from a bad dream.

Except it wasn't a dream. They'd crashed in a snow-covered wilderness, and his surroundings were deathly quiet except for the booming voice of a male snow owl desperately seeking a mate before breeding season ended.

Darkness surrounded him as the night sky was obliterated by the blowing snow. He unbuckled his seatbelt and slid out of the plane until he could touch ground. He landed calf-deep in the marshy conditions that existed beneath the blanket of snow. The freak snowstorm hadn't been preceded by below-freezing temperatures, so the ground underneath still had the characteristics of late summer.

Levi immediately regretted wearing sneakers for the flight northward to Smoky Falls. He turned back to crawl onto his seat in search of his backpack and gun case, but both had been thrown clear of the plane when it crashed. Despite his need to change into his hunting boots, he had to find the others.

"Karl! Eddie! Are you guys okay?"

The wind picked up, causing the wet snow to blow off the canopy. The whispering pines were stifled by the weight, but the sound of the wind inhibited his hearing. He yelled louder this time.

"Hey! Are you guys okay?"

Levi tried to recall the moment of impact and the way the plane had reacted to crashing into the trees. He closed his eyes and replayed the sudden demise of their flight in his mind. They'd clipped a wing, flipped over, and then tumbled. He couldn't make sense of it, so he decided to look for debris.

He'd been fascinated by the work of the National Transportation Safety Board's investigations of airplane crashes ever since a Cessna Citation crashed across the Ohio River onto Paradise Bottom in Kentucky when he was a boy. He'd paddled his canoe across the river and stood just outside the yellow caution tape, watching the investigators pick up and catalog every piece of debris, including body parts.

He tried to determine what direction the tail section had come from. It had plowed through the snow and broken-down pine saplings as it went. Levi was concerned about getting disoriented in the dark. It wouldn't take but one wrong turn and, within minutes, he could be lost in these conditions. Also, he was keenly aware of how difficult it was to survive in a snowstorm without adequate shelter. As soon as he found the others, that would have to be their first priority.

The wind intensified and Levi was beginning to feel the chill in his bones. Up ahead, he saw a faint, flashing red light. *Part of the wing*, he surmised. Excited, he picked up the pace and trudged through the snow and the murky ground beneath it. The forest floor was the worst of both worlds. Muddy and cold from the snow.

"Hey! Can you hear me?" he shouted again as he got closer to the shining beacon.

"Over here!"

"Karl?"

"Yeah! Levi, this way. Eddie's hurt and the pilot's missing." His voice drifted off.

Invigorated at the prospect of reuniting with his friends, Levi tried to jog-slog through the snow. This turned out to be a mistake, as his sneaker stuck in the muck and came off his foot. He turned to retrieve it, soaking his sock and foot in the snow in the process. He dropped to his knees in the dark and crawled on his hands and knees, plunging his arm into the eighteen-inch holes left by his steps.

"Got it!" he exclaimed as he wrenched the shoe out of the cold sludge. He replaced the shoe, but now he was soaking wet. By the time he reached the nose section and the first row of seats, he was beginning to shiver from the damp cold.

However, it was the gruesome discovery that sent chills up and down his spine.

CHAPTER 4

Northwest Ontario
Canada

Levi had seen death, but only after hunting animals. This was the first time he'd seen a human being dead. When his grandpa died, he was only a child, and Sarah had shielded him from the open-casket funeral that Grandpa Chapman had requested in his will. Even then, after the mortician had worked his magic, his grandfather appeared to be in a restful sleep. This kind of death was far different.

The French-Canadian pilot had been mangled and pummeled by the forest. As the aircraft crashed through the trees, limbs and trunks battered the man's body beyond recognition. His horribly twisted body hung in his seat harness, but his head had been ripped open by a tree branch that still protruded from his neck.

Levi stopped and immediately dropped to his knees, retching. His stomach convulsed as it emptied into the snow. Every attempt he made to control it was overridden by the sight of the pilot's mutilated corpse, which would forever be embedded in Levi's mind.

"Levi! You all right?"

Karl Tate's shouts came from deeper into the wreckage, but only thirty feet away. The blowing snow prevented the two friends from seeing one another.

Levi continued to cough, but his stomach had been emptied. He scooped up two handfuls of snow and frantically shoved them into his mouth, hoping the wet substance would clean out the vomit. He swished the water around in his cheeks before spitting it out. Levi would give anything for a bottle of Scope mouthwash at the moment.

18

"Yeah. The pilot's dead," he replied matter-of-factly.

"Shit! Are you sure?" asked Karl.

Levi didn't bother to look again. The man's corpse left little doubt. Without answering, he moved through the blizzard toward Karl's voice.

The entire row of seats behind the cockpit had been ripped from the airplane's floor and thrown clear of the fuselage. The fact that all three of the guys survived was a miracle. Levi slowly approached Karl and patted him on the back.

"Are you in one piece?"

"By the grace of God," he replied. "Eddie's kinda banged up. I think he's got a broken arm, and he's lost a few teeth."

Levi walked around Karl and knelt in front of Eddie Cramer, who was doubled over in pain, clutching his left arm. "Did you clip a wing?"

Eddie chuckled, spitting out bloody sputum as he did. "Very funny, asshole. When the wing clipped the tree, the tree clipped me. I'm pretty sure it's broken."

Levi looked over at Karl. He always used humor to diffuse a tense situation, even though sometimes it was snarkier than others.

"I don't know, Karl. He ain't cryin'. If it was broken, he'd be squallin' like a baby, don't you think?"

"Yeah, you're right," said Karl with a chuckle. He played along. "Maybe you should give it a squeeze to make sure?"

Eddie immediately protested and pulled away from his friends. "Screw the both of ya! Nobody's squeezin' my dang arm!"

Blood trickled down Eddie's forehead and over the bridge of his nose. More blood trickled out of the side of his mouth, where he'd been smacked hard enough to lose his two front teeth.

Levi struggled to see his friend in the dark, but he had to find a way to assess his head wounds. The broken arm could wait. He turned to Karl for assistance.

"We gotta find our gear."

"I know, but the shit could be anywhere. I can't see ten feet in front of me."

"You gotta try, Karl. Listen. Don't wander far. Go straight out and straight back. Use your footprints to guide you back. Seriously, if you get lost, we're screwed."

"Got it. What about Eddie?"

"I'm gonna try to check him out, and I need to get him warm. The loss of blood could lead to shock, especially in this dang snowstorm. Man, you gotta hurry."

"I'm on it," said Karl as he walked off into the darkness.

Levi turned his attention to Eddie. "Okay, buddy. We're gonna get you fixed up. The first thing I need to do is keep you warm. I told you the weather could change up here."

"Yeah, I know," said Eddie apologetically. "Levi, you're always right about this stuff. I should've listened."

Levi stood to remove his jacket and immediately felt the chill. It didn't matter; he wasn't bleeding profusely like his friend.

"Okay, I've gotta wrap this around you, but I don't wanna move your arm. It's gonna hurt enough just jostling you around."

"I can deal with the pain, but I gotta tell you my neck really hurts, too. I got whipped around pretty bad, you know?"

Levi gently pulled Eddie forward in his seat and slipped his hunting jacket behind him. Eddie let out a groan as Levi wrapped him in the coat.

"Where's the pilot?" he asked Levi.

"Deader than dead. But we're not, and I intend to keep it that way."

More blood poured down his forehead, prompting Levi to focus his attention on Eddie's scalp.

"Dude, I'm really sleepy. How 'bout I rest my eyes for a bit until they rescue us."

Eddie's words were slurred, and his eyes began to flutter open and closed. Levi knew that he had to keep him awake, so he came up with a solution that might draw Eddie's ire, but it would be effective.

He created a pancake of snow to use as an icy cold washcloth. Without warning, he wiped the blood off Eddie's forehead. The act immediately snapped the injured man out of his stupor.

"What the hell, Levi? A little warning would've been nice!"

"Oh, sorry about that. I missed that class in nursing school."

"You mean torture school. You're really sick, dude."

"Yeah, I know. Hold still for a minute."

Levi began to examine Eddie's scalp. A small strip of metal was embedded near the crown of his head, slicing into the scalp. Steady gushes of blood were coming out of the wound.

Levi sat back on his heels and considered his options. He needed to remove the sliver of metal, but he also needed to have something to put pressure on the wound to control the bleeding. He also needed to be honest with his friend.

"Okay, here's the deal. You've got a piece of the airplane stuck in your head, and you're losing a lot of blood."

Eddie reached up to feel for the wound as if to confirm the diagnosis for himself. Levi quickly, but gently, pulled his good arm back down.

"Don't do that," he ordered. "I think I can easily remove the metal, but I've gotta find something sterile to stop the bleeding until we can find our bags or a first aid kit or something."

Eddie was slipping out of consciousness again. "What are you gonna do?"

Levi took a deep breath and exhaled. He was about to become the second Boone to drop his drawers out in the open in the last week.

He quickly kicked off his sneakers and unbuckled the leather belt holding up his jeans.

"No, dude! No way!" protested Eddie, who was suddenly fully aware of what was happening.

"Just relax, Eddie. They were clean when I put 'em on this morning."

"Dude, did you shit yourself when we crashed?"

"No, idiot."

"Are you sure? Did you check yourself?"

"Yes. Will you calm down? Your gonna make your head bleed more."

Levi undressed, quickly pulling down his Fruit-of-the-Loom white cotton briefs and mooning his friend in the process.

"Get that out of my face!"

"Would you rather I turn around?"

"Dude, I hate you right now," Eddie lamented.

Levi was as anxious to get his pants back on as Eddie was. A man's parts don't fare well when being exposed to a blizzard.

He folded his underwear to allow for a large section of white cotton to be used as a compress. Now he had to remove the metal and keep Eddie from squirming.

"Ready?" Levi asked.

"For what?"

"I'm gonna remove the metal and then cover your wound with this compress. Don't jerk around, or it'll make it worse."

"Jeez. Shouldn't we wait until we get to a hospital or somethin'?"

"Eddie, I think we're miles off course. Plus, it's been at least an hour and I haven't heard any type of aircraft in this mess. They're not looking for us. Heck, they may not even know we're missing."

Eddie sighed and hugged his broken arm a little tighter. "All right, make it quick."

Levi stood over his friend and found his scalp in the dark. He gently traced his fingers through Eddie's hair to make sure this was the only wound. Other than a knot that was growing near the crown of his scalp, the protruding metal was the only point of bleeding.

"Eddie, are you ready?"

"Yeah."

"On three, okay?"

"Do it," he replied, his body tensing for the pain that was likely to come with the extraction.

Levi found the best place to grip the metal and the proper angle to pull it out without creating further damage. Then he began the countdown, stretching the words out for effect.

"One. Two."

He quickly pulled the metal out and immediately pressed his cotton underwear over the wound. Changing the countdown to *two* was the oldest trick in the book, but effective.

Eddie grumbled, but he didn't shout in pain. "Asshole. I knew you were illiterate."

Levi smiled. His friend would survive the injuries if they could stop the bleeding and keep him from going into shock.

He heard the sound of feet shuffling through the snow, and he inwardly hoped that Karl had found their gear.

That was when the wolves began to howl.

CHAPTER 5

Riverfront Farms
Southeast Indiana

The Boone family came to America to escape religious persecution in England during the mid-seventeenth century. In the 1600s, the Society of Friends, or Quakers as they were better known, flocked to the New World, settling mostly in the colony of Pennsylvania founded by William Penn. Known for their inventive minds, they played a central role in forging the Industrial Revolution in America.

Squire Boone was the first of his family name to arrive, and he married fellow Quaker Sarah Morgan in 1720. They had eleven children, including Daniel and Squire Jr. Daniel and Squire Jr. became pioneers and trailblazers, establishing the Wilderness Road through Kentucky, Tennessee, and beyond to the Mississippi River. The family survived Indian attacks, became involved in local and state politics, and created homes for thousands of settlers in Kentucky and Indiana.

For two hundred fifty years, the Boone family lived off the land, and Squire was proud to have carried forward that legacy. Riverfront Farms paid homage both to his heritage as a Boone, and Sarah's as a Chapman, by combining a farming operation with extensive apple orchards.

Moreover, Squire and Sarah had assisted families in getting settled in Southeast Indiana along the Ohio River, where they worked at Riverfront Farms, worshiped in churches built by the Boone family in the past, and taught their kids in a historic schoolhouse built by Squire's grandfather.

Squire was an extremely proud man and was generous to a fault.

Pride made him stubborn, and his generosity pushed him to the brink of bankruptcy. Still, he slept at night without worry. He'd adopted a means by which he lived his life in the way of his pioneer ancestors— *do and deal*. Sometimes, he'd said to Sarah, you just have to do what's necessary and deal with the consequences of your actions later.

It was not an excessive-risk, living-on-the-edge approach to life. Rather, it was a take-things-as-they-come mindset drawing upon personal experiences and genetics to problem-solve.

So when Chapman rang the warning bells, Squire shrugged them off. He'd called Chapman's theories *wild-eyed*. As he'd told Sarah, the Boones and Chapmans had lived without power back in the day just fine. They could do it again.

Sarah had been adamant, chastising him for potentially putting the family at risk all because he was ignoring their son's warning. He didn't agree with her totally, but he certainly wasn't going to stand in her way if she wanted to pick up a few extra things at the grocery store.

Squire, who hated watching the news on television, nonetheless surfed through the channels to learn more about Chapman's pole-shift theory. Coincidentally, at least in Squire's mind, there was a massive power outage in parts of Europe, but none of the newspeople said anything about pole shifts or the sun's radiation.

Sarah rushed through the living room, carrying an armful of cookbooks. "Have you heard anything new?"

Squire watched her frantically scurry about as she gathered notepads, pens, and books to spread out on the dining table. "Sarah, I think you need to relax. There's nothing on the TV remotely related to some kind of pole reversal or magnetic field weakening."

"What about the power outage? And did it effect Paris where Chapman was?"

"They say the power did go out, but it was probably caused by the heat wave they're havin', and they hope to restore it shortly. I don't know about Paris, but I'll check. Say, why don't you take a break and sit with me? We'll watch together."

Squire was concerned about his wife's mental state. She was prone to bouts of anxiety and was secretly seeing a doctor about it. She tried to hide a medication called buspirone from him, but he'd stumbled across it in the bathroom vanity one day. When he saw the name of the doctor who'd prescribed it, he assumed she must be taking it to calm her nerves. At the moment, in her overexcited state, he doubted the medicine was working.

"Squire, there's no time for television. We've got to get ready like Chapman suggested. Now, I've already called Carly, and she's on her way over with the kids."

Squire muted the television and turned to his wife. The distraction caused him to miss the representative from NASA, who was responding to questions about a possible solar flare.

"Sarah, why do you have to drag Carly into this nonsense? Doesn't she have enough on her plate handling the kids while Levi is gone?"

Sarah stopped and took a deep breath before responding, "This is not nonsense. I feel it in my gut, Squire. The signs are all there."

"Honey, it's just, um, I think maybe your anxiety is getting the best of you. You know, causing you to overreact. Maybe you just need to relax a little."

Sarah gritted her teeth and stuck out her jaw. She removed her apron and slammed it on top of the dining table. "First off, anxiety is not a choice, so don't tell me to relax as if that will make it go away. Second, this is not about being anxious. It's about having a sense of urgency. You heard that in Chapman's voice, right? He's not making this up."

Before Squire could address her statement, the front door opened and their grandkids hopped through the foyer, each choosing a grandparent to hug first.

Carly Boone followed close behind. "Hey, guys. Everything okay? I mean, I could hear y'all from outside."

Carly had married Levi almost ten years ago, and they'd hoped to have a big family. However, complications during her second pregnancy with daughter Rachel forced them to accept the realization that any future pregnancy would put her in grave danger.

Life went on happily for the young couple. Seven-year-old Rachel was growing up to be as feisty as her mother and grandmother, while eight-year-old Jesse was a chip off the old block, as he developed into a *mini-me* of his father.

"Yes, honey, everything's fine. Squire's being stubborn."

Carly laughed and gave her father-in-law a hug together with a kiss on his razor-stubbled cheek. "Hi, Dad. I don't believe a word of it."

"Well, maybe she's just partly right," he mumbled, still salty over being dressed down by Sarah.

Carly, a petite brunette who could roar like a lion and fight like a tiger, was a member of the Boone family by marriage but fit in like she was blood. Her relationship with Squire and Sarah was better than the one she had with her own parents, who'd divorced and moved to different parts of the country soon after she married Levi. Sarah had taken Levi's bride under her wing, and the two Boone women had become best friends.

Sarah hugged Jesse and then reached for Carly's hand. "He's an awnry old cuss sometimes, but I still love him with all my heart. Now, come on. You and I have some work to do."

"Awesome!" exclaimed Jesse. "They'll work and we'll play, right, Grandpa?"

"You betcha, young man."

Sarah and Carly smiled as the two grandkids copped a squat on both sides of their beloved grandfather on the sofa. He switched the television monitor input to reveal the latest video game download for PlayStation. Each of the kids grabbed a controller and the games began.

"Carly, let's slip outside and talk on the front porch. I have a voicemail message from Chapman you need to hear."

CHAPTER 6

Riverfront Farms
Southeast Indiana

Carly listened closely to Chapman's voicemail message. She pursed her lips and shook her head from side to side as she took in every word. When the message ended, she walked a few paces away and looked out across the farm.

"That sounds like the old Chapman, you know, from the tornado-chasin' days."

"I agree," said Sarah as she motioned for Carly to take a seat on the white swing that was suspended from the wraparound-style porch. Sarah would never want Squire to catch her taking a moment to *relax*, as she knew he was right when he made the statement. She needed to calm her nerves in order to think rationally about the task at hand.

"Whadya think we should do?" asked Carly.

"Chapman said get ready, so I think we should. I've got a few ideas, but I need your help. Squire's attitude isn't very helpful, and you're very organized. We'll need that to get prepared for whatever might happen."

Carly thought for a moment. "When I was growing up, you know, my parents lived in Elwood just west of Muncie."

"Right. I remember."

"Well, as a kid, I went to school near an LDS community."

Sarah interrupted. "Church of Latter-day Saints. The Mormons."

"Yes. Anyway, they were all homeschooled and it was a good thing, too. The other kids around Elwood used to bully them and make fun of them. I hate to admit it, but I didn't defend them like I

28

should have. You know how it can be when a rabid mob decides to pick on someone. If you speak out against it, then they brutalize you, too. I stood silent when I should've stood up. That was wrong."

Sarah reached for her hand, puzzled why this conversation was necessary right now. "Honey, that was a long time ago."

"I know, um, sorry," said Carly. She took a deep breath and continued. "Anyway, the LDS families were known as preppers. Their religion taught them to be prepared for emergencies in every possible way. They lived within their means and stayed out of debt."

Sarah laughed nervously. "Well, that eliminates the Boone family right there."

Carly shrugged and continued. "Mostly, they believed in having a good supply of food, medicine, and essentials. They were also taught to be self-reliant. They honestly believed their community could live well and survive any scenario without the help of the government."

"What do you think? Based on what you saw, anyway."

"I absolutely believed they could. I became friends with a girl from their community. We'd hang out by Big Duck Creek and skip stones while we talked. She'd tell me about all the chores each family member had to do and why. Sarah, they were always growing food, canning, and stockpiling more for the future."

Sarah nodded and patted her daughter-in-law on the knee. "Honey, we may be a little late to this preparedness game, but there's no time like the present. We don't have the time, or the rainfall, to grow our own food and whatnot, but I have a credit card and a big SUV that can do some damage at the Corydon Walmart. Whadya say?"

Carly replied, "I'm in, but do you know what we need to buy?"

"Not completely, but sort of. Let's go inside and I'll tell you how I think we should approach it. Let's use your recollection of the LDS folks to help me create a big ol' shopping list."

The two women went inside, where Squire and the grandkids were having a great time playing video games. Sitting on the sofa, focused on the game, they were oblivious to Sarah and Carly's discussion at the dining table.

Nonetheless, the two women spoke in hushed tones so they didn't unduly concern the children or unintentionally solicit the input of Squire.

Carly began first. "Let's look at it from a common-sense approach. Water is very important, not only to keep us hydrated, but also to cook and bathe with."

"We have the wells," interjected Sarah. "Plus, they're solar powered because they're spread all over the farm and orchards."

Carly pointed out something Sarah hadn't considered. "Yes, but what do we need to keep the wells functioning while keeping the water stored and purified?"

Sarah started a list for a stop at Capitol Feed & Farm. She jotted down seeds, fertilizer, medications for the chickens, and well supplies.

Carly continued. "Water is most important, followed by food. We will can everything that we have growing in the fields now, including apples. I saw you write down seeds. I remember from talking with my friend back in Elwood that the LDS people used heirloom seeds."

"Of course, so do we, but I'll make a note."

"Then the next thing we should focus on are foods that don't require refrigeration or electricity to prepare. Let's make a Walmart list."

Sarah began to jot down a list of dry goods like beans, rice, and pastas. She expanded the Walmart list to include canned goods and jotted a note in parenthesis that read *check shelf life*.

Over the next thirty minutes, the two women huddled over the dining table and thought of every aspect of their daily lives, from drinks to food to medicines and hygiene.

Lastly, they discussed weapons. Sarah said, "Squire's father used to always say, if you can't defend it, it isn't yours. He believed in teaching his kids, and grandkids, how to properly handle weapons. They grew up learning which guns were best used for what situation, and then he trained them so they were always comfortable using them."

"Levi remembers all of those lessons, and he's passed them on to those two," added Carly, nodding at the superheroes playing the most recent version of *Spiderman*. "Heck, they even learn from those video games, eighty percent of which are ridiculously violent. I try to shield them from it, but Jesse seems to find a way to play them anyway."

Sarah grimaced and shook her head. She disapproved of the video games for her grandkids, although she'd enjoyed them when she was a kid. "Well, we're gonna need to stock up on ammunition, and it's gonna be hard with the new rules restricting how much we can buy. I have an idea that might work. Give me a minute while I run to the bedroom. Then we'll go."

While Carly recruited Jesse and Rachel to warm up barbecue leftovers for their grandfather, Sarah slipped off into the master bedroom to open the safe hidden away under a pile of shoeboxes in their closet. She retrieved a stack of hundred-dollar bills and shoved them into her purse.

"Money talks and ..." She smiled as her voice trailed off.

CHAPTER 7

The White House
Washington, DC

Grant Houston had enjoyed a meteoric rise to the presidency. A California native and fourth-generation San Franciscan, he'd been born into a family of attorneys on his father' side and scientists on his mother's. His childhood was difficult as he battled the emotional stress of his parents' divorce and the complications associated with a severe dyslexia condition.

After graduating from the University of California at Berkeley with a degree in political science, Houston chose to go into business with a family friend rather than pursue a law degree, as demanded by his father.

The liquor store he opened with his partners was certainly not what his mother had planned for his life either. She, however, supported him in his endeavors, and within a few years, the *mom-and-pop* enterprise became a chain of twenty-three liquor stores, restaurants, and boutique hotels.

Politics was never on Houston's radar although he was keenly interested in matters that related to the environment and animal rights. He grew up with an otter, an unusual pet by any measure, but one that taught him that all animals, not just the typical domesticated ones like cats and dogs, deserved love and protection.

His first foray into politics was in his late twenties when he worked on the San Francisco mayoral campaign of a local political heavyweight. He hosted private fundraisers at his restaurants and actively promoted his candidate's cause in social media. When the election campaign was successful, he was rewarded with a vacant seat on the city's Parking and Traffic Commission.

Certainly, an unknown quantity with a political start on the Parking and Traffic Commission wasn't necessarily considered presidential timber, but Grant Houston was a different breed. He was driven and saw an opportunity to use his handsome appearance and eloquence to promote causes that were dear to his heart.

Soon, he became the youngest member of San Francisco's board of supervisors, which then vaulted him into the local news spotlight. With the blessing of the mayor who started him in politics, he finished first in a nine-candidate field and became one of the youngest mayors in San Francisco history.

But Houston wasn't done yet. As mayor of San Francisco, he began to get noticed by national party leaders and was honored with a speaking slot at their national convention during a presidential election cycle. He wowed the crowd with his soaring rhetoric and was soon well known around the country.

Successful campaigns for both lieutenant governor and later governor of California set him up for national prominence. And now, barely nine months after he took the presidential oath of office, he was sitting in the Oval Office at the White House facing a monumental crisis the likes of which no president before him had faced.

"Mr. President, they're waiting for you in the Roosevelt Room," announced Angela O'Donnell, his longtime chief of staff from his days in California government. O'Donnell had been challenged often during her early days in Washington because she, like the president, was an outsider. To complicate their early days in office, the media alleged the two had a tryst during the presidential campaign just a year prior. The cloud of controversy had swirled over their heads for months, yet they'd effectively circled the wagons in an attempt to govern. Hugely protective, she'd become a tenacious gatekeeper preventing unfettered access to the president.

"Ang, you know I've been up to my eyeballs with this gun legislation on Capitol Hill. I haven't had time to look at this situation in detail. Seriously, is this much ado about nothing? I know they've experienced outages in Eastern Europe and into France from this solar storm, but it's happened before, and the grid was repaired soon thereafter."

O'Donnell shut the door leading into the secretary's office. She approached the president and gently ran her fingers down his chiseled jawline. "Don't let this distract you. Whatever it is, we'll deal with it together, just like always. Past presidents on both sides of the aisle have allowed their domestic agendas to get distracted by international events and media hype. Not yours. This is an opportunity to right the wrongs of the past and create a legacy to be proud of."

Houston bent over and kissed his chief of staff. The tryst reported by the media was much more than that. For all intents and purposes, the two were husband and wife except for one minor detail—his legal spouse was still living in California, pursuing her career as a Hollywood producer.

"I love you," he whispered in her ear, always concerned that his office was being surveilled by someone. "Let me hear them out, and if it appears it requires more of my attention, then I'll shift gears."

"Grant, it's more about what the media thinks. We'll make sure they believe you're on top of the situation, you know, *closely monitoring events*, etcetera. In reality, this could provide the perfect distraction for you to ram the gun bill through Congress."

"This is why I need you by my side twenty-four seven."

She reached behind him and pulled him closer to her body before passionately kissing him. She whispered in a sexy voice, "No, this is why you need me twenty-four seven."

A gentle tap at the door interrupted their moment, and the two quickly put some distance between them.

"Yes, come in," said the president.

"Sir, I'm sorry to interrupt," said his secretary. "Apparently, something is developing in relation to your briefing, and they have requested your presence immediately."

President Houston took a deep breath and exhaled. "Thank you." With his lover in tow, he marched toward the Roosevelt Room across the corridor from the Oval Office.

The meeting room was often referred to as the *Fish Room*, a moniker hearkening back to the day of President Franklin D. Roosevelt, who used it to display an aquarium and some mementos of his fishing expeditions. Later, President Richard Nixon named the conference space the Roosevelt Room to honor Theodore Roosevelt, who built the West Wing, and FDR, who expanded it.

Inside the windowless room, which served to hold daily briefings and multimedia presentations, every chair was full of representatives from NASA, NOAA, and the USGS—the triumvirate of the planet's earth sciences. As the president and O'Donnell entered the room, the attendees all stood out of respect, and President Houston casually waved to them to sit.

O'Donnell took the floor, as had come to be expected in the Houston administration. The president always allowed her to set the stage for any briefing. She dispensed with the pleasantries and got right to the point.

"It's oh-dark-thirty and we've delayed the president's daily briefing on matters of national security to meet with all of you. I trust what you have to say trumps his duty to protect our nation."

Several of the attendees gulped and appeared to sink into their chairs. Only one sat a little taller. It was Nola Taylor, a rising star within NASA's organizational structure. A former astronaut and climatologist with an expertise in analyzing climate patterns and the geological effects on the world's weather, Taylor was on the fast track to become the head of the agency's Space Technology Mission Directorate. In recent years, the directorate had shifted its focus from exploration to using space technology to study the climatic impact of humans on the planet.

She was calm and collected as she addressed the president. "Mr. President, Chief of Staff O'Donnell, my name is Nola Taylor, and I can assure you this is a matter that may be directly related to the national security of our country."

CHAPTER 8

The White House
Washington, DC

President Houston gave O'Donnell a look as he leaned forward. "I'm intrigued, Ms. Taylor. Go on."

"Sir, just a few hours ago, a geomagnetic storm, or geostorm for short, struck an area of Eastern Europe stretching from Ukraine, through the former Czech republics, and into France. This storm, one that had been predicted by our SWPC in Boulder, was recorded as a G1."

The president held his hands up and leaned back in his chair. "Ms. Taylor, please, provide this layman with a little more context here."

"Yes, sir, my apologies. The Space Weather Prediction Center, or SWPC, is the division of NOAA that continually monitors and forecasts space weather alerts and warnings for the U.S., and the world, really. Space weather consists of conditions on the sun that emit solar winds, plasma, and particles that could have a direct impact on our planet's spaceborne and ground-based electronics."

One of the attendees began to cough, so Taylor paused her response until the fit was over. The man was offered a glass of water, but the coughing continued until O'Donnell nodded to an aide to remove him from the Roosevelt Room.

"Please continue," said the president.

"Yes, sir. Space weather, in the form of coronal mass ejections and geomagnetic storms, can damage satellites, navigation, Earth-based telecommunications, and can cause damage to the electrical systems we rely upon for energy. Just as we need early warning systems in place to monitor hurricanes, tornadoes, and other naturally

36

occurring events on Earth, we need to monitor the Sun for possible solar flares that can damage our electronics."

"Ms. Taylor, I'm familiar with the impact solar flares can have on our power grid. In California, we established solar arrays that were independent of the PG&E grid after the sophisticated sniper attacks in 2013. These arrays harness the power of the sun while being hardened and independent of the main grid."

"Yes, sir, I'm familiar with your work on that project when you were lieutenant governor. However, what I'm talking about today could have a far-reaching impact on the entire country."

"A larger geostorm than what we customarily experience?" he asked.

"No, sir. There is no current threat of a Carrington-level solar storm event. The threat of an ordinary storm wreaking havoc has emerged." In 1859, a powerful geomagnetic storm struck the planet for two days. The coronal mass ejection spewed electrified gas and subatomic particles that breached Earth's atmosphere, causing telegraph wires to catch on fire and early electronics to malfunction.

"How?" asked O'Donnell.

"Geostorms occur when a coronal mass ejection or a high-speed solar wind stream engulfs the Earth, causing the magnetic field to become unsettled. We can predict when a CME will sweep over Earth's magnetic field, creating the conditions for a geostorm, but we cannot always be accurate as to the strength.

"Once the geostorm hit Eastern Europe overnight, the SWPC, as confirmed by NOAA, was able to identify it as a G1 storm. Now, G1 storms occur approximately seventeen hundred times every eleven years, which is the typical length of a solar cycle. A G1 storm is manageable, meaning that it can cause weak power grid fluctuations, minor satellite malfunctions, and can confuse migratory animals in the northernmost regions of the planet."

The president interrupted her. "And aurora."

"Yes, sir. Periods of active auroras are most vibrant across the northern territories of Canada and can also be seen at middle latitudes depending on atmospheric conditions."

The president glanced down at his watch. O'Donnell picked up on the gesture and pressed Taylor to move it along. "How does all of this relate to our national security? I mean, I recall a geostorm knocked the power out in Quebec many years ago, but it was restored within a few weeks."

"Yes, I'm glad you brought up the Quebec event. That geostorm was caused by a massive X15 solar flare, resulting in a far greater impact on the province's electric grid. Some studies indicate that geostorm was a level G3. That is many times greater than the G1 experienced in Europe."

O'Donnell was growing impatient. "Okay, last night's solar storm was an irregularity. Again, it begs the question, why does this require the president's immediate attention?"

Taylor looked around the room, hoping to gather strength from her fellow scientists. She found the words and was blunt in her delivery.

"Because geologic conditions exist for it to happen again, and very soon."

The president motioned for an aide to bring him a bottled water. He pulled his Montblanc pen out of his shirt pocket and laid it on the conference table. In an odd act of irony, he mindlessly twirled the pen on the polished tabletop, mimicking a compass spinning out of control.

"May I?" A man seated across from Taylor asked to address the president. With the wave of a hand, he was encouraged to continue by the president.

"Mr. President, Ms. O'Donnell, my name is Professor Gerald Lansing with the USGS. If I may, let me give you the bottom line, and then I'll provide you an explanation."

"Please do," encouraged an impatient President Houston.

"The Earth's magnetic field has weakened considerably. This appears to be happening because the planet is experiencing what is known as a superfast magnetic reversal."

The president grasped the pen to stop it from spinning. The professor had his full attention. He began to place the pen back in his shirt pocket, but the professor boldly stopped him.

"Actually, Mr. President, may we use your pen to illustrate my point?"

The president shrugged and then asked, "Sure, but don't you have your own pen?"

The professor boldly smiled. "I do, but yours is nicer. And because it is a Montblanc, it is apropos. Let me explain."

The president laughed, as did others in the room, taking the edge off the tense moment. The president slid the pen across the table, and Professor Lansing began.

"We have evidence that a pole shift is in progress and is occurring much faster than the geologic record has shown in the past." He took the pen and pointed it toward the president. "Sir, magnetic north and true north, as we know it, are not the same. Magnetic north will wander based upon what's happening within the Earth's core.

"Deep beneath the planet's surface, liquid iron is sloshing around at its core, causing the North Pole to move away from Canada and towards Siberia."

As the professor spoke, he wiggled the Montblanc slightly to indicate a compass needle fluctuating.

"In recent years, this movement has significantly altered where the magnetic north pole is located, and has caused global geomagnetism experts to undergo an urgent update of the World Magnetic Model. Ordinarily, this is done every five to ten years, but because of the rapid movement, we are monitoring it daily now."

"So you're saying the North Pole is in Siberia?" asked the president.

"No, sir. Now it is closer to Kazakhstan and is approaching the Caspian Sea just east of Georgia."

"The fast motion of the north magnetic pole is most likely linked to a high-speed jet of liquid iron beneath Canada. In fact, and please excuse the hypothetical because we are in the early stages of studying this phenomenon, the location of the north magnetic pole appears to be governed by two large-scale patches of the magnetic field. One is located beneath Northern Canada, and the other is in Kazakhstan."

The president's demeanor changed considerably. Suddenly, legislative battles in Congress seemed petty by comparison. "Are you saying we are experiencing a change to the Earth that may result in two north poles?"

"Yes, Mr. President, and possibly more. For now, based upon our data, there are two distinct magnetic north poles. One is based in Canada, the other in Kazakhstan, but the patch of liquid iron beneath Eastern Europe is winning."

The professor slid the pen back to the president, who rolled it through his fingers. "You said this has some relation to Montblanc. What did you mean by that?"

"Sir, for decades, the rising global temperatures was causing the massive Mont Blanc glacier in Northern Italy on the border of France to melt. This five-hundred-square-mile mountain of ice was losing large chunks of ice and causing flooding throughout Southern France and Switzerland."

"Okay?" the president asked, seemingly unsure of the relationship between the melt-off and the pole shift.

"Sir, Mont Blanc is experiencing a rapid refreeze. We have reports that the mountain is experiencing high-speed, frigid upper-level winds coming from the eastern parts of Europe, resulting in subzero temperatures. These winds bear all the similarities to an Alberta clipper, the fast-moving low-pressure systems that come from Canada and invade the United States from time to time. Only, the winds experienced across Northern Italy are coming from the east.

"Further, the Caspian Sea, which is near the current magnetic north that is moving across Kazakhstan, is beginning to freeze over in its shallowest regions."

O'Donnell interrupted the professor. "The Caspian's strategic importance lies in its energy resources. It is oil and natural gas rich and has been tapped by Europe as part of the Trans-Caspian Pipeline to avoid dependence on Russian or Iranian energy. A disruption in the flow of natural gas, for example, would devastate the European economy."

Nola Taylor spoke up. "Ms. O'Donnell, this brings us full circle to the realistic threat our nation, and the world, faces. With the weakened magnetic field, we are more susceptible to these geomagnetic storms. Every week, a G1 storm, like the one that hit Europe, passes over our planet. It's just a matter of time before the United States receives a direct hit of a geostorm and we suffer the same fate as Eastern Europe."

The president raised his hand to stop the conversation. "If I understand you both, not only is this pole shift going to generate significant changes in our weather patterns, but the weakened magnetic field could cause our power grid to collapse due to a geostorm?"

"Yes, sir," Taylor and Lansing replied in unison.

CHAPTER 9

The White House
Washington, DC

Chief of Staff Angela O'Donnell had been listening to the discussion while checking messages on her smart phone. World leaders were asking to speak with the president as the situation in Europe was unfolding. Words like *permanent, long-lasting, catastrophic,* and *deadly* were used by her counterparts in Europe. She scowled as she read message after message, as the realization came over her that the president was about to be distracted, but rightfully so.

The president continued his inquiry. "Okay, I understand this is a rapidly developing situation, although for the life of me I don't understand how it could go undetected for however long it took for the north pole, or poles, I guess, to begin moving across Russia. With that given, what are we facing here?"

Taylor responded, "A geostorm of the level that hit Eastern Europe could come our way within days or weeks, depending upon the Sun's activity. The Solar and Heliospheric Observatory, SOHO, is a spacecraft designed to study the internal structure of the sun and its extensive outer atmosphere.

"SOHO takes snapshots of activity on the Sun's surface, such as coronal holes, the low-density regions of the Sun's atmosphere that are the source of the high-speed winds of solar particles emitted into space. As these coronal holes release this solar matter, soaring up and away from the Sun's surface, conditions are created for massive solar flares.

"At the moment, we are monitoring one such active region, AR4111. Seventy-two hours ago, this active region released a series of

42

non-Earth-directed X-flares, with the most powerful being an X1.4. Now, in the scheme of things, this is a relatively benign solar flare and not likely to cause damage to our planet's critical infrastructure.

"However, just over thirty-six hours ago, a more powerful X2.2-class solar flare was emitted. The SOHO data revealed this to be the brightest, most powerful of the year. Although it was much weaker than the X-flare that took down the Quebec power grid in eighty-nine, it still managed to cause extensive damage in Eastern Europe when it hit the Earth's atmosphere last night."

"Do these coronal holes close up?" asked the president.

"Yes, sir, they do," replied Taylor. "We've all studied the reports from the Joint ALMA Observatory in Chile. ALMA is the world's largest radio telescope array in the world. The images and recorded data are conclusive. As the sun's surface rotated out of view, it was expanding, not contracting. That means as the sun rotates on its axis over the next twenty-seven days, this active region could become larger. Or, as these things are somewhat unpredictable, it could disappear altogether."

"That's good," remarked O'Donnell, seeking a glimmer of hope that this bad news might just disappear from their to-do list.

"True," continued Taylor. "But there are more active regions coming into view in the coming days, any of which could yield the same potentially devastating result as the one that occurred last night in Europe."

O'Donnell snarled, "Well, why don't you let us know when a *real* threat exists?"

"We are," replied Taylor. "In the same hemisphere as AR4111, another very large active region was noted twenty-six days ago. It too, was expanding and was responsible for several major X-flares. Fortunately, none of those were Earth-directed, meaning we dodged a bullet. We may not necessarily be as lucky next time."

"When will you know if we are facing a threat?" asked the president.

Taylor pulled out her iPhone and launched her SSEC – GOES app developed by the University of Wisconsin, which now included

43

solar activity. She studied the various images produced by GOES, the geostationary operational environmental satellite system operated by NOAA. She showed the images to the president and his chief of staff.

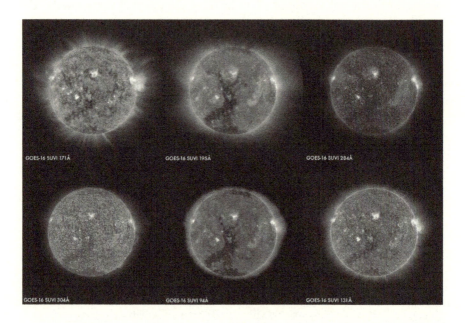

"The infrared technology provides us six different views of the sun at this precise moment. At the top left, you can see the sun's ejection activity. As you can tell, it's quite active. We'll be monitoring these images as the active region rotates back into view."

"When will that be?" asked O'Donnell.

"Tonight, late evening," replied a NOAA representative who hadn't spoken yet.

"And when will we learn if there is the potential for a geostorm?"

"In twenty-four to thirty-six hours," the NOAA representative replied again before adding, "Then we'll watch for the next one, and the one after that. Mr. President, we'll have the potential for a geostorm every few days. There will be no rest."

CHAPTER 10

Aboard American Airlines Flight
Atlantic Ocean

The massive American Airlines Boeing 777 steadily rose to its cruising altitude of forty-one thousand feet, soaring through the sky at five hundred seventy miles per hour. Chapman Boone allowed the turbulence to toss his head back and forth against the spacious seats he and Dr. Isabella Dubois shared in business class. The combination of three bourbons and Isabella's soothing words helped him put the catastrophe that would soon be unfolding across France and Eastern Europe behind him. His entire focus was now protecting this beautiful new woman in his life and getting home to his family.

He felt no regret for his inability to convince his executive producers at The Weather Channel to act on his warnings. Their reaction was almost identical to that of Isabella's coworkers at the research institute in Paris—ambivalence and doubt.

He chuckled to himself as he considered the old proverb that dated back to the twelfth century. You can lead a horse to water, but you can't make it drink. It's one of the English language's oldest proverbs, first found in the *Old English Homilies* written in 1175. Like so many idioms adopted by cultures around the world, the descriptive phrase applied to many situations, including this one.

That said, Chapman was silently cursing himself for not thinking outside the box. All the signs were there. Tropical storm systems were on the move as hurricanes and typhoons migrated away from the equatorial regions and toward the North and South poles. Over the past forty years, the total number of storms had remained constant although what had increased was the number of successful storm births and their subsequent intensity.

It was natural for the media and climate scientists to define a storm by the amount of damage it had caused—monetarily and in human loss. Chapman looked beyond the hype and focused on the data. A major hurricane that reached the other upper levels of a Category 5 storm was disregarded by many as uneventful if it didn't make landfall. The fact that the storm originated in an unusual location and followed a track that was out of the ordinary was not widely reported.

Chapman spent some time studying the formation and build of Atlantic hurricanes, but he was more interested in the expansion of the Pacific hurricane season. In the past decade, more tropical cyclones were forming off the Baja Peninsula and making their way into the Pacific Ocean. Historically, these storms would eventually lose their intensity because they feed on warm seawater over eighty degrees. The ocean water temperatures up the coast of California toward Washington were generally under seventy-five degrees.

As those readings began to rapidly rise in the last five years, climate-change alarmists blamed greenhouse gases despite the fact that carbon emissions had been steadily decreasing for decades. Nobody, including Chapman, bothered to look for alternative theories for the rapid change. Well, most people, anyway. There were a few, like Dr. Harry Pruitt in Greenland, who suspected a shift of the poles might be responsible. Even now, Chapman wondered if the geostorm that struck Eastern Europe really opened any minds to the pole-shift theory.

Be that as it may, Chapman, while still intrigued by the dramatic changes the planet was undergoing, needed to focus on survival. It was easy to get comfortable in the spacious business-class seats of the American Airlines jet and forget about these things that weighed heavily on his mind. However, geomagnetic storms, many much stronger than what just hit Europe, occur all the time.

The world was playing a dangerous game of Russian roulette with the Sun, and the Earth's star was holding all the firepower.

*Ladies and gentlemen, the captain has turned off the fasten seat belt signs, indicating we've reached our cruising altitude. You may now move about the cabin, and we will begin cabin service shortly. I regret to inform you that our in-flight internet connection will not be available for the duration of this flight, but we will be showing a movie momentarily. Our feature tonight is an American political thriller—*The Boston Brahmin, *featuring Ryan Reynolds and Ben Affleck.*

"No internet," Isabella whispered into his ear. "Do you think it's the storm?"

"Hmm?" Chapman was still deep in thought. "Um, maybe. Airplanes use satellite-powered Wi-Fi through an antenna mounted on top of the plane. When over the water, they connect to satellites."

"Maybe the satellites have been knocked out?" said Isabella.

"Or the airline has been informed of what really happened back there, and they're initiating a communications blackout until they figure out what to do with us."

"Chapman, what do you mean? Do you think the power is off in America, too?"

"No, I don't think so," he replied as he sat a little taller in his seat. He reached for her hand and gave it a gentle squeeze in an attempt to reassure her. And himself, too. "My guess is that American Airlines doesn't want over two hundred panicked passengers and crew. I imagine the news will be exploding with this story over the next several hours."

"You were deep in thought. Are you okay?"

Chapman managed a smile and nodded. "I'm punishing myself for not seeing the signs, or at least speaking out about the abnormal weather I observed."

"Weather signs?"

"Yes, because that's what I know. I was thinking about the number of hurricanes that were forming in the Pacific Ocean. The weather patterns in the western United States have changed considerably because the El Niño effect has returned."

El Niño and La Niña were opposite phases of temperature fluctuations between the ocean and surrounding atmosphere in the east-central Pacific Ocean. A decade prior, La Niña, the cold phase, had overtaken the Pacific, having large-scale impacts on global weather. El Niño, Spanish for *The Little Boy* or *Christ Child*, was originally recognized by fishermen off the coast of South America in the seventeenth century with the onset of unusually warm waters.

Chapman continued. "The phases of El Niño and La Niña swap places every nine to twelve months. That changed a few years ago when the much warmer waters of El Niño became the norm. Looking back on it now, I should've questioned why the pattern didn't follow its customary nine-to-twelve-month cycle. It all makes sense. The pole shift was changing the dynamic of the planet and her weather."

Isabella gently kissed Chapman on the cheek as the movie began. They both watched the opening scene.

"I have been there," Isabella began, interrupting the silence between them. "That is in Ukraine near Mariupol. I attended a conference there years ago."

Chapman nodded and tilted his head back in attempt to process all the events.

Isabella leaned over and whispered in his ear, "You should not bear this burden alone, *mon amour*. I am guilty as well."

CHAPTER 11

Aboard American Airlines Flight
Atlantic Ocean

"My mind has been wandering from one scenario to another," began Isabella. "I have wondered what our lives will be like under the constant threat of the Sun. There is no period in history to study. This has never happened to modern humanity."

Chapman was philosophical. "Our star gives us life and it can take it away."

"I have considered the psychological aspects of a world without power. How will civilization react to a world without lights? Sadly, it is electricity that dictates our daily activities. It defines us as being superior to all other forms of life on Earth in history."

Chapman shook his head. "We will lose control figuratively and emotionally. Without electricity, supply chains will come to a halt. Food will not be delivered, and medical care will suffer. Police and fire departments will be overwhelmed as the strong assert their will over the weak."

"People do not always play nice together," said Isabella.

"No, they don't. Our fellow man may be the least of our concerns. As the magnetic field weakens, the atmosphere that protects us from harmful rays will dissipate. We will be susceptible to acute radiation sickness similar to the way people die when exposed to a nuclear bomb. It will overwhelm the body's ability to fight the high radiation levels."

"We can go underground," offered Isabella.

"Yes, maybe. But for how long? And how do we eat? We won't be able to grow food. We may have to walk around the planet holding a

Geiger counter to determine if it's safe. We can also consider avoiding high-risk factors such as high altitudes, the lower latitudes, wherever they may end up being, and reflective geographical attributes like sand, water, and snow."

Isabella tried to offer words of encouragement. "I will do that to survive. We will buy lots of sunscreen and long-sleeve clothing to avoid ultraviolet rays."

Chapman grimaced. "There is a difference between living and surviving. The question is what kind of sacrifices is mankind willing to make to survive? It will be a world without entertainment or luxuries. There will be no modern conveniences that people rely upon. It will be gritty, difficult, and dangerous."

The conversation between the two began to place them in a dour mood. Chapman, who wasn't a heavy drinker, nonetheless decided another cocktail was in order. It just seemed liked a good time to catch a buzz.

He glanced toward the flight attendants, who were gathered in the galley. They were giggling as they whispered to one another and looking in his direction. Isabella noticed, too.

"It appears you have a fan club," she said as she leaned closer toward the window to allow some space between them. "Those women are smitten with you, *oui*?"

"No," Chapman lied. He tried to downplay the attention that he was accustomed to in public. "Well, maybe. I don't know. I get that a lot."

"You do, do you?" asked Isabella, a hint of jealousy in her voice.

Chapman was attempting to avoid eye contact with the flight attendants and Isabella. He nervously fiddled with his fingers as if he were trying to map his fingerprints for future reference.

He shrugged in response to her question, squirming in his seat at the awkward situation. Finally, Isabella moved closer to him and whispered something to him in French.

He smiled and nodded, pretending to have some inkling of what she just said to him. He didn't, but he loved to hear her voice, so he gave the impression he understood. Then he couldn't help himself.

Turning to her, he asked, "That sounded very sexy. What did you say?"

Isabella leaned over and whispered into his ear as she squeezed his thigh. "I said, if you ever think about touching another woman, I will castrate you with a butter knife." She gently kissed his cheek, but her piercing eyes proved she was sincere.

Chapman immediately clamped his knees together and gulped.

CHAPTER 12

Riverfront Farms
Southeast Indiana

Sarah drove, taking the country back roads that meandered northward, generally following the serpentine path of Indian Creek, which bisected their farm and led to Corydon. The fifteen-mile drive to Walmart took about twenty-five minutes through the farmland of Southeast Indiana. During the ride, Carly listened to Chapman's message two more times, pausing it occasionally to research some of the terminology he'd used on Google.

"Um, Mom, some of what Chapman is saying is considered, you know, *out there*. Conspiracy theory stuff."

Sarah continued to drive toward Corydon, undeterred. "Okay, by conspiracy theory, I take it you mean tinfoil-hat thinking?"

"Yeah, actually. The media and scientists say pole shifts have occurred since the beginning of time, and they don't necessarily cause the end of the world."

"Okay, when was the last time it happened?" asked Sarah.

"Three-quarters of a million years ago," replied Carly. "That said, this one article says the planet is overdue for another one, and even another website claims we might be starting one now."

Sarah looked over at Carly. "That doesn't sound like conspiracy theory to me."

"Well, they say the compass needles will change, but that's about it."

"Chapman mentioned the compass needle, too. But he went on to say that the planet's protection will be weak, making us vulnerable to the sun's rays."

Carly nodded as she continued to navigate to different websites on her cell phone.

Sarah continued. "Here's the thing. The last time this happened, man didn't exist. Things are much different now. Heck, look at what you're doing. When I was growing up, there was no such thing as a cell phone, much less the internet or the ability to connect to it out here in the middle of nowhere. The pole shift may not have impacted the doggone dinosaurs, but it may have a huge effect on us, like Chapman said."

"Yeah, you're right. I guess it's like anything else. Until you see it happen with your own two eyes, there will always be a bit of doubt as to whether it's real."

Sarah laughed. "Listen, Squire is the same way except he's too stubborn to open his mind to the possibility. I believe the threat is real because I trust Chapman's judgment. He wouldn't have been frantic like that if he wasn't genuinely concerned. Squire prefers to stick his head in the sand, and Levi is off in Canada chasin' down Bullwinkle. It's up to us Boone women to take care of them."

"We all have our roles to play, right?" added Carly rhetorically.

"That's right," replied Sarah. She turned up State Road 135 toward Corydon. "Do you remember the talk we had about having a husband before you married Levi?"

"Yes, and I really appreciated it. My mother wasn't interested in giving me any advice, not that I would take it from her anyway. My parents hated each other and stayed in a loveless marriage until I graduated high school. They shoved me out the door to find my own way, and they promptly got divorced and flew the coop."

Sarah smiled and squeezed Carly's hand which rested on the console. "I said the key to making your marriage a happy one was learning how to take proper care of your husband even if he doesn't think you need to."

"You get what you give, right?"

Sarah nodded. "Exactly. When I was unreasonable and insufferable, I'd get the same back from him. Now, it wasn't right away, of course, but in due time any man can only take so much, and then they let us have it."

The women laughed.

"Levi is more patient with me than I am with him," said Carly.

"That's because he loves you, and he hates to see you unhappy. It's ingrained in most men's genetics. Do you remember what I said?"

Carly laughed. "You bet. You said men are putty in the hands of a woman they love."

"That's the truth. Now, there are times that men try to blow off their responsibilities of taking care of us. If their minds are made up that some task is unnecessary or a certain chore can wait, if you bug them about it, they bow up because they think you're nagging. When really you're just trying to be a loving wife by keeping your home neat, organized, and operating smoothly."

"Yup. I did exactly what you told me to do—train him like a puppy."

The two women began laughing as they entered the small town.

"Sit. Good boy." Sarah could hardly say the words through her laughter. "Here's a cookie."

"Or something else," added Carly as tears began to stream down her face.

"You betcha. That's the ultimate treat, missy, and you should wield it like a mighty sword!"

"I save it for only the best behavior!"

The two were in a jovial mood as they pulled into Capitol Feed & Farm. After they exited the truck, Sarah got to the point.

"We have something going for us that most men don't—intuition. They're logical to a fault. We have the ability to draw on past experiences, our genetic makeup, and events around us to analyze and process things. Now is one of those occasions in which our gut instincts tell us to get ready. And despite Squire's grumblings, that's exactly what we're gonna do."

CHAPTER 13

Walmart
Corydon, Indiana

After a quick stop at the feed store, they arrived at Walmart, which was no busier than normal for this time of day. The two women each grabbed a cart, and Sarah led the way into the produce section. Sarah explained what she was thinking in buying produce in addition to harvesting their own.

"At this point, we only have enough produce on the farm for a few months if you include feeding Kristi, Chapman, and his new friend."

"He's got a girlfriend?" asked Carly.

"Maybe, or something else. I don't know. We'll have to wait and see. Anyway, buying produce at retail prices and then spending the money on canning supplies, plus our time, seems like a waste. However, if Chapman is correct, we have to move quickly and gather as much extra food to store as we can. So I wanna focus on the produce that helps us the most."

"Like what?"

"I thought about the fruits and vegetables used in the majority of the dishes I cook, including sauces, casseroles, and stews. For example, let's start with the vine-ripened tomatoes. Then we'll make our way to the string beans and cukes."

Sarah was reaching for a vine full of tomatoes when a woman cackled behind her. She recognized the voice immediately and rolled her eyes.

"Well, imagine that! If it isn't the Boone women gracing us with their presence. What's wrong, life down on the farm not going so well? Is your crop so bad you gotta come buy tomatoes like us city folk?"

Sarah sighed and turned to face the mouthy interloper. "Hello, Wanda," greeted Sarah because she had to, not because she wanted to. Wanda Clark was the rotund, motormouthed wife of Bully Billy Clark, the Boones' banker and nemesis.

"Sarah, Carly, I never thought I'd see the day when you two would have to resort to shopping in the Walmart produce department. I sure hope that farm is producing lots and lots of vegetables and apples and such. Are things not going well?" Sarcasm oozed with every word.

"Things are just fine, Wanda," replied Sarah dryly. She scowled and turned back to the tomatoes, but the banker's wife wasn't done yet.

Like all bullies, Wanda sensed weakness on the part of Sarah, who was keenly aware of the large note that was owed by Riverfront Farms to her husband's bank. Wanda continued to make passive-aggressive remarks and poignant questions. Sarah tried to hang in there, but was becoming visibly upset at the interrogation.

Wanda went for the jugular, much like her husband had done to Levi in the feed store a couple of weeks ago. "I sure hope you people are taking care of my apples, too. Billy says that due date is looming large on the calendar, and I'm curious to see if you can work some kind of miracle to pay it."

Carly, who was standing to the side next to a large display of apples, began dropping them one by one into a grocery basket—Wanda's. With a death stare aimed at Wanda, Carly continued to load apples into the woman's shopping cart.

Wanda, who was preoccupied tormenting Sarah, didn't notice at first. Until, that is, Carly dropped several at once on top of a dozen eggs on the bottom of the cart. Wanda finally released her jaws from Sarah's throat and snapped her head at Carly, who continued dropping apples into her cart.

"Hey! What the hell do you think you're doin'?" Wanda snarled.

Carly smiled and allowed several more apples to roll out of her hands so that now over two dozen were plunked on top of Wanda's other groceries. She sneered at the rude woman and grabbed another couple of handfuls.

"Keep talkin', bitch, and I'll fill the whole dang thing up with apples, and then—" Carly paused and inched closer to Wanda, whose eyes grew wide "—I'll stuff one in that big, fat mouth of yours like a hog on a spit."

Wanda, although frightened, stood her ground. "You can't talk to me like that."

Carly's eyebrows rose and she set her jaw. She dropped all of the apples in Wanda's cart but one—a big, juicy Red Delicious—and held it at chin level to the heavyset redhead.

"Not another word," she growled.

Sarah snickered as she imagined her daughter-in-law stuffing the Red Delicious into the woman's big mouth. Apparently, several bystanders, who'd gathered around to watch the scrap unfold, thought Carly's threat was funny too.

Wanda left in a huff, abandoning her cart and marching straight for the exit doors.

Carly turned to Sarah, and the Boones exchanged high fives. This battle was won by the good guys. But the war would prove to be a long one.

CHAPTER 14

Corydon, Indiana

Sarah and Carly were in an upbeat mood as they traversed the aisles of Walmart, loading up on supplies to help them survive the gathering storm. Their primary focus was on food that could be stored in the short to medium term—canned goods, boxed foods like cereals, rice, and pasta, and then bulk items that could be prepared over an open fire. They also stocked up on spices and condiments to give the potentially mundane meals a little flavor. Soon, two baskets became four.

Their last stop at Walmart was in the sporting goods section, where they purchased their maximum allotment of ammunition. Since 2020, Walmart had stopped selling handgun ammunition, opting to cater to hunters instead. Each customer was limited to purchasing one hundred rounds of rifle ammunition per day.

The entire family enjoyed hunting deer and feral hogs, so they bought an equal amount of ammunition for each of their rifles. Levi had taken his two best rifles with him to Canada, along with the maximum amount of ammunition that the FAA allowed to be checked with his luggage. He was the Boone family's best hunter, so they made sure he had the most ammo.

The Boone women were viewed with suspicion as they checked out. People are naturally curious, and those stuck in the checkout aisle behind them were annoyed by the wait. However, Carly and Sarah ignored the subtle pressure coming from the strangers and made their way through the checkout.

Each basket was paid for using a different bank debit card, and was accompanied by obtaining a hundred dollars cash back from the register. They also stopped by the ATM located near the customer service center on the way out. They withdrew the maximum amount their cards were allowed. Sarah recalled the stories told by Squire's father of cash shortages during the near-collapse of the American banking system in 2008. She was determined to withdraw as much cash out of the family's accounts as she could before the catastrophe Chapman predicted came to pass.

The last stop was Gun World, which was located on the highway leading back to Riverfront Farms.

"Mom, aren't we gonna run into the same problem with limits here?" asked Carly as Sarah caught a glimpse of the clock on the dashboard.

"I've known Allen for twenty years," replied Sarah. "He's a straight shooter, pardon the pun, and a good guy. He also owes me and Squire a few favors. His kid had a run-in with the sheriff's office over hunting without a license. Squire lied and said Allen's son was on our land even though he'd actually encroached onto the state park up by Indian Creek."

"I remember that," said Carly. "The Clarks and the Edmunds have always had issues with each other. Do you remember when Sheriff Clark tried to set up a sting operation and sent that twenty-year-old with the fake ID to buy handgun ammo?"

"Yeah, I sure do. That was six months after we helped Allen's son. It's been an ongoing feud."

They pulled up to the front door of Gun World, where the owner was in the process of locking up for the night. He immediately recognized Sarah's truck and waved them in.

"Hey, Sarah! It's kinda late for y'all, isn't it?"

"It is, Allen, but we've got a lot going on. Listen, you remember Carly, Levi's wife, right?"

The two exchanged pleasantries, and Allen quickly locked the door behind them because he was closed for the day.

Allen shook Carly's hand. "Of course. How's that boy gettin' along up in the frozen tundra? Has he bagged himself a moose yet?"

Carly laughed. "I wouldn't know. He's off with his *boys*," she began sarcastically. "Heck, they're probably laid up in the hunting camp, playing poker and throwing back shots of Knob Creek."

"I sure hope so," said Allen. "I was just watching the news, and I guess a freak blizzard hit that neck of the woods today. The weather people said it was unheard of for this time of year."

"Great," Carly groaned. "When he calls, he'll be begging me to let him stay an extra week because of the weather."

Allen walked behind his sales counter and rapped his knuckles on the counter like a bartender. "Well, what'll it be this evening, ladies? I've got a special on the latest TriStar Viper semiautomatic twelve gauge. Also, if you want something a little more excitin', I've got our Smith & Wesson AR-10 chambered in .308 Winchester on sale for thirteen hundred dollars. It includes a soft-side case and two standard magazines. It's the same round Levi uses in his rifles, if I recall."

Sarah wasn't in the market for weapons, but then she thought for a moment. It made sense to have the bulk of their rifles using the same type of ammunition so their stock could be shared. She was unfamiliar with an AR-10 rifle other than the fact it was semiautomatic, which might come in handy if they were to run into difficulty someday.

"Squire's gonna flip his lid, but do you have two of those Smith & Wesson rifles? One for me and one for Carly?"

"I do, actually. I can give you another ten percent off if you buy them both."

He reached under the counter and pulled out two clipboards with the requisite federal paperwork. While the two of them filled out their forms, Sarah nonchalantly added, "And we'll need five hundred rounds of ammo for each. Plus, we each need five hundred shells of double-ought buck and another five hundred rounds each for our two Remington 700s. They use two-two-three."

Allen hesitated. "Um, Sarah, you know I can't sell more than a hundred rounds per person per day."

Sarah stopped and reached into her handbag to recover a stack of hundred-dollar bills wrapped in a rubber band. She hated using that much cash when she really needed to hold on to it, but Allen would never fulfill her request with a paper trail like a credit card receipt.

"I also know that you keep your own stash back in the safe for your best customers."

Allen appeared nervous and looked past the Boones toward the front door. He rushed around the counter and peered through the blinds before closing them. He turned to address Sarah, who stood leaning against the counter, locking her eyes on his.

"Sarah, you're asking me to sell you three thousand rounds of ammo. I'm not even gonna try to explain what that could do to my business, but just as important, I have to know what's goin' on." He hesitated before adding, "And, Sarah, our families go way back, so please don't blow smoke up my ass, pardon my French."

Sarah stood firm under the pressure. She knew she was asking a lot, but her gut told her it was necessary to call in this favor. Allen, by referencing the fact that their families had a history, understood he owed the Boones. He was just concerned.

"Allen, I've come to see you tonight for a couple of reasons. First, Riverfront Farms needs to restock its ammunition. Just the other day Carly was attacked by a wild pig. We've had other instances of coyotes coming down out of the state lands to harass our livestock. Second, we've never asked you for a favor, and now I am. We'll be square after this."

Allen, who was also the Boones' nearby neighbor up Indian Creek, didn't want to say no. "Well, I get it, so I'm gonna help you out. I'm glad you came in late when the store was empty."

He turned and went to the back office. He returned with a Rubbermaid push cart containing the three thousand rounds of ammunition.

"Looks heavy," commented Carly.

"It is and bulky, too. I'm gonna have to figure out how to get it to your truck without puttin' on a show for one of Clark's deputies drivin' by."

Edmunds sighed and began to process their firearms application. While he did, Carly pulled Sarah aside and pretended to show her the new shotguns hanging on the wall.

"Mom, he's the only gun dealer in town besides Walmart and the feed store, and they don't carry much. Maybe we should give him a heads-up?"

"Tell him about Chapman's warning?"

"Yeah. If things get awful, his inventory will be far more useful to those of us who live in the south end of the county than a few extra dollars in his pocket, don't you think?"

Sarah leaned back and studied her daughter-in-law. "What's going on in that head of yours?"

Carly took a deep breath and exhaled. "Maybe I watch too much television, or it could've been that run-in with Wanda earlier. I don't know which, but I do know that some people really suck. Look at how people treat one another sometimes. Imagine how desperate they'll be if the power goes out and Walmart trucks stop delivering food and a man's kids are starving to death. Where do you think they'll come lookin' for food?"

"The farms," Sarah quickly replied.

"Exactly, they're gonna come for our food that we need to feed our family and the people who work for us. At first, we might politely give 'em a little, or even turn 'em away. But they'll keep comin' back out of desperation. When we say no, they'll get angry, and things could escalate. Do you know what I mean?"

Sarah rolled her eyes and emitted a long, deep breath. "You're right. We're gonna need allies and who better than the guy with the most guns."

"Whadya gonna do?" asked Carly.

"It's time to recruit some like-minded thinkers, starting with Allen."

CHAPTER 15

Northwest Ontario
Canada

Wolves howl for a variety of reasons. Members of the pack will chorus howl, a ritual used to defend their territory and rally the pack together. It will begin with a single howl, which is relatively simple in structure. After a second or two, a second wolf joins, followed by one or two more until the rest of the pack follows en masse.

The gradually accelerating start to the chorus howl makes it possible to pick out the first three or four members of the pack, the leaders, but after that, there will be too many to count. Once the entire pack is howling, the sound becomes more modulated, changing pitch rapidly in what the human ear might assume to be chaotic disorder. That would be an incorrect assumption, as the members of the pack are very much attuned to one another.

Wolves are social creatures and therefore recognize the voices of others. The howl of a packmate, a neighboring pack, or a complete stranger to their territory will all solicit different responses.

Levi was not used to the howls of wolves. There were no known wolf populations in the state of Indiana except, on occasion, areas bordering the northern part of the state near Michigan. There was an urban legend in the state that coywolves, a coyote-wolf hybrid, inhabited areas southwest of Indianapolis, although Levi had never seen or heard of one.

Karl raced back to the clearing created by the wreckage. He'd slung Levi's backpack over his shoulder and was toting a gun case under each arm. "Did you guys hear that?" he asked apprehensively.

"Yeah, but I think they're a ways off," replied Levi. He reached out for his backpack, which Karl happily unloaded off his shoulders.

"That damn thing's heavy. Whadya have in there, Levi?"

"Lots, but most importantly, something that'll keep the one-armed bandit alive."

Levi rummaged through his pack and found his first aid kit. Anytime he traveled, he carried certain essentials in his gear regardless of where he was headed. His grandpa and Squire had instilled in him that he should always be prepared for anything. Levi was no Boy Scout, literally or figuratively, but he was a Boone. Boones were explorers and wilderness wanderers. They knew better than to leave home without the means of getting back there under any circumstances, including walking.

Karl set Levi's gun case by the airplane seat and set the other one next to Eddie. "How ya doin', compadre?"

"*Muy bueno*," said Eddie with a chuckle. "Say, um, Karl, do you reckon ya should get one of those rifles loaded in case the wolves decide to come around?"

Karl stood and shook his head. "We had to keep the ammo separate from the weapons, remember?"

"Oh, yeah."

"Use mine," said Levi. "But y'all don't forget, we only packed fifty rounds per rifle. It was too heavy otherwise."

"Crap, that's right," remembered Karl. "Smoky Falls had plenty for us to purchase."

Levi found his first aid kit and unzipped it. He added, "Right, so don't be shooting at ghosts, but be ready in case the *neighbors* decide to come for supper."

"Should I go look for Eddie's guns and our backpacks?" asked Karl.

"Hang tight," said Levi. "Let me get our boy cleaned up, and I need to get some dry clothes on."

Karl slowly walked in a circle around the bench seat while Levi got down to business. He shared what was troubling him. "Levi, we'll freeze to death in this weather."

"That's a nice thought," quipped Eddie. "Let's see, I've got about five ways to die tonight. I could freeze, bleed out, or get eaten by wolves. Then there's always sasquatch."

"That's only four," interrupted Karl.

"The fifth way is death by bacteria or plague or whatever Levi has on his underwear."

"Huh?" Karl was perplexed.

"Never mind," interjected Levi. He applied Polysporin ointment to Eddie's gash and covered it with gauze. Then he used a camouflage ballcap to cover Eddie's scalp. "There, keep that on."

"Better than your underwear," said Eddie with a chuckle. Levi gently wiped his friend's face off, and then Eddie muttered, "Thank you."

"No worries, brother," said Levi. He took a deep breath and looked at the sky. He was capable of navigating by the stars, but he wasn't familiar with Canada and not sure which way led to civilization. His instincts were to head south, back the way they came, and away from the inclement weather. Plus, Hudson Bay lay to the north, and the shores were sparsely populated, from his recollection.

"We need to hunker down," said Karl, interrupting Levi's thoughts.

"I agree," said Levi. "It would be nice to have your sleeping bag. Do you wanna try searching again?"

"Sure. I haven't been in this direction yet, or the area where you came from."

Eddie interrupted them. "Guys, I'm really getting cold, and this arm is starting to ache."

Levi furrowed his brow. Eddie was right. Shelter was the first priority in any survival situation. In extreme conditions like these, they could die of exposure in a matter of hours.

"I have an idea," he began. "My seat and the tail section are still intact. It'll be like squeezing ourselves in a drain culvert, but at least we can use our body heat to stay warm."

"Oh, sure, nice and snug," said Eddie with a sarcastic moan. "I've already had to sniff your undies, now you think you're gonna hold me? I can't wait to tell Carly about this."

"Shhh!" admonished Karl.

"You know I'm just—" said Eddie before Karl repeated himself.

"Shhh! I hear something out there," he whispered.

Levi scrambled to his gun case and loaded his other rifle. He and Karl immediately dropped to a knee, flanking the bench seat, where Eddie curled up to stay out of their way. The guys listened as the sounds of crunching snow could be heard over the ever-present wind.

"I hear it, too," whispered Levi. "We've got to get to cover before it's too late."

"Whadya think it is?" asked Karl. "It sounds too heavy to be a wolf."

"I don't plan on waiting for it to show itself. Let's go!"

CHAPTER 16

Northwest Ontario
Canada

The guys followed Levi through the woods. First, they stopped by the part of the wreckage where the pilot had died. Karl showed remarkable intestinal fortitude as he approached the pilot's body and rummaged through his pockets, looking for anything of use. He found a lighter, a Victorinox Swiss Army multi-tool, and a pocket compass.

Karl could feel an inscription engraved on the back of the brass compass. He cupped the device in the palm of his hand and flicked the Bic lighter to illuminate the words.

"Every adventure requires a first step."

"Ain't that the truth," commented Levi. "So let's get to steppin' before the wolves chase us down for supper."

Levi's rifle led the way as he did his best to locate his previous footsteps in the snow. Between the additional accumulation and the wind blowing the frozen moisture across the forest landscape, it was slow going.

"I think I see it up ahead," he announced as they entered a small clearing created by the wreckage. The guys picked up the pace, and a minute later, they were surveying their options.

Karl shouldered his rifle and stood in front of the opening with his hands on his hips. "Well, the first thing we have to do is scoop out the snow. He held his arms wide to gauge the width of the tail section. "I'm guessing six feet. If we lay on our sides, we can all squeeze in there."

"Like freakin' sardines," complained Eddie. He reached down and made a snowball and shoved it into his mouth.

"Eddie! No!" Levi said in a loud whisper. "Spit that out."

"Why? I'm thirsty."

"I know, but you can't melt snow that way. Your body has to use a lot of heat to melt it into water, which will make your body temp drop a bunch. We need to keep you warm."

"Levi, I'm parched, dude."

"I've got this, trust me. I've got two squeeze bottles in my pack. We'll fill them with snow and use our body heat to melt it into water."

"Makes sense," said Karl. Although there was never a particular hierarchy among the three friends, Levi was always looked up to when it came to matters regarding the outdoors. Whether it was his Boone lineage or practical experience learned from his father and grandfathers, Levi always seemed to know what to do when the guys were hunting or camping in the woods. "What's next?"

"First, let's clear this thing out, and then we'll squeeze in together. We'll use my backpack to shield us from the wind and snow."

"What about the wolves?" asked Eddie.

"We'll point our barrels out and shoot 'em if we have to," replied Levi.

"Dude, that'll blow our eardrums out!" Eddie warned.

"Maybe, or maybe not," Levi shot back. "At least we won't be some wolf's puppy chow."

Karl and Levi worked together to clear the tail section, and then they dried it using a fleece sweatshirt in Levi's backpack.

"Okay, before we go in, let me try to splint Eddie's arm," Levi said as he rummaged through his backpack again. "First, take these Advil."

"All four of them?" asked Eddie.

"Yeah. That's eight hundred milligrams, the same as a hospital would give you. We need to reduce your inflammation."

Eddie swallowed the pills and then asked, "What else?"

"Obviously, lie on your right side and keep your left arm tucked against your body. Karl and I will do our best not to bump you."

"Do your best? How 'bout don't?"

"I'm gonna make a splint for you," continued Levi, ignoring his questions. He looked around the wreckage and found a pine tree limb that was two inches in diameter. "Karl, up ahead is my row of seats. Take that pocketknife and cut loose the seat belts. We'll use the tree limb to keep his forearm immobilized and the seat belt webbing to hold it in place."

Karl quickly retrieved the seat belts, and Levi began to splint Eddie's broken forearm. "Now, please don't cry or I'll stop."

"Shut up, dude."

When Levi was finished, he gave Eddie some instructions. "In a perfect world, I would have included your elbow to immobilize the whole lower part of your arm. We just don't have the supplies for that, so it's gonna be up to you to hold your arm as still as possible until we can get you to a hospital."

Eddie was humbler than earlier. His moods tended to swing like that. "Thanks, Levi. I can do that."

The guys talked about how to shimmy into the tail section together without causing any more trauma to Eddie's battered body. After a few jokes about passing gas, you know, guy stuff, the three of them entered their temporary shelter.

Levi had removed the largest articles of clothing from his backpack to be used as makeshift pillows and blankets to lie on top of. The metal tail section was lying on top of the snow and quickly cooling marsh of the Hudson Bay Lowlands. Insulating them from the ground was more important than covering their bodies.

When they were finally settled, and after some moanin' and groanin' from Eddie, the guys were able to relax. The silence lasted about ten minutes until there was a complication.

Eddie said, "I gotta pee."

"I'm gonna kill him."

"No, I am."

CHAPTER 17

American Airlines Flight
Atlantic Ocean

A pair of flight attendants stopped by their aisle, and Chapman gave them their drink orders. They were also given a light snack of brie cheese coupled with a package of crispy French waffle crackers made by Tresors Gourmands. While they waited for their drinks, Isabella made a suggestion.

"The blonde woman was giving you *the look*."

"What look?"

Isabella playfully slugged his arm, causing his brie to fall off the cracker and into his crotch. She picked up the plastic knife that came with their snack. Twirling it in her hand, she asked, "Would you like me to get that for you?"

Chapman quickly reached down and plucked the morsel of cheese off his pants. He set it on the tray and shook his head rapidly from side to side. "Um, no, thanks," he replied, and then he admitted he'd noticed the blonde girl was unashamedly giving him the once-over.

"Here is what I am offering you, *Monsieur Boone*. It is a onetime pass to flirt in my presence. Only, I am going to leave you for the lavatory. This will allow you a few moments alone with your blonde admirer."

"Why would you do that? Is this a setup so you can use that knife?"

Isabella enjoyed watching Chapman squirm. "No, this is not a ruse. She will be more open with you while I am away. I know blonde women all too well. They have no shame."

Chapman laughed at her statement. "What am I supposed to do while you're away?"

"Ask her about the internet and what she knows about the power outage. She will open up to you because you are cute."

"I am?"

"No," she said teasingly. She picked up his snack tray and shoved it in his chest. Then she raised his tray table and slowly pushed her way past him to enter the aisle of the wide-body jet. She flipped her long hair over her shoulder and marched off to the lavatory.

The two flight attendants who'd taken their drink orders immediately descended upon his seat with an extra snack tray and their drinks. After some playful banter between them, Chapman tried to garner some information.

"Hey, guys, I really need to check my emails. Why won't they let us have the internet?"

The blonde shrugged, but her fellow flight attendant replied, "Other transatlantic flights have reported difficulties connecting with the new Ka-band satellites. The older Ku band like Panasonic are too slow, and passengers just complain about it."

"Wow, I'm impressed," said Chapman, flashing his signature smile bracketed by his dimples. "You know, I'd be okay connecting to the slow satellite. Can you guys help me with that?"

She shook her head. "No, I'm sorry, Mr. Boone. Only the pilot can do that and, well, you know, if I tell him that you're on the flight, he might allow it. Shall I ask him for you?"

"Yes, please. Thank you." Chapman thought for a moment and then he asked, "What happened in Paris as we were leaving? It looked like all the lights went out."

She didn't have a definitive answer for him. "The pilot mentioned it briefly when he gave me instructions to start cabin service. He thought it had to do with the unusual warm weather in Europe. You know, air conditioners overwhelming the system."

Chapman knew that wasn't the case because temperatures had fallen back to slightly below normal in the last few days. He studied the woman's face to determine if she was lying to cover the truth. She seemed to genuinely believe her statement, so he didn't press her any further.

The pause in their conversation created an opening, so the blonde flight attendant got down to business. "Would you mind if she takes a picture of us? You know, for my Instagram?"

Chapman shrugged. "Yeah, sure."

She handed her coworker a small Canon compact camera and quickly sat on the armrest next to Chapman. She cozied up against his shoulder and provided him a sultry smile. Chapman joined in the fun until the photo was snapped, and he noticed Isabella standing in the galley with her arms crossed, giving him the death stare.

The flight attendants were about to leave him alone until he stopped them. "Hey, um, if you don't mind, will you take these with you?"

He gathered up the snack trays and all the plastic knives, just in case.

Isabella returned as the flight attendants departed, and she immediately claimed her guy by bending over to plant a kiss on his cheek. She got settled into her seat, and Chapman handed her their next round of drinks.

He was about to speak when she raised her hand to stop him. She reached into the seat pocket in front of her and retrieved one of the small plastic knives.

"You forgot this one, *amoureux*," she said with a devious smile to her lover. "It is a lesson learned, *Monsieur Boone*. Always let your adversary think he has taken something, while keeping a secret for a later time."

"Is that an old French proverb?" he asked.

"No, it is a rule of survival. Now, what did you learn? And I want to hear every detail. Are we in agreement?" Isabella tapped the plastic knife on the tray table next to her drink.

"Oh, absolutely."

CHAPTER 18

Amundsen-Scott South Pole Station
Antarctica

It's like no other place in the world. At the center of the Antarctic, the geographic South Pole was a barren desert of snow. It was literally the coldest place on Earth, and the U.S. scientific research station located high atop an icy plateau nine-thousand feet above sea level was considered the leader among the scientific community on the desolate continent.

The South Pole was the only place on the planet where the sun would shine continuously for half the year and remained completely out of sight for the other half. However, despite the harsh and unwelcome conditions, it was a much sought-after assignment for climatologists and geologists.

Half the year, the South Pole station housed around two hundred scientists and support personnel. There was a restaurant-grade commercial kitchen, a mess hall, a gym, and a greenhouse within the climate-controlled facility.

The South Pole winter was extraordinarily dull for the inhabitants of Amundsen-Scott. During the South Pole winter, the sun sets in February and doesn't rise again until November. Only a skeleton crew inhabits the station during this period of time, known as *winterovers*. The temperatures outside are so cold that most aircraft couldn't land. The hydraulics on the plane's skids were only rated to minus-sixty degrees and were subject to catastrophic failure in the event temperatures dropped below that, as they frequently did.

Or used to, anyway.

For the past year, Dr. Amber Hagood had watched the planet self-destruct with the help of man. The polar ice caps were melting at an alarming rate, at least as far as scientists were concerned. Together with her associates at the Geophysical Institute at the University of Alaska, Dr. Hagood had developed an ice sheet model several years prior that revealed in the next two hundred years, the melting would occur at an ever-increasing rate due to climate change. The projections revealed the planet would experience a sixty-three-inch rise in global sea levels.

During a presentation to a group of NASA oceanographers at a conference in Pasadena, she warned that humanity should've been retreating from the coastlines decades ago. Yet homes and businesses crowded the world's seashores nonetheless.

She stared at the four computer monitors mounted on the walls of her cubicle. They revealed a series of graphs depicting sea levels at various monitoring stations around the planet. Next to these graphs, average temperature readings were shown. The correlation simply wasn't there. The amount of sea level rise didn't match any known models associated with the overall warming of the planet. In fact, average temperatures had been dropping around the globe in the last several years.

Her job was to figure out why.

Daily life at the South Pole was taxing on the mind and the body. For some reason, this particular winterover had been especially difficult for Dr. Hagood, despite it being her tenth. She was dedicated to keeping the world abreast of the threats we faced from climate change, and therefore she committed her life to her work. That meant remaining on the job every day of the year, regardless of the warnings her superiors and psychologists gave her.

She hadn't slept well for the last couple of months. She frequently tossed and turned at night, wondering what the monitoring stations around the world would reveal the next day. Hoping new data might reveal an answer to the weather anomalies.

On this particular morning, she found herself especially alert and aware of her surroundings. She began to see her job at the South Pole to be of extraordinary importance. A feeling of empowerment came over her that she couldn't quite understand. It was like an awakening.

She was dressed in a pair of fleece shorts and a tank top she'd received for Christmas last year from a not-so-secret Santa, a married man who let the isolation of his first time as a winterover get to him and had become lonely at night. She'd rebuffed his advances, but kept the gift nonetheless.

Dr. Hagood raced out of her sleep pod and made her way into the operations center, the central research and communications hub of Amundsen-Scott. She banged away on the keyboard until she'd produced the research results that were now before her. She searched the data for clues. The team at the South Pole research center had always focused their efforts on the floating monitoring stations found in the world's oceans. After all, their goal was to identify rising sea levels and use the results to confirm the conclusions reached by decades of researchers before her.

All of a sudden, her brain told her to look outside the box, as they say. Beyond the usual suspects. Find the needle in haystack. The odd man out. The clichés for an inconsistency were endless.

Dr. Hagood's mind was operating like a supercomputer that just got a kick in the pants by a power surge. Her fingers frantically beat on the keyboard as if her time was about to expire. It wasn't, at least not today, anyway.

She searched the databases of the world's most prominent environmental research partners. The McMaster Institute in Canada. Australia's Cooperative Research Centre. The Helmotz Centre in Germany and the Grantham Institute in London.

"There have to be anomalies in the other direction," she whispered aloud although she was the only scientist in the operations center. Everyone's attention, their primary focus, had always been instances of warming around the planet. Warming temperatures meant melting ice. Melting ice meant rising seas. The narrative had been set in stone.

But what about abnormal cold? What if there were instances of extraordinary cold trends to counteract the warming?

As she downloaded the data and began to plug it into the

propriety software she'd developed to create a model utilizing hundreds of research stations around the globe, her eyes grew wide and perspiration began to form on her forehead. The software triangulated areas of the planet that had been experiencing unusual freezing trends over the last five to ten years. She linked the locations together to create a pattern.

Dr. Hagood shook her head repeatedly as the numbers began to reveal a new theory. A model began to take shape on her center screen.

"How can this possibly be? Have we been making the wrong assumptions all along?"

She leaned back in her chair and tapped the top of her mouse with her index finger. She leaned forward to create a global map view of her results. This only resulted in her becoming more perplexed.

The map revealed both hot spots, or areas where temperatures had been trending much warmer, as well as cold spots, where temperatures were continuously moving toward subantarctic norms or below.

Yes, Greenland, the Arctic Circle, and Antarctica had all been experiencing warmer temperatures. But areas of Eastern Europe, Southeast Asia, Australia, and even West Central Africa were experiencing frigid temperatures.

"Quadropolar? Is that even possible?"

The Earth has more than two magnetic poles, but only two of them were dramatically obvious—North and South. This was known as a dominantly dipolar system. The basic physics of magnetic fields, whether on a large scale like the planet, or on a small scale like a horseshoe-shaped magnet, resulted in a dipolar system.

What was not commonly known was the fact the Earth actually had several weaker magnetic poles—eight of them, in fact. Known as octupoles, these localized geographic regions barely affected life on Earth, with the lone exception of the South Atlantic Anomaly.

Dr. Amber Hagood had begun to piece together the puzzle of the profound impact the pole shift was having on the planet. She sought answers and she was beginning to find them.

The only problem was that there was nothing she or anyone could do about the coming catastrophe for humanity.

CHAPTER 19

Riverfront Farms
Southeast Indiana

Squire was exhausted from playing video games with his grandkids. He wished he could bottle their energy and sell it, or drink it up for himself. As he reached his sixties, he was still able to handle his duties around the farm, but he found himself tiring at night. He'd begun experiencing diarrhea, loss of appetite, and he was now pulling his belt a notch or two tighter.

Squire blew it off as an age thing or stress related as the farm suffered from the prolonged drought. The note coming due was hanging over his head, and that consumed him throughout the day.

After dinner, he allowed the grandkids to play a little, and then he shuffled them off to bed. He wanted to check the news for updates on the situation overseas and to make his own determination if Chapman's concerns were warranted. He got settled in his chair with a mug of decaf coffee and began flipping through the channels. He quickly learned the situation in Europe had taken a turn for the worse.

CNN International was broadcasting live from Paris, where looters and rioters were out in force. The country was under siege as young people took advantage of the power outage and the overwhelmed Police Nationale, who were responsible for Paris and other nearby urban areas.

The French national guard had been called out to protect the historic museums, churches, and points of interest, leaving shop owners to largely fend for themselves. The scene was similar in Southern Germany, Hungary, Romania, and Ukraine as opportunists sought to disrupt government operations and enrich themselves.

The scene shifted back to the CNN Atlanta studios, which featured a roundtable discussion with three scientists, including one from Australia. Squire turned up the volume so he could listen to the exchange.

"Without being overly dramatic, but by simply stating facts, if a geostorm of this magnitude hits the United States, you can kiss modern life goodbye. It's hard to overstate the importance of the Earth's magnetic field as protection against the Sun. It is, quite frankly, a ruthless solar-wind-shredding machine that enables us to maintain life on our planet.

"You see, Earth cruises around the Sun at about sixty-seven thousand miles per hour, constantly bombarded by a constant stream of plasma particles ejected by our star. It's akin to a speeding motorboat displacing water as it steams across the ocean. In the scientific community, we call it *bow shock* because of its similarity to a boat forcing its way through stubborn waves."

The interviewer interrupted with a question. "How does the magnetic field work against these solar winds?"

"As the solar wind crashes into Earth's magnetic field, the bow shock slows it down, resulting in a nice warm breeze. When the magnetic field weakens, as it appears to be doing, the Earth will continue to be bombarded by a hot, soupy plasma of protons, ions, and electrons ejected from the Sun. These winds blow all day and in all directions, blasting out of the Sun at speeds up to five hundred miles per second and temperatures approaching three million degrees."

"My god," exclaimed the interviewer. "You'd think that would be more than enough to bake our planet into a pile of ashes."

"Well, actually, it is. Venus is a prime example of that. Our planet and its atmosphere remain largely unscathed thanks to the strong magnetic field. However, as is being reported, that may be changing as a result of this pole shift."

The interviewer took a deep breath, and the camera zoomed in on her concerned face. "Let's shift gears for a moment. Assuming this pole shift is the root cause for the magnetic field weakening, we can now tie it into the leaks from the White House that all air traffic in the United States will be grounded within the hour."

The Australian scientist interrupted. "Yes. The pole shift has disrupted our global positioning systems, and the functionality of our satellites in low-Earth orbit can be disrupted by the solar matter. Furthermore, if North America were to take a direct hit from a geostorm similar to the one experienced in Europe …" His voice trailed off before continuing. "Well, it would be lights out."

Squire stood and began to pace the floor in front of the television. He moved quickly to the stairwell and took a couple of steps up toward the bedrooms to listen for any activity from the grandkids' rooms. It was quiet, so he made his way back to the television.

CNN was continuing to show images depicting societal collapse. Police in riot gear used water cannons to repel protestors, who countered by throwing Molotov cocktails and rocks. Fires were burning out of control. Images of looters racing out of retail stores with arms full of merchandise ran on a continuous loop with a chyron at the bottom of the screen that read *Paris in Chaos.*

Squire had seen and heard enough. He muted the television and tossed the remote into his chair. He checked his watch and was astonished when he realized how long Sarah and Carly had been gone on their shopping trip.

He wasn't annoyed at the length of time they were taking. He was glad and proud that his wife had persevered despite his obvious pushback. He regretted his bad attitude and would let her know by apologizing as soon as she got home.

He wandered through the downstairs, soaking in the information that he'd garnered from the news reports. He tried to imagine a world without power and closed his eyes to shake away the visuals.

Squire stopped and smiled as he recalled the words attributed to his ancestor Daniel Boone. He whispered to himself, "All you need for happiness is a good gun, a good horse, and a good wife. Thank you, Lord, for blessing me with all three."

CHAPTER 20

Northwest Ontario
Canada

"Karl, you awake?" asked Levi in a whisper. He'd lain awake for hours after the guys finally calmed down. He'd replayed the events of the day in his head, trying to make sense of how the pilot could've flown so far off course that he mistook the wilderness for a lake.

"Are you kiddin'? Eddie snores like a moose in heat." Karl adjusted his body so he could look in Levi's direction although it was pitch black inside the cramped tail section of the airplane.

Levi laughed. "I tried nudgin' him from time to time, and he'd stop for a minute. Then the freight train came rollin' down the track again."

Karl chuckled. "Whadya thinkin'?"

"A million things, but mainly I'm tryin' to figure out where the hell we are. That old pilot seemed to know what he was doin'. How did he miss a lake as big as the one at Smoky Falls?"

"Do you think he got distracted talkin' about that planet Nibiru garbage?"

Levi subconsciously shrugged. "I dunno, maybe. I remember he said it was taking longer to get to Smoky Falls than he expected."

"Blamed it on the headwinds, right?" added Karl.

"Yeah. He talked about terrain warning systems or somethin', and then he said the GPS would guide him to the lake."

"The plane was all over the place," said Karl.

"I was watching the altimeter. He had a bead on his landing strip, or lake. At least according to the GPS."

"Well, all I know is the trees grabbed a wing, and the next thing you know, here we are, splat."

"And lost," said Levi. "Hey, did you bring your Garmin?"

"Nah. I didn't think we'd need it since the guides would be taking us everywhere. Eddie didn't either. Said he forgot it."

"Eddie forgot everything," said Levi as he gently whacked the back of his head against the inside of the airplane. "Including winter clothes. We've gotta find your—"

A loud thump against the tail section of the plane stopped Levi from speaking.

"What was that?" whispered Karl as he jostled Eddie in an attempt to stop his snoring.

THUMP!

"Shit!" Levi rolled over on his belly and readied his rifle. Karl quickly followed his lead and pulled the bolt action on his .308.

The sound of heavy feet walking outside the back half of the airplane could be heard until the entire tail section rocked back and forth.

"What the hell?" said Eddie, angry at being awakened.

"Shhh!" admonished Karl.

Levi joined in. "Something's out there. Quiet."

The crunching in the snow stopped, and then the loud-pitched, earsplitting sound of something clawing the outside of the plane frightened the guys.

Eddie started to squirm, and then he felt the pain of his broken arm. "Oh, gawd, that hurt."

"Shut up, Eddie," ordered Karl just loud enough to be heard.

The movement outside stopped. The guys held their breath and remained completely still, waiting to see what would happen next. It only took a second for them to find out.

THUD!

Something large rammed the side of the tail section, causing Karl's side of the plane to dent inward. Eddie screamed and the guys began shouting a ripe mixture of profanities.

BOOM!

The next attack on their shelter was harder this time.

"What do we do?" asked Karl.

Levi replied calmly, "Keep your rifle trained on the opening. Shoot anything that moves!"

"What if it's a bear?" asked Eddie.

"Then we frickin' kill it!" shouted Levi. Then he began to implement some defensive measures. Animals in the wild aren't interested in human interaction. He'd watched survival shows on the National Geographic Channel that revealed the things to do if being attacked by bears. "Pound the top of the plane and yell. That should scare it off."

The guys began to bang the top and sides of the tail section with their fists while Eddie stomped his feet to assist. All three yelled in an effort to frighten away whatever was pounding Karl's side of the wreckage. After a moment, they stopped and listened.

Thirty seconds passed and they couldn't hear a sound. Eddie was the first to declare victory.

"I think we scared him off."

Karl agreed. "I think you're—"

BOOM!

The noise reverberated in their ears like a bass drum being pounded with its felt-covered beater.

The creature slammed into Levi's side of the plane, denting the tail section so hard that it jabbed into his ribs.

Levi was pissed. "That's it!"

He forced the backpack out of the opening and scrambled out of the wreckage, using his arms to pull himself forward. He rolled out onto the snow and immediately rose to one knee with his rifle trained on his side of the aircraft.

But there was no target in sight.

"What is it?" asked Karl.

Levi replied, "Hold on." He rose to a low crouch and began to inch toward the side of the plane. His eyes darted into the dark forest, searching for signs of movement. As he got closer to the point of impact, he swung back and forth, thinking he heard footsteps. He wished he had his night-vision scope, but they were now illegal in Ontario.

The snow had stopped falling and the skies were beginning to clear, allowing the stars to peek through. Levi steadied his nerves and took in a deep breath of fresh Canadian air. It would've been invigorating had it not been for their circumstances. It was getting colder as the storm passed over them, leaving them at great risk of exposure.

"Levi!"

"Yeah, sorry! I think it left, whatever it was."

Karl shouted back, "I'm comin' out."

Seconds later, the two guys were walking around the plane, feeling the fuselage as they used their hands to guide them in the low light.

"This had to be a moose," said Levi.

"Maybe even a bull," added Karl. "Something, maybe antlers, scratched the side of the plane. It was like nails on a chalkboard."

Eddie chimed in, "Yeah, well, I've had enough of this shit. I'm cold, my arm is killing me, and nobody's comin' for us. I vote we head out of this snow-swamp crap and find help."

Levi approached the opening to the tail section and reached his friend, who was standing several feet away.

"Eddie, we can't go anywhere right now," said Levi. "If it stays clear, we can try in the morn—"

Levi never finished his sentence. The thumping of hooves in the snow preceded the throaty, airy grunt of an animal approaching them. Levi reacted on instinct.

He raised his rifle and fired in the dark toward the clomping sound. The bullet whizzed past Eddie and struck a tree, shattering the bark and embedding with a thud.

"Run, Eddie!" shouted Karl, who also raised his rifle.

Eddie ran between the guys, who both fired into the darkness toward the baritone grunting creature.

One of their bullets found the target. The animal let out a cough, followed by a groan before it hit the ground so close to the guys that white, powdery snow flew onto their faces.

"Got him!" said Levi.

"No, I hit him," said Karl as he pushed ahead of Levi to confirm the animal was dead.

"Come on, I fired first," argued Levi.

"And missed."

Levi joined his side and Karl flicked on the lighter. Two gaping bullet holes appeared between the bull moose's massive velvety antlers. The eleven-hundred-pound male was dead.

The guys spontaneously tried to exchange high fives but missed each other's hands due to the darkness.

"Team effort, right?" asked Levi.

"I'll take it. Our first kill. But how are we gonna get it back to camp?"

Karl and Levi began to laugh when Eddie joined them.

"This ain't over," he began, causing Karl and Levi to notice the seriousness in his voice. "Listen."

Levi held his breath to listen to the sounds of the Hudson Bay Lowlands. The wolf chorus had begun again.

CHAPTER 21

American Airlines Flight
United States Atlantic Seaboard

For some unknown reason, a chill came over Chapman and the hair rose on the back of his neck. A feeling of dread overcame him, but he fought it off, visibly shaking his shoulders and sitting a little taller in his seat. Neither he nor Isabella had been able to sleep. In part because they were hyped up as they flew toward a new adventure with unknown challenges, but mostly because they were enjoying each other's company.

Their whirlwind romance had developed at lightning speed and with an unexplainable urgency. It was based in part on physical attraction, but it first developed out of mutual respect for one another's intelligence.

Chapman wanted to keep the conversation going to avoid worrying about what would confront them once they landed at John F. Kennedy airport in Queens, New York. They'd been holding hands for hours, bonding in a way that allowed for physical touch and subdued public intimacy. To the casual observer, they looked like a nice couple who'd enjoyed the trip of their dreams to Paris and were exhausted from taking in all of the sights at once.

He tilted his head toward Isabella and asked, "May I ask you an honest question?"

"Yes, of course. There should always be honesty between us."

"Isabella, you're a beautiful, brilliant woman. I find you extremely attractive and funny at the same time, especially with the thing about the butter knife."

"That was not a joke, Chapman."

"Okay, let me add badass to the list of things I adore about you."

"You are preparing me for something. What is it?"

"No, no. I promise. No surprises from me. It's just that, um, you are perfect in every way."

She laughed and kissed his hand. "In your eyes, yes."

"I think it would be in any man's eyes. Have you ever married or had a serious relationship?"

"I could ask you the same thing, Prince Charming," she replied with a joke. "I saw you in action earlier, remember?"

"Oh, that was just an act for your benefit. I saw you watching."

"Liar!" she exclaimed loud enough to attract the attention of a man seated across the aisle. She lowered her voice. "You didn't see me. You were flirting."

Chapman blushed. He was busted. "Okay, I do flirt too much. But it's harmless, usually. Truthfully, I've never wanted to have a serious relationship. Have you had any?"

"No. I have taken lovers, but it was not emotional."

Chapman didn't understand French women, so he treaded lightly as he broached the subject of their first night together. "Is that what you thought about me, you know, the first night?"

Isabella laughed. "No, you are different. You are a man who has my interest beyond sexual attraction. Perhaps a man who has something much more."

"So you decided to try before you buy?"

Isabella was confused. "What?"

"It's an American saying. Retail stores offer the consumer the opportunity to purchase their products without commitment. If the customer keeps the product, then their credit card is charged. If they return it, then they don't pay. It's called *try before you buy*."

Isabella stuck her chin out and shrugged. "I suppose it is the same. I want to know someone better before I invest any time with them. In the past, no man has caught my attention to be more than a *try before you buy item*."

Isabella paused and then asked, "Have you been married or had a serious love in your life?"

"Not really. I love my job, and in my free time, I enjoy learning about the planet. I always thought a wife or even a girlfriend would get in the way of that. You know, pull me away from my passion."

Isabella laughed and bent across the armrest to kiss him. "You see why I have never taken a husband. Men are demanding of my time. They get jealous of my career and research. They want me to have babies and stay home to cook dinner. That is not who I am, so I have remained single."

Chapman digested her statement and decided to avoid the topic of children. They'd just met, and it was far too early to talk about things like marriage and kids. He relayed his true feelings. "I think you and I are the same. We love what we do, and our greatest fear is that a relationship would stand in the way of our aspirations. Before you, I'd never met a woman who would be my partner as well as the love of my life."

Isabella looked into his eyes in the dimly lit cabin. "Do you think I am that woman? A partner?"

"Yes, and the love of my life."

Isabella began to shake her head, feigning disagreement. "Chapman Boone, you do not know me. I am very difficult to be around. I am strong headed. Have you noticed that I am always right?"

"Yes, so?"

"Well, sometimes I am not right. I need a man who will remind me when I am, um, too much."

"I will do that for you."

"You must also remember that I am my own person capable of making my own decisions. I do not need a man to tell me what to do or take care of me. I have been independent for too long."

Chapman loved to hear her open up. "Okay, that is a fair request. However, will you let me pretend to take care of you?"

"*Oui*, of course. I hope that you will. I just do not want you to feel an obligation."

Chapman reached out to touch her face. He kissed her and then whispered into her ear, "Equal partners."

"It is agreed, equal partners, um, as you Americans say, with benefits."

"Oh, yes. I like the benefits."

She pushed him away and then suddenly blurted out, "STEVE!"

Isabella was looking across the aisle through the portholes on the north side of the aircraft. Chapman's first assumption was that she'd seen an old boyfriend in the midst of their intimate conversation. He pressed his back against his seat so she could lean across his lap. Then he saw what she was referring to.

STEVE was an acronym for strong thermal emission velocity enhancement, a mouthful to be sure. STEVE was an atmospheric phenomenon that created a rare aurora-like glow that appeared as a ribbon of light in the sky. It was a somewhat rare occurrence caused by a wide ribbon of superheated plasma creating the streak of light purple and green light extending across the night sky.

"Impossible," she muttered.

"This doesn't make sense," added Chapman. "If the pole has shifted as we suspect, then this aurora can't be happening in Canada unless—"

His sentence was cut off by his partner, Isabella. "Dipoles. The north magnetic pole has shifted across Siberia, but a second geomagnetic pole has remained closer to true north."

"This could explain the severe weather anomalies," added Chapman. "And animal confusion."

"Do you know what else this means? The South Pole is likely shifting and may have, in fact, split into two regions like the north magnetic pole."

"The hot ribbon of ionized gas that everyone on the plane is admiring is bad news for our planet," cautioned Chapman. He lowered his voice so he wasn't overheard. "Isabella, this could have a catastrophic impact on the balance of the Earth's geologic formations. We've always known the Earth to have two dominant poles and several very weak quadrupolar poles, of which there are, mathematically, about eight. However, in modern history, these weak departures of the local geographic field have little physical impact on the planet. From what I can see of the intensity of this STEVE, the dipolar effect could possibly create movement in the tectonic plates."

Isabella whispered back, "Volcanic, earthquake, and wide temperature swings."

Chapman grimaced. "Yes. The upheaval could change the face of the planet."

They sat in silence, digesting the ramifications of what other passengers were declaring to be *the most beautiful sight they'd ever witnessed.*

Chapman noticed the sky brightening toward the east, and he checked his watch. He craned his neck to search for lights along the Atlantic Seaboard, but couldn't see any. He performed the time calculations in his head. Either the aircraft was woefully behind schedule, or America was in the dark.

CHAPTER 22

American Airlines Flight
United States Atlantic Seaboard

Long-haul transatlantic flights can be exhausting for crew and passengers, even aboard the massive luxury airliners like the Boeing 777. The crew, including flight attendants, were encouraged to take periodic breaks in the lounge and six tiny windowless bedrooms known as crew rest compartments, or CRCs.

A secret staircase leads to the bedroom area nestled behind the cockpit and above the first-class passenger rows. The crew members could stretch out, pull a curtain closed, and immerse themselves in quiet solitude courtesy of sound-blocking BOSE headsets.

Captain Chuck Whittaker decided to take a respite during the final hours of the Paris to New York flight. He stretched his six-foot-three frame into a bunk bed that felt more like a coffin than a place to sleep. It was cramped but better than trying to nap in the body-hugging seat in the cockpit.

He'd been flying American Airlines jets for twenty-seven years. Retirement was on the horizon, and he'd become more excited about spending the rest of his life on his farm outside Charlotte, North Carolina, than flying his final hours as a commercial pilot.

Captain Whittaker had received a message from American Airlines dispatch in Fort Worth, Texas, that flights originating out of Europe would be blocking passenger access to the internet. Initially, there was no explanation, and he spent the first half of the flight speculating with his copilots about the reasons.

When he decided to lie down and rest, he assumed the internet restrictions applied to the CRC as well. Nonetheless, he picked up one of the iPads provided in each bunk and launched the Safari app. He was shocked to find complete access to the web.

He was even more shocked to learn what had happened in Eastern Europe. Rumors were rampant as to the cause of the widespread power outage that had thrust much of the continent into darkness. He scoured the web looking for credible, verifiable reporting on the reasons for the widespread collapse of the European power grid. Theories ranged from cyber attacks to excessive heat conditions to squirrels eating through electrical lines.

He was devouring every article he could find when the lead flight attendant came to the CRC and advised him that the first officer needed him back on the flight deck immediately. She didn't know why, only that it was urgent.

Whittaker checked his watch. They were an hour and a half from their later-than-scheduled arrival at JFK due to unusual headwinds. He slipped on his shoes and shoved the iPad under a pillow. He told the lead flight attendant to advise all of her crew to be prepared to wrap up cabin service quickly if notified.

He raced back to the cockpit and was greeted by First Officer Connor Shields, who got right to the point. "Chuck, we've just been advised by JFK tower to divert."

"Why?"

"The FAA, on orders of the president, has grounded all commercial and private aircraft across the continental U.S. Once all inbound flights are on the ground, air travel is suspended until further notice."

"Any explanation?"

"Nope, and I pressed them."

Whittaker ran his fingers through his hair and sighed. He got settled into the captain's seat and buckled up his harness. "Okay, where are we headed?"

"Um, we don't know yet. All they would tell us was that JFK will not be able to accommodate our landing there and to stand by for another destination."

"Not be able to accommodate? Seriously? They used those words?"

Shields nodded and held his hands up with a shrug. "It takes a lot of runway to land one of these birds. There aren't that many in the vicinity of JFK that can handle us."

"Sir, fuel is also an issue," added the other copilot of the enormous aircraft. "We pretty much fought upper-level winds during the entire trip across the ocean. We're not in a position to go runway shopping."

Whittaker took a deep breath and exhaled. "Okay, let's get AA operations on the line and try to get some answers from our people. Meanwhile, raise JFK tower and—"

"Chuck," interrupted Shields, "they've just advised us to continue this circular holding pattern. It extends from Long Island southward along the coast to the mouth of Delaware Bay and back up again."

Whittaker was both incredulous and concerned. "What? What is that? Three miles round trip? Do they think we're equipped for aerial refueling? Get me our flight ops on the line now!"

*****

As the airplane banked to the left for its second circuitous trip along the New Jersey coast, Chapman leaned into Isabella and snuck a look out the window. The sun was rising and the weather appeared to be clear.

"I don't get it. They've got us in a holding pattern, and weather doesn't appear to be a factor."

"It's been over thirty minutes," added Isabella.

Suddenly, a commotion could be heard from the coach section of the aircraft. The business-class flight attendants rushed past their row and entered coach, pulling the curtains together to block the business passengers' view.

However, the curtains could not mask the excited, loud voices coming from the rear of the aircraft.

"I just caught a signal on my cell phone. All hell's breaking loose in Europe!"

"Me too. My wife texted me and said Russia started a war with a cyber attack of the power plants."

"That's bullshit. I read the French officials blamed it on squirrels!"

The flight attendants could be heard trying to calm down the passengers. As voices grew louder, one of the flight attendants raced up the aisle into the crew galley that separated first class from business. She spoke with a woman who appeared to be the lead flight attendant. After a brief conversation, the lead picked up the phone to contact the flight deck.

The shouting continued, with mostly male passengers arguing about what might be happening in Europe.

"Why would Russia cut off the power?"

"They're probably about to invade."

"That's ridiculous."

"No, it's not. Ask Ukraine."

"Yeah, Estonia and Georgia, too."

An older woman asked, "Georgia? My daughter lives in Savannah."

Chapman shook his head in disbelief and muttered, "You can't fix stupid."

Isabella had a puzzled look on his face. "They are wrong and stupid?"

He squeezed her hand and laughed. "They're all making assumptions and then shouting it out at the top of their lungs like they're the authority on what happened. None of them are right, and I feel like going back there to straighten them out."

"Do you like to argue? I mean, debate?" she asked.

"No, not really," he replied, and then he acknowledged what she meant. "I get your point."

She rubbed his shoulders. "Like you said, you can't fix stupid."

"Good morning, this is Captain Charles Whittaker from the flight deck. As many of you have noticed, we've been placed in a temporary holding pattern by the JFK tower. JFK has been temporarily closed to further arrivals for an unknown period of time, so they have been looking for an alternative airport in the region.

"We've now been cleared for landing at Teterboro, New Jersey. On behalf of American Airlines, I am sorry for any inconvenience this has caused you. This is a situation that is totally out of our control, but I can assure you that American will have gate agents to greet you at the departure lounge to assist you in getting back to Queens. At this time, I'd like our flight attendants to stop all cabin service and prepare for landing."

Chapman sighed. "I don't know about this."

"Why?" asked Isabella.

"Teterboro is not that far from JFK, maybe thirty miles. But it's very small by comparison. This is a big aircraft, and it needs—" Chapman was interrupted by an argument between one of the flight attendants and a male passenger.

"There's no way that he'll stop this thing at Teterboro. I know that airport. The runway will never hold it."

"Please, sir, take your seat. The captain has illuminated the fasten—"

"I don't give a rat's ass about that seat belt sign. He needs to understand that the runway is too damned short for a seven-seven-seven. He's gonna crash and get us all killed!"

It was his last statement that sent the coach-class passengers into a panicked frenzy. People began to demand answers from the flight attendant, and when she didn't have any, she started screaming at them to calm down and remain in their seats. Chaos ensued.

Several flight attendants raced down the aisle to assist. The first officer, Shields, came back on the aircraft's communications system and demanded that everyone take their seats. As he spoke, a flight attendant's voice could be heard begging him to do something to calm the passengers. The entire conversation between the copilot, the captain, and the flight attendant was overheard by the passengers.

Some listened intently to their discussion while many in the coach section argued amongst themselves or with the flight attendants. But somehow, above the fracas, these words by the first officer were heard by everyone—*We can't circle around again, we'll run out of fuel.*

All two hundred twenty-two passengers collectively became unnerved.

CHAPTER 23

North Lawn
The White House
Washington, DC

Rudy was an ordinary guy. Wife. Two older kids. Georgetown graduate who landed a job within the White House as an administrative aide many years ago. His work ethic and adherence to strict confidentiality practices resulted in a nonpartisan staffer position within the West Wing of the White House through multiple presidential administrations.

He didn't have any pressures—marital, career, or financial. He did his job. He loved his family. He played golf on Saturdays and worshipped on Sundays.

Then things began to change. Mental things. Unexplainable, head-pounding, I'm-so-confused kinda things.

Rudy quietly went to see his physician assistant, who checked his bloodwork annually and monitored his cholesterol. Routine, mundane, healthy-as-a-horse type stuff.

He complained of headaches that were increasing in frequency. They talked about his diet, caffeine intake, and sleep habits. All of that was a-okay.

Weeks later, Rudy felt compelled to go back when, without his wife's knowledge, the brutal headache he'd experienced resulted in a blackout episode. He was immediately referred to a neurologist, who spared no expense ringing up Rudy's government health care plan to look for the root cause of his condition. The results came back.

Nothing. Nada. Zippo.

"Rudy," the doctor had said, "have you considered taking some time off? Perhaps a little vacay is in order. You know, recharge the batteries." Blah-blah-blah.

Rudy wasn't tired. He wasn't stressed. He didn't need a vacation. He simply needed *relief*.

One Saturday, after a round of golf, his wife texted him and told him to pick up a few things from the grocery store. She thought it might be nice to grill some steaks, have a few beers, and relax in the backyard. Since the kids were off at her parents' lake house for the weekend, she thought it might be nice to spend a little special quality time with her man.

Rudy, the dutiful husband, gladly hustled off to the market and picked out the steaks. Scheele's Market in Georgetown was having a BOGO sale on rib eyes. Proud of his frugal shopping, he quickly selected his twofer, times two. Four steaks for the price of two. What a deal!

Rudy would never be able to explain why he bought four steaks for two people, not that it mattered because two of them never made it to the house. Something came over him in the car that day. An insatiable hunger that prompted him to pull into a 7-Eleven parking lot and eat the BOGO steaks—raw.

By the time he arrived home, his memory of the Jenny Craig moment, a temporary lapse in judgment characterized by stuffing food in one's mouth, in which he devoured the raw meat had faded, and so had his constant headache.

In fact, he'd never felt better. Euphoric, in fact. And virile. He made love to his wife like a porn star, and a glorious weekend in the sack was the first of many.

As long as he ate raw meat.

Over the summer leading up to this fateful day, Rudy consumed more and more raw meat. Rib eyes. Always the eye of the rib. Bone in, of course.

His headaches ceased. His constant doctor visits ended. His wife smiled. A lot. And Rudy became a functioning drug addict whose choice of medication was raw meat.

As the summer wore on, and the heat index rose, and the poles shifted, Rudy began to unravel. He felt frustration. Anger. There never was enough meat to consume. Soon he stopped trying to hide his insatiable appetite for raw steak from his family. They began to become concerned, but after two heartfelt attempts to discuss it with Rudy, they gave up because he exploded in rage.

Four days ago, while Rudy was supposedly at work, which he wasn't since he'd been terminated the week before due to excessive absences, his wife and kids fled their home to the safety of her parents'. She planned on getting a restraining order in addition to filing for divorce.

She never got the chance.

Last night, Rudy made a little road trip to Roanoke, Virginia, to have a discussion with his wife. He thought perhaps dinner and a bottle of wine might smooth things over so she'd come home to him.

Rudy packed a light snack for the four-hour drive to his in-laws'. A Yeti cooler was purchased, as were a dozen rib eyes. As he traveled across the Francis Scott Key Bridge to start his journey, Rudy did the math with remarkable clarity.

"Let me see. Twelve steaks. Four hours. Three per ..."

He dipped into the cooler and fumbled with the packaging until he had a piece of the cold, raw meat in his hand. He began to chew. Rudy's digestive system was in a rage as well. When he chewed on raw meat, the meat didn't break apart. It stayed like a wad in his mouth until he swallowed it. It moved through his large intestines over a period of thirty-three hours until it passed. He was frequently constipated, which contributed to his inhospitable demeanor.

Two hours later, he was out of steak. So much for intricate calculations. Determined to make things right with his wife, he soldiered on, fighting the rage and headache that began to build as he approached his in-laws' neighborhood.

He parked across the street and waited, summoning the courage to go inside. He thought of what to say, although he'd rehearsed his opening statement for hours. He simply couldn't remember. Everything was a blur. One long confusing dream that he replayed over and over, without sleeping.

Just as he was about to exit his car and go inside, his wife appeared on the front porch. She was crying and needed comforting. She got it, from another man. A small, wiry, no-skin-on-the-bones guy was hugging Rudy's wife.

And he didn't like it.

The next thirty seconds were straight out of a horror movie. Rudy flung the driver's door open, raced in front of an oncoming car, and crossed the lawn in a flash. Before his wife and the skinny guy could break their embrace, Rudy had crashed into them.

He hovered over the man, growled and promptly bit off the man's right cheek.

His wife screamed for help, but that only served to distract Rudy and return his attention to the task at hand—kiss and make up with his bride. Only, he didn't kiss her. He grabbed her hair, exposed her neck, and bit into her jugular vein, causing her blood to spew all over the soon-to-be-formerly-married couple.

Rudy fell on his knees and howled like a wolf. Madness had overtaken him. The skinny guy made a lame effort to tackle Rudy, an effort that resulted in the man's death by cannibalism.

He never heard his in-laws scream for help. Nor did he stick around for the police to arrive. His instincts told him to flee, and he did. Without any consciousness of what he had done, or why, he took off for DC. His mind was returning to its new-normal state, one that allowed him to function as long as it was fed.

However, four hours was a long time for Rudy the Unraveled. He needed relief. He needed to eat raw meat. And he wanted to take his next meal at the place where he'd worked until the day he was fired—the White House.

Covered in blood, Rudy managed to reach the White House complex unnoticed by law enforcement. There were several times that the Virginia State Police missed him driving back to DC in his black Prius. Luck was on his side.

He made his way down Seventeenth Street, past McDonald's and Peet's Coffee, where he used to be a regular. He ditched the Prius in a fire lane and scampered across Pennsylvania Avenue in a hop-along gait that resembled a young girl playing hopscotch in a park.

Then his adrenaline kicked in as he ran under the tree-lined canopy toward the North Lawn. He found what he was looking for—a little snack. Two tourists were casually walking in front of him toward the statue of General Rochambeau, the French general who helped America gain its independence.

Somehow, seeing the Frenchman made him think of steak tartare, which oddly, was a Mongolian dish, not that it mattered. French. Mongolian. The tourists would provide him a welcome snack and energy on the way to his objective.

He lunged at the woman, who was slightly overweight. He sank his teeth into her meaty arms. Her husband tried to fight Rudy off with a camera bag.

It had no effect as the crazed former White House staffer gnawed away at the woman's flesh.

Screams from bystanders startled Rudy, and he abandoned his appetizer. He fled across Pennsylvania Avenue, ignoring the shouts of the Capitol Police, who were racing in his direction.

Rudy stood on top of a bike rack outside the perimeter fence protecting the North Lawn. He tore off his clothes and reached deep within himself to let out a bloodcurdling yell, hoping to release the demons. Hunks of bloody flesh fell out of his mouth as he triumphantly raised his fists in the air.

Voices. Shouting. They're coming for me.

His head pounded.

Rudy didn't hesitate. He jumped onto the fence, ignoring the bands of concertina wire that were designed to block an intruder from climbing over. He felt no pain as his skin was ripped open to the bone.

In a bear-hug motion, he embraced the razor-sharp deterrent and rolled over it, landing with a hard thud on the lush grass. The wire ripped open ribbons of sliced flesh on his chest, across his groin, and down the fronts of his legs, yet he managed to get to his feet.

Rudy was on a mission, although now he didn't know what it was. He just knew. Once again screaming in a language that even he couldn't comprehend, he began to run toward the White House.

He ran like the wind, parts of his body falling as he went. The blood loss was incalculable, but somehow his strength remained—even as bullets began to rip into his body.

The Secret Service and Capitol Police moved toward him, methodically plugging round after round into Rudy until finally his life was mercifully over.

At the time, an explanation for his derangement couldn't be determined. Autopsies and interviews revealed nothing but a troubled man who'd descended into madness. No one thought to consider the profound impact the reversal of Earth's magnetic field had on the human brain and how it functioned.

No, that would come later.

CHAPTER 24

The White House
Washington, DC

President Houston was in the Oval Office, arguing with his wife on the phone, when he heard a commotion emanating from his secretary's office. He was thankful for the distraction, as his mind was focused on matters of state, not the state of his failed marriage.

"What the hell is all the racket?" he shouted after he disconnected the call.

His secretary hustled into his office, followed by two members of his Secret Service detail. They pushed by her and positioned themselves between her and the president, a maneuver that didn't go unnoticed by the leader of the free world.

"What's the meaning of this?" he demanded.

"Sir, we have reason to believe a credible threat to your safety exists," replied one of the agents.

"We're evacuating the West Wing, sir," added the other.

"What's happened?"

"Mr. President, there was a breach at the North Lawn. A man scaled the fence and charged the White House until he was killed."

"Did he have a gun?"

"Um, no, sir," replied the other member of the detail. "He was naked, sir."

The president shoved his hands into his pockets and wandered toward the windows behind his desk that overlooked the South Lawn. He despised the unnecessary use of force, even if it was ostensibly used to protect him.

"They shot a naked guy?" he asked sarcastically.

The agent glanced at the secretary and back to the president. "Sir, he was covered with blood. He scaled the concertina wire and it ripped his torso to shreds. The man, um, who was identified as a former West Wing employee, had just attacked a woman on Pennsylvania Avenue."

"Attacked?"

"Yes, sir. He tried to eat her arm off before entering the White House grounds."

"Come on," began the president, who didn't appreciate unnecessary drama with the strain he was under. "A naked man, a former staffer who walked these halls, attacked a woman and then crawled over the razor wire installed by the last administration?"

"Yes, sir," the agent responded. "If I might add, sir, it took nearly fifty rounds to bring him down. He just kept coming toward the building, unfazed."

The president sighed and made his way to his desk. Beads of sweat broke out on his forehead. He'd dealt with his share of crazies as mayor of San Francisco, and for some reason, California had been a magnet for lunatics since the days of Charles Manson, but this was beyond belief. "Gentlemen, I appreciate your concern for my safety. However, this sounds like an isolated incident that doesn't require the West Wing to be evacuated."

"Sir, our orders came from the chief of staff upon advice of the White House Medical Unit."

President Houston slumped in his chair. He was clearly perplexed and wanted some answers. He barked at his secretary to summon O'Donnell and the White House physician immediately. "Thank you, gentlemen. Please wait outside."

"Sir, our orders are to remain by your side at all—"

"There's no one in this entire government whose orders overrule mine. Now, please. Out!"

The two agents looked at one another and slowly exited the Oval Office. One took up a position in the president's secretary's office, and the other positioned himself in the study on the opposite side of the Oval Office.

The president sat in silence for several minutes. Over the past twenty-four hours, he'd taken the time to review his security briefings a little more closely. He also took a moment to peruse the news online. While the news from Europe dominated the headlines, several stories had caught his eye related to animal activity, bizarre weather events, and two nearly disastrous plane crashes. Thus far, he hadn't seen any reports of people eating one another.

An urgent knock at his door preceded his chief of staff and the White House physician entering with a Secret Service agent in tow.

"Mr. President," greeted Dr. Francis Randolph, a Georgia native who'd been the chief White House caregiver for the last three administrations.

"Francis," the president said as he shook hands with the elderly doctor, "did you clear my building?"

"I suggested it to Angela, yes."

"Because some crazed fool jumped a fence. From what I'm told, he's deader than dead. They found it necessary to kill the unarmed idiot forty or fifty times."

"Mr. President," interjected O'Donnell, "that's what it took to bring him down. Despite what he'd inflicted upon himself, and the severe injuries and blood loss as a result, he was still able to run nearly a hundred yards while being shot."

"Was he on drugs or something?" asked the president.

"Sir, we don't know, but there's been a development that prompted me to suggest this," replied the doctor. He took the next several minutes to relay the background of the dead man, his relationship to the West Wing, and the attack upon his estranged wife.

"All of that happened last night and into this morning?"

"Yes, sir," replied O'Donnell. "Secret Service investigators gleaned all of this from a brief phone call with the man's in-laws, who witnessed the attack. Apparently, he'd been descending into this mental state for many months, including while he was employed down the hall as a research aide to the senior political strategy team."

The president turned his attention to his physician. "Francis, I still don't understand why this isolated event requires shutting down the business of the White House."

"Because, sir, it's not isolated. At least not in our opinion."

President Houston assessed O'Donnell's demeanor. The two were lovers, but were also political partners in tune with one another. Her dour look spoke volumes.

"Okay, okay. Please, let's sit down, and explain how you arrived at this conclusion."

The three of them took up seats on the couches that faced one another across from the Resolute Desk in his office. The presidential seal separated the president from his trusted aides.

Dr. Randolph began, "After your briefing yesterday from the folks at NASA and NOAA, Angela provided me the packet of materials they disseminated to the attendees."

O'Donnell eased up onto the edge of the couch. "I had a hunch, Mr. President, that a geologic event of this magnitude might involve more than wonky compass readings or power outages. I thought Francis should be aware, you know, just in case."

"I'm glad she brought me into the loop, sir," continued Dr. Randolph. "I've known for years that geostorms and solar activity in general have an effect on human consciousness and well-being. These massive releases of energy spew plasma with tens of millions of superheated electrons, protons, and heavy ions close to the speed of light all over our solar system.

"This is not commonly discussed, but animals and humans have a magnetic field that surrounds them, not unlike the Earth's magnetic field, which protects the planet from potentially harmful solar matter. Studies have shown that our magnetic activity peaks during high incidences of anxiety, depression, and emotional disorders like bipolar or general mood swings.

"Ordinarily, the effects of these coronal mass ejections are of short duration. Headaches, palpitations, mood swings and fatigue are all symptoms of the pineal glands in the brain producing excess melatonin hormones."

The president interrupted. "Are you saying that the geostorm that struck Europe caused the guy to do this?"

"No, not necessarily," replied Dr. Randolph. "However, it may have exacerbated something else that was going on within his brain."

"Please explain," said President Houston.

"Our body has an emotional response to almost anything. Animals do too. Every emotional reaction is the body's response to waves of energy. Sometimes these emotions may appear all of a sudden with a clear reason, and other times they may be a stress response. It's something akin to the phenomenon known as barotrauma."

The president leaned forward. "I was once a PADI-certified diver. Are you referring to decompression sickness?"

"Related," replied the doctor. "Studies have shown that following deep, undersea earthquakes, massive amounts of energy are released, generating waves and currents that slam submerged creatures and even divers. The force of this energy damages any animal's brain and circulatory systems. As the injuries progress over weeks or even months, some of the ocean's animals experience such severe, intense pain that they commit suicide by beaching themselves."

"Hey, wait a minute," interjected O'Donnell. "I saw a report the other day that pilot whales had beached themselves onto the coast of France. It was just before the solar flare hit Eastern Europe."

"Francis, could this be related?" asked the president.

"Yes, it could," he replied. "Now, I have a theory that is outside my wheelhouse, but certainly something that should be addressed by the geologists at NASA's Jet Propulsion Laboratory in cooperation with the USGS. Undersea quakes have links to movement of the tectonic plates. After reviewing the materials from yesterday's briefing, it's possible that the significant changes in the Earth's magnetic field, a direct result of fluctuations in the spinning liquid core, may be moving the tectonic plates."

"Which is resulting in the possible mental instability of both animals and humans," concluded the president.

"Well, I will say there is precedent for magnetic field fluctuations initiating abnormal animal behavior. To me, it's logical that the permutations of the geomagnetic field can also affect human brain rhythms and throw off normal hormonal balances."

"Making billions of people go batshit crazy," said O'Donnell.

Dr. Randolph chuckled and smiled. "Not exactly the medical terminology I would've chosen, but aptly descriptive of what we experienced on the White House grounds today."

The president stood and wandered around the Oval Office. He removed his jacket and pulled his arms behind his back to stretch his chest and relieve some tension. "Francis, we've evacuated the West Wing, and the media will be demanding answers. I've got to be able to address this without scaring three hundred twenty million Americans into thinking their neighbors are all going to turn into zombies."

Dr. Randolph grimaced. "Mr. President, I understand your dilemma. Please keep in mind that I've posited a theory based upon my medical background and scientific fact. That said, the pole shift impacting our planet, while not unprecedented, has never occurred to this magnitude in the history of modern man. Frankly, it's never been thoroughly researched because there isn't a means to create a test environment."

"So what do we tell them?" asked the president.

O'Donnell answered, "We tell them nothing. Internally, we minimize the number of staff present to essential personnel only. Also, we keep a Secret Service detail at the side of the president at all times until we can get some answers. We'll use this morning's intrusion as a logical explanation for that."

The president studied both of his trusted advisors before he spoke. "And what do we do if one of them loses their mind?"

Nobody had an answer for that question.

CHAPTER 25

The Situation Room
The White House
Washington, DC

President Houston marched through the bowels of the West Wing, with a small entourage in tow consisting of Chief of Staff O'Donnell, the White House press secretary, his speech writer, and an equal number of Secret Service personnel who'd been assigned to watch each member of the president's staff who were in close proximity to him, as well as each other.

He entered the hallway that led to the Situation Room. He greeted the watch officer, a lieutenant commander in the United States Navy, who was assigned to approve access inside. He was dressed in a sharply pressed black uniform and saluted the president.

After returning the salute, the president approached the secure door with a camera mounted above it. A black-and-gold plaque inscribed with the words *White House Situation Room: Restricted Access* reminded visitors of the room's importance.

The White House Situation Room was a five-thousand-square-foot complex of rooms located on the ground floor of the West Wing.

The Situation Room was born out of frustration on the part of President John Kennedy after the Bay of Pigs debacle in Cuba. President Kennedy felt betrayed by the conflicting advice and information coming in to him from the various agencies that comprised the nation's defense departments. Kennedy ordered the bowling alley built during the Truman presidency removed and replaced with the Situation Room.

Initially, before the age of electronics, President Kennedy required at least one Central Intelligence analyst to remain in the Situation Room at all times. The analyst would work a twenty-hour shift and sleep on a cot during the night.

Other presidents, like Nixon and Ford, never used the Situation Room. In most cases, a visit from the president was a formal undertaking, happening only on rare occasions. President George H. W. Bush, a former CIA head, would frequently call and ask if he could stop by and say hello.

When there had been a foreign policy failure, such as when the shoe bomber boarded a flight on Christmas Day in 2009, the Situation Room became a forum for a tongue-lashing directed at top-level intelligence and national security personnel. Fortunately, the Houston administration had not yet experienced a crisis requiring a high-level national security briefing like this one, until now.

The lock on the door buzzed, and the president entered the main conference room. Updated in 2006, the room was surrounded by flat-screen monitors used for secure video conference, and computer terminals that linked the president to world leaders, as well as his military personnel. The once ornate mahogany walls that made the space resemble a big corporate boardroom were now replaced by sound-friendly whisper walls designed to block sophisticated listening devices.

President Houston immediately recognized some of the same faces that had initially briefed him on the pole shift and the weakening of the planet's magnetic field. Chief of Staff O'Donnell had already given him a heads-up on the subject matter of the briefing and the need for urgency. Now, the president hoped to pin down the brightest scientific minds in America to offer solutions as to how he could best protect the nation.

"Well, ladies and gentlemen, I understand we're at the moment of truth," began the president. "The fate of an entire nation is based upon what you're about to tell me, and what I do next."

Just as in the prior briefing, Nola Taylor from NASA took the lead. "Sir, the active region that had been on our radar appeared as expected and immediately generated an X-class solar flare. The data is still being analyzed, but it appears to be a magnitude X2 to X3."

"What level of geostorm activity can we expect?" asked the president.

"G1 or G2," she replied. "Very similar to the one that engulfed Eastern Europe and Paris."

"Do you have an ETA on when it will reach Earth?"

"Thirty to thirty-six hours, sir."

"Marvelous," he muttered to himself as he closed his eyes momentarily. Then he asked, "Do you have a projected location of where it might hit Earth?"

Taylor leaned forward and clasped her fingers together as she rested her arms on the conference table. "Sir, at this juncture, it's impossible to definitively answer your question. While this solar flare is directed toward Earth, the timing of its arrival could result in a direct hit, or perhaps a glancing blow, or maybe even miss the planet altogether."

"Well, Ms. Taylor, that's a lot of coulds, perhapses, and maybes."

"I understand, sir, but unfortunately, the closer the solar flare gets to the planet, the more accurate our predictions become. We needed to brief you now so that you can prepare any possible countermeasures."

"Countermeasures?" he asked.

"Yes, sir," replied Taylor. "We can reposition satellites in our low-Earth orbit. Because of the potential effect on our global positioning systems, you might consider grounding air traffic. And, although this is outside my purview to suggest, you might consider repositioning the nation's military assets."

"Why?" asked the president.

"Um, sir, to deal with the, you know, aftermath."

"Aftermath of what?"

"The potential damage caused to our infrastructure by the geomagnetic storm."

The president rubbed his temples. This had all been thrust upon him so quickly. He was furious with previous presidents and Congress for not establishing an action plan to deal with a catastrophic event like this one. Certainly, nobody anticipated a pole shift causing the weakening of the Earth's magnetic field. However, solar flares happened all the time, and it was just a matter of time before the *big one* came along.

The awkward silence allowed another voice to enter the discussion. An older woman sat quietly at the far end of the table from the president. She raised her hand respectfully.

"Mr. President, may I speak?" she said in a calming voice.

He looked at her and waved his hand in a by-all-means gesture. "Who are you, and do you have anything positive to add?"

"I believe you have the answer, Mr. President," she replied.

The president appeared both perplexed and annoyed. "Ma'am, I'm not in the mood for riddles."

"Understood. My name is Cassandra White with FERC," she began as she sat a little taller in her seat. FERC was an acronym for the Federal Energy Regulatory Commission, an agency of the government that regulates electricity and other forms of power resources. "I imagine that you're not in the mood. You do have the answer, sir. You've implemented the solution in your home state."

The president took a deep breath and tried to figure out what the woman was referring to. Then he furrowed his brow and began to point in her direction. "Yes. Yes. I know where you're headed. You're referring to the wildfires, aren't you?"

"I am."

"We had a *black start* plan. Truthfully, I pushed back against it at first, but PG&E had the right idea."

"Yes. Do you see what I'm suggesting?" she asked.

"Can we do it on a national scale?"

"In part, yes. It's never been done, naturally. But we've game-planned it."

After years of massive wildfires and damage to electrical substations and associated infrastructure, California, under the suggestion of Pacific Gas and Electric, with the reluctant blessing of then-Governor Houston, began to implement a plan to avoid the constant expense associated with rebuilding the grid when the fires were doused.

As the height of fire season approached California, typically a period of dangerously strong winds mixed with temperatures approaching triple digits, communities began to implement preemptive blackouts to reduce the fire risks.

In years past, downed power lines operated by PG&E contributed to the fires that spread across the state. The *black start* plan was designed to eliminate adding fuel to an already roaring fire, so to speak, while protecting other critical aspects of electricity delivery to the state's users.

The power shutoffs were not without their critics. Many argued that losing access to the news networks put lives in danger, as warnings weren't getting to certain communities. There was also heightened concern about those with health issues who relied upon medical equipment to stay alive.

Mostly, citizens screamed bloody murder about the inconveniences they incurred due to the short notice provided by the utilities and the mere fact that they had to live their lives for a brief period of time without electricity.

Nonetheless, during President Houston's tenure as governor, the black start plan, formerly known as Public Safety Power Shutoffs, worked to reduce the spread of wildfires and the longer loss of power caused by the outbreaks.

O'Donnell, who was the president's chief of staff while he was in Sacramento, spoke up first. "There were grumblings at times, but overall, the black start plan worked. We were able to work with the utilities to target specific substations and then use flatbed-mounted generators to jump-start them after the threat was over. As long as we can find a way to protect that equipment, we can get the grid back on its feet in short order."

The representative from FERC spoke up. "The nation's military installations have been hardened against electromagnetic pulse events, whether man-made due to a nuclear weapon, or naturally occurring, as in the geostorm that concerns us all. They have buildings that are shielded and capable of protecting the equipment. The biggest problem we face is the lack of generators capable of restarting these massive substations. It could take weeks to fire them up again after the black start plan is implemented."

The president nodded. "California was different. We only cut the power to the communities directly impacted by the fire. The equipment wasn't at risk because it was kept far away from the wildfire and not subjected to the likes of a solar flare."

Another attendee of the briefing raised his hand to speak. "May I add something, Mr. President?"

"Of course. And you are?"

"Nathaniel Arnold with the Department of Energy."

"Go ahead, Mr. Arnold."

The young man gulped and began, "Sir, if I understand correctly, the potential for a geostorm knocking out our grid can come as frequently as twice a week during the peak of a solar cycle like the one we're in right now. Exactly how often are you going to have to turn the power grid off and then back on again? Also, what kind of toll will that take on the equipment, as well as the psyche of the American people?"

Nathaniel Arnold's words hung in the air as everyone in the Situation Room contemplated a world without power.

CHAPTER 26

Outside the White House
Washington, DC

Nathaniel Arnold was on cloud nine when he exited the White House and summoned an Uber to drive him the short three miles to the James V. Forrestal Building. Arnold had been a last-minute stand-in for the Energy Secretary, who'd fallen ill and was under a physician's care for kidney stones.

Recently divorced right after he turned forty, Arnold had jumped headfirst into the DC dating scene, choosing to look outside the Energy Department for prospective mates. He'd met his first wife at work, and the two found they couldn't be with each other virtually twenty-four seven.

He'd met Maxie, an attractive woman nearly fourteen years his junior, who was a research assistant at the *Washington Post*. The two hit it off and frequently met for drinks at Johnny's Half Shell, a seafood restaurant just blocks from the Capitol that was known for hosting the political movers and shakers of Washington.

Arnold really didn't care much for politics, trying his best to stay out of partisan bickering in the workplace. He was a career bureaucrat and intended to retire that way. Maxie liked to perform research and rarely got involved in the news reporting side at the *Post*, although recently she'd cozied up to a new hotshot named Eric Bradley, who'd shown more than a passing interest in her.

Arnold wasn't aware of Maxie's interest in the new reporter, as he was smitten with the younger woman. While the two frequently acknowledged they weren't *exclusive*, Arnold just assumed that Maxie was as infatuated with him as he was with her.

116

In any event, he was very excited to share the news of his contribution to this high-level meeting that involved the president. He recounted the events to his girlfriend and excitedly bragged how he might have an impact on the president's decision.

Naturally, Arnold had already told Maxie during their morning pillow talk about his attending the meeting. When she pressed him to disclose the nature of the briefing, he was somewhat aloof, but felt like all of the details would be coming out soon anyway. He wanted to impress her with his importance, and therefore he might have been a little loose with his tongue.

Now, it's possible that Maxie kept her promise and didn't repeat any of Arnold's words to her coworkers at the *Washington Post*, especially the secret lover she'd taken on the side—the hotshot reporter.

But when a headline story came out later in the day on the website of the *New York Times* that the president was facing an existential crisis that might require him to shut down the nation's power grid for an extended period of time, Arnold never imagined that the devastating leak came out of his mouth. After all, his girlfriend worked for the *Times'* principal competitor, the *Washington Post*.

The Uber driver's wife, however, was on the staff of Maggie Haberman, the White House correspondent for the *New York Times*.

Loose lips sink ships.

CHAPTER 27

Teterboro, New Jersey

Anger and shouting were replaced by fear and praying. Many passengers were gripping their armrests, knuckles white as the aircraft began its slow, prolonged descent into the Teterboro Airport. The captain, seemingly aware of the short runway, had been cleared for a flatter descent that allowed him to slow his airspeed considerably.

Like many of the passengers who preferred to see their potential demise unfold, as opposed to closing their eyes, waiting for it to be over, Chapman and Isabella monitored their progress through the porthole-sized window adjacent to their row of seats.

Tension was high between them, but they supported one another as the plane dropped closer to the ground. The closer the aircraft got to the Teterboro runway, the tighter Isabella's grip became on Chapman's hand.

Chapman never relayed the story that he recalled involving a plane crash in Teterboro when he was growing up. A corporate jet had overshot the runway, hurtling off the end toward a busy highway in the midst of morning rush hour. The plane had careened across a culvert, rammed into twenty cars, sending the burning wreckage across the road into a warehouse, where the crew members and passengers calmly walked away.

Chapman considered using this as an example to calm her nerves, but she was astute enough to know no two plane crashes were alike. And there was a big difference between an eleven-passenger corporate jet and a Boeing 777—*big* being the operative word.

The captain brought the aircraft lower to the ground, seemingly grazing the top of the MetLife football stadium at the Meadowlands

118

as he made the final turn into the runway. The aircraft was brought to a near stall as it soared toward landing. It was eye level to a car dealership when the rear wheels touched down just as the runway began.

Now for the fun part. The captain deployed every available measure to produce rearward thrust after touchdown, rapidly slowing the Boeing 777 as its momentum fought against the pilot's tactics. Using brakes, spoilers to increase wing drag, and thrust reversers on the General Electric engines, the plane fought to come to a stop.

Emergency vehicles had gathered on both sides of Runway 19 as the powerful aircraft shuddered and shook, throwing passengers forward in their seats and luggage bins open. A suitcase dislodged from across the aisle where Chapman was sitting and landed on the floor next to him. He bent down to stabilize it, which helped him avoid the laptop computer sailing over his head.

Isabella wasn't so lucky. The edge of the laptop landed on top of her thigh, causing her to scream in pain. A scream drowned out by the spontaneous cheer that erupted when the aircraft came to a stop with its front wheels resting in the grass at the end of the runway.

Chapman immediately turned to check on her. "I'm sorry, I could've stopped it."

She was rubbing her leg and eased his concern. "I will be fine. It is Charley's horse."

Chapman laughed and kissed her. "Yes, Charley's horse. Don't worry, if you can't walk, I'll carry you."

"See, I will let you take care of me," she said with a smile before becoming serious. "Chapman, how far are we from your home?"

"I'm not exactly sure. Maybe eight or nine hundred miles?"

The captain addressed the passengers, interrupting them. "Well, folks, this is Captain Whittaker again from the flight deck. My apologies for the rougher-than-usual landing. This runway is much shorter than what we're accustomed to with this equipment. Um, we are most likely stuck in place here, but the ground personnel are bringing the portable stairs to help you disembark. You may take your carry-on luggage with you, and the rest of your bags will be available at baggage claim. Again, my apologies for the delay and the adventure at the end. We hope you have a great rest of your day, and thank you for flying American Airlines."

Two hours later, Chapman and Isabella were inside the terminal. The chaotic scene inside was not unlike the near-melee that almost took place on board the plane. Thousands of passengers were stranded, angry, and confused. Airport personnel were overwhelmed and getting frustrated as passengers demanded answers they were unable to provide.

Isabella was able to walk, but she wasn't able to put full pressure on her leg. As they moved with the throngs of passengers along the concourse, television monitors were turned on to the CNN news feed. They listened to the host and his guests opine as to what happened in Europe and how that related to the president's decision to ground air travel.

"Our sources with NOAA are confirming that a geomagnetic storm struck Eastern Europe. It immediately impacted the power grids of several countries and spread across the easternmost regions of Europe like a wave, causing cascading power outages.

"While there has been no official word from the White House as of yet, we do believe that the executive order grounding all air traffic was directly related to this solar activity. Let me turn to our veteran CNN weatherman, Chad Myers. Chad?"

Chapman led Isabella into a gate area that was relatively empty. Several people were gathered around the television monitor suspended from the ceiling of the terminal. Chapman had experienced charley horses and leg cramping on the farm. He needed to get blood flow to Isabella's thigh muscle so she could move without causing further damage to her leg.

"Here, sit and get comfortable," he began to explain. "I'm going to stretch your thigh muscle and massage it. As I do, flex your foot by rolling it around on your ankle, and then pull your toes toward you. Okay?"

Isabella smiled and nodded. Chapman removed her shoe and gave her right foot a quick massage. Then, while he rubbed the top of her thigh and gently massaged the muscle, being careful not to cause her any pain, he monitored the CNN broadcast.

"Reports from the European Space Agency and NASA have confirmed that a G1 geomagnetic storm struck an area near Central Romania."

The host interrupted Myers and asked him to explain for the viewers how these geomagnetic storms develop.

"If you think of the Sun as a giant bubble of boiling water, then the solar wind would be the wisps of steam that float away from the surface. The Sun is always simmering, sending off clouds, or tendrils, of high-energy puffs of particles called coronal mass ejections.

"These solar wind particles are what create the aurora phenomena in Earth's northern latitudes. Now, what is unusual about this particular geostorm is its relative weakness to storms of its type in the past.

"Ordinarily, a G1 storm might cause minor inconveniences and, of course, the beautiful aurora. By minor inconveniences, I'm talking about ham radio disruptions perhaps, GPS devices providing misleading data, and the occasional localized power outage at rural electricity providers who don't have the most up-to-date equipment.

"What I am hearing from our contacts at NASA has not been made public, at least not officially yet. You see, in times of intense geomagnetic storms, when the Earth's magnetosphere is weakened, the solar wind and these particles slam into the planet. It's like releasing the energy of several nuclear weapons detonating simultaneously.

"These missile-like groups of matter are capable of opening a gate in the Earth's magnetic field, allowing the energetic particles to enter the atmosphere and send currents all the way down to the planet's surface. They can induce currents in the electrical grid, overheat transformers, and cause them to fail. These enormous transformers that are part of our power grid can take months or years to replace. You can't exactly buy another one at Home Depot."

Chapman smiled up at Isabella and stood with his arms outstretched. "Are you ready to give it a try?"

She nodded and stood.

Walking with one shoe on and one shoe off, she swayed along the wall of the terminal away from other stranded passengers.

"So much better, Chapman. Thank you."

She hobbled back to her seat and retrieved her shoe. Chapman assisted her with putting it back on, and then he looked up to her.

"The president must be aware of the solar flare, and now the question is whether our contemporaries at NASA and NOAA will piece together the pole shift as being the cause. I believe they have; otherwise the president wouldn't have grounded all air travel."

"Should we get a hotel room for the night and start our travels tomorrow?"

Chapman helped her onto her feet and grimaced. "I don't think we should wait. Believe me, I'm exhausted like you, and I'd like to see you get some ice on your leg. However, as the scientific community and the news media continue to arrive at the truth, the public will become aware of the seriousness of this. I believe the president knows that the next geostorm could be the one that takes down our grid, so he took the initial step of getting the planes out of the sky."

"I will do my best to keep up with you. Should you call your family?"

Chapman pulled his cell phone out of his pocket and tried, to no avail. After several attempts to place a call, only to get alternating messages that all circuits were busy or simply a fast busy signal, he shoved the phone back in his pocket and pointed Isabella in the direction of baggage claim and the car-rental counter.

"We'll try again later. First, let's get our transportation."

CHAPTER 28

Teterboro, New Jersey

The two travelers made their way to the rental-car counters at Teterboro and were greeted with a hostile mob. Chapman pulled Isabella to the side, where she would be away from the scrum taking place around the kiosks. He looked over the top of the animated rental-hopefuls and saw the same eight-and-a-half-by-eleven sign that appeared to have been printed for every company. It read, quite simply, *NO CARS*.

Chapman shook his head and questioned his own sanity for hoping otherwise. Naturally, with flights grounded nationwide and every airport within a hundred miles of the city accepting diverted aircraft, the rentals would be sold out. He returned to Isabella to explain.

"I should've known. The rental cars are all leased out. Now that I think about it, we'll be lucky to find a taxi or an Uber."

She hobbled slightly toward him until she reached his side. "We could walk," she said with a chuckle.

"Yeah. Um, no. You know, I saw a car dealership just as we touched down on the runway. It may be two miles to walk there."

Isabella looked around and pointed toward the baggage carousels. "The wheelchair. Can you push me? I will carry the bags."

"Brilliant!" exclaimed Chapman as he pushed his way through the angry mob looking for a rental-car agent to scream at. Chapman pictured them all huddled under a desk locked in a back room somewhere.

He reached the wheelchair and bulled his way back through the uncooperative crowd like a dad pushing a stroller through the Magic

Kingdom. "Excuse me, pardon me. Coming through. Wheelchair. Make way, please." He didn't wait for some people to react, opting instead to give them a gentle nudge, drawing nasty looks before the victim turned their ire back toward the unmanned rental counters.

Isabella was laughing as he returned, pointing to the top of the wheelchair. "Look, it has an orange flag. Very stylish."

"Sporty, too."

He loaded her up and got her legs positioned on the footrests. He piled their bags in her lap and off they went. None of the airport personnel gave them a second glance as he wheeled her through the glass front doors and onto the sidewalk.

Within minutes, he was pushing her down Industrial Avenue to make the two-mile-long trek to where Runway 19 began at the intersection of Moonachie Avenue and Redneck Avenue (seriously, no kidding). It took them almost an hour, but they managed to joke and laugh the entire way. It was an adventure that would create lifetime memories of their first days as a couple.

Chapman pushed Isabella to the front of Bergen County Auto Group, a used-car dealership specializing in used BMWs. Chapman wasn't surprised that the two of them arrived unnoticed by a swarm of car salesman. Their wheelchair trade-in wasn't particularly attractive to a dealership that dealt in *bimmers*.

He helped Isabella inside and approached a young woman at a sales desk just inside the plate-glass doors. "Hi, we need to speak to someone about buying a car."

Without looking up from her tablet computer, where she scanned Yahoo! News stories, she curtly responded, "Cash or cash equivalent only. No credit."

Chapman misunderstood. "Not a problem. I have excellent credit."

The gum-chewing salesperson looked up and made eye contact with her prospects. "No credit. The owner cannot get any of our financing sources to make decisions right now, you know, considering everything that's goin' on. Cash or cash equivalent only."

"What does that mean?" asked Isabella.

The woman rudely replied, treating Isabella as if she couldn't comprehend English. She stretched out her words as she spoke. "Caaassshhh. Gooollldddd. Or maaajjjor credit card. Got it?"

Isabella's first impression of people from New Jersey wasn't a good one.

"Did you say gold? Really?" Chapman rolled his eyes.

"That's right. Now, feel free to look around if you can pay by one of these three methods. Keep in mind, credit cards carry a four percent administrative charge."

"Come on, Chapman. Let us leave this rude—"

Chapman firmly grabbed Isabella by the arm and tugged her away from the gum chomper before a catfight broke out.

"I agree," he whispered. "Let's try to make a deal before we get going."

They walked arm-in-arm through the small showroom and then strolled outside. They were shocked by what they found. The regular window stickers of the cars had been marked through with a red Sharpie and increased by fifty percent. All of the cars were well over twenty thousand dollars.

"I don't have that kind of availability on my credit cards," Chapman complained. "This is ridiculous. They must have something less expensive." He marched back inside, leaving Isabella on the sidewalk alone. He approached the salesperson again.

"Um, these are kind of pricey for my credit card. Don't you have anything under ten thousand?" Chapman laughed to himself. He couldn't believe he was going to use his Discover card to purchase a vehicle.

"Around the side," she replied, once again without taking her attention away from the computer. She made no attempt to mask her snide attitude. "Motorcycles are all you can afford."

Chapman couldn't resist. "I can afford plenty. You just insist upon getting paid with gold or some such."

The woman shrugged and pointed toward the side of the building.

Chapman retrieved Isabella, and they made their way to the motorcycle inventory. As they walked through the neatly arranged bikes, she asked, "Do you know how to drive one of these?"

He hesitated. "Well, I drove a friend's dirt bike on the farm once. I rode a perfect wheelie until I ran into a barbed-wire fence."

Isabella abruptly stopped. "Chapman, maybe we should try another car dealer."

"No, I've got this. I mean, how hard could it be? Besides, we need something with good gas mileage in case ..." His voice trailed off as he walked briskly away from her. He'd found the perfect solution, and he was on a mission to check it out.

At the back of the building sat a gently used BMW R1200GS, which included a complete sidecar mounted to its side. He was like a little kid in a candy store.

"Isabella, this is the one. It's perfect and it's under ten grand!"

Ninety-nine ninety-five, to be exact.

She caught up to him and stood with her hands on her hips. "You expect me to ride in that sidecar like some German officer in World War Two? No, Chapman, I can't do it. Let's go find a real car."

He plead his case. "No, you can ride behind me on the padded seat. We'll use the sidecar for our bags and whatever else we need to travel. Come on, it'll be fun!"

She rolled her eyes and then giggled. "Okay, maybe a little bit of fun. I need sunglasses, a scarf, and toothpicks."

"Why do you need toothpicks?"

"To pick the bugs out of my teeth as we ride to Indiana."

Chapman couldn't help himself as he rushed to her, lifted her in a bear hug, and twirled her around and around. He loved her more than life.

CHAPTER 29

Brookfield Zoo
Chicago, Illinois

Kristi leaned back in her office chair, with her feet propped up on the corner of her desk. Her computer keyboard was in her lap and the mouse in her right hand as she navigated the World Wide Web in search of research papers discussing other instances of unusual animal behavior similar to the ones they'd experienced.

Tommy mimicked her posture by slouching in a chair, feet propped up on the other corner of her desk, researching the zoology journals on the Wiley Online Library website for more information on the phenomenon they were witnessing. Interestingly, they remained singularly focused on studying their scientific resources and took no time to glance at the news headlines.

Occasionally, Tommy complained about the bandages she'd wrapped around his hand and the throbbing pain the wound caused. She'd acknowledge his complaints with the occasional grunt or *I'm sorry*, but mostly they resembled an old married couple lounging in their respective easy chairs, pointing out something of interest from time to time, but not necessarily hearing one another.

The two had stayed at the zoo the entire time since Tommy had been attacked, hunkered down in Kristi's office, searching for answers. They'd consumed anything edible from her small refrigerator and cupboard full of snacks, occasionally walking outside to stretch their legs and get fresh air. Otherwise, they were oblivious to the events transpiring around them. They were intent on confirming their theories about the animals' behavior. Just as important, the two were looking for any scientific research that might help alleviate the mental suffering and confusion being experienced by the creatures they lovingly cared for.

Someone, or something, began to pound on Kristi's office door, causing both of them to jump out of their chairs in fear. They didn't say a word as they stared at each other, wondering what to do.

Thump! Thump! Thump!

A steady three-knock demand to be opened. Its constant beat was unlikely an animal and more likely a cop. They were right, sort of.

The door handle turned, and a gust of fresh air preceded the head of the zoo's security team as he entered her office.

He was curt and to the point. "Dr. Charles, um, I mean Boone, you're needed in the administration building."

His brusque approach struck Kristi the wrong way, considering the circumstances. She directed her ire at the security chief. "Yeah, well, *your* presence was required at the big cat's habitat yesterday. Where were you and your team when one of our zookeepers was being mauled and Mr. Bannon was being attacked?"

"I'm sorry, ma'am. I didn't know anything about Mr. Bannon, and our patrols came across the other situation late in the evening." He began to make his way toward the door, when Kristi stopped him.

"That's all you've got to say? *I didn't know?* Where are your people? Why aren't the phones working?"

The security chief stopped and stared outside. Without turning around, he said, "Most of them quit after the incident at the bear habitat." He didn't elaborate, nor did he address the issue with the telephone lines.

"Wait. What happened there?" asked Tommy.

The man simply shook his head and reminded them both to go to the administration building immediately. Then he walked away.

"What the heck was that all about?" asked Tommy as he wandered to the door and watched the security chief walk along the sidewalk with his head hung down.

Kristi leaned over her computer keyboard and exited her programs. Her research had yielded everything from beached dolphins off the coast of West Africa to an unusual feral hog migration from Canada into the U.S. To be sure, abnormal animal behavior was not unexpected, but the frequency and number seemed to be increasing. It certainly was at the Brookfield Zoo.

She stood and pulled her lab coat off the back of her chair. She checked to make sure the masking tape was still in place covering the name of her ex-husband. She pulled it down and brushed out the wrinkles. "Let's go find out."

The two of them walked briskly through the zoo complex. It was eerily quiet and desolate. Normally after hours, zoo personnel scampered about, cleaning up after the visitors that day and caring for the animals at night. The zoo would come alive in the evening hours as the animals sensed they were alone for the most part. They knew they were captives and, over time, grew tired of being on display. It was only the newcomers to Brookfield who were animated for their human watchers upon arrival, but as time passed, they gradually became disinterested in their surroundings.

Tommy opened the double glass doors for Kristi as they entered the administration building. In stark contrast to the nondescript block and brick buildings that housed the zoologists and the veterinarians, the admin building was ornately designed and impeccably decorated. As part of the Chicago Zoological Society, the executive team at the zoo had to kiss many a rear end in order to keep the zoo funded. Like most zoological parks in America, they couldn't operate on gate receipts and tee shirt sales alone. It took government money, private donations, and legacy grants via animal lovers' estates to stay afloat.

A security guard pointed Kristi and Tommy in the direction of a small auditorium at the end of the hallway that stretched the entire length of the building. As they walked toward the open doorway, Kristi glanced at the photography of Marsel van Oosten, four-time winner of the prestigious Wildlife Photographer of the Year competition.

The Dutch photographer was known for taking risks in order to capture the best shot in the wild. His photographs depicted animals in a peaceful, tranquil state. Kristi wondered if van Oosten would be interested in photographing the current state of the animal kingdom at Brookfield Zoo today.

As they entered, Dr. Barbara Boston, the zoo's executive director, waved to Kristi and pointed to two chairs in the front row of the auditorium.

"I think we're all here now," she announced as all eyes were on the two until they took their seats. As they made their way down the aisle, several attendees commented on Tommy's extensive bandaging and shrugged, as they were unaware of what had caused his injuries. As everyone settled down, Dr. Boston began.

"I'm sorry for the late hour meeting. Frankly, I assumed all of you were home at this point, and it took a little while to locate our late arrivals, who were still at the zoo. Let me tell you what's happening."

Tommy and Kristi exchanged glances and then looked around the room at their coworkers. Most of them were dressed in casual clothes as if they'd just been dragged out of their easy chairs. Tommy and Kristi were the only ones who appeared disheveled and exhausted. What they were about to learn transcended the difficulties they'd faced in their small part of the world.

CHAPTER 30

Brookfield Zoo
Chicago, Illinois

"Please, let me continue," admonished Dr. Boston as she implored the attendees to stop chatting among themselves. "Although there has not been an official announcement from the president, it appears that the recent power outage caused by solar activity across Eastern Europe has led the administration to believe that a similar event could occur in our country. There are far more questions than answers at this point, but I must tell you this is very disconcerting for all of our lives."

The group began to talk again, and Kristi turned in her chair to study their faces. She was exhausted, but they were also frightened.

The executive director continued. "If the reports are true, the president intends to turn off our electricity, perhaps as early as tomorrow."

Another murmur rumbled through the attendees, many of whom had been home with their eyes glued to the news. Kristi and Tommy had been on the internet all afternoon, but their focus was on scientific research, not perusing the news websites.

"Please, everyone, allow me to finish. Now, as I said, this is strictly rumor and conjecture based upon anonymous sources, but many experts are saying this is a distinct possibility. The reason I've called you all here this evening is to discuss how this impacts Brookfield Zoo and especially the animals within our care."

One of the attendees from the rear of the room shouted out a question. "How long will the power be off?"

"I heard it could be weeks or even months," another attendee replied.

Another person chimed in. "That was FoxNews and their conspiracy theorists. CNN said it would only be temporary."

Dr. Boston grew frustrated. "Listen up, people. I don't know how long it will be turned off, or whether it will be at all. But, as a group, we need to discuss our options in all scenarios."

"What do you mean by options?" someone asked.

"Well, first of all, the zoo is not equipped to operate without power. And by operate, I'm not referring to opening up for visitors. By the way, on that note, we'll be closing to outsiders until further notice."

The room burst into an uproar. Even those who'd been glued to the television all afternoon and were aware of the White House leaks hadn't realized their jobs were directly affected by this.

One person shouted their questions. "What about us? What are we supposed to do?"

Dr. Boston was glad to reply and get back on point. "Well, for one thing, I hope that all of you report to work, as we intend to continue paying you. Now, if the power grid is down, we don't expect those of you who live some distance away to be here. But if you can walk or ride a bicycle, for example, I would expect you to come and help out."

A man stood up in the middle of the aisle. "Dr. Boston, with all due respect, I believe you're being naïve about this. When the power is shut down, this city is going to descend into chaos. Heck, it practically is lawless on a normal day. There's no way I'm leaving my house when the power is cut off."

A number of voices joined in his sentiment.

"Yeah, same here!"

"I've got my own to care for!"

"It'll be too dangerous."

Kristi was becoming angry. She stood, turned to the group and began firing off a series of very logical questions. "If we stay home, who will care for the animals? Are you gonna let them starve? What about water? If the power is off, the city can't pump water to us."

"Everyone," interrupted Dr. Boston, "Dr. Boone raises valid points, which is why I've called you all here. We have to come together to address our responsibility to care for these magnificent animals."

The panicked, angry members of the zoo's administrative staff continued to bombard Dr. Boston with questions.

"Do you mean like the bear that mauled the security guard?"

"Or the lions that ate half my staff?"

She responded, "Yes, all of them. I don't have a handle on why these accidents have occurred at the zoo of late, and frankly, I look to some of you for an explanation. But that is a discussion for another day. For now, we have to come up with a plan of action to care for all of them."

Tommy raised his hand. "Why don't we divide into teams and work in shifts? I think I can speak for Dr. Boone in saying that we'd be glad to care for them." Tommy turned to the others in the auditorium and conducted a quick, albeit approximate head count.

Thirty-three were in attendance.

He asked, "How many will join us and commit to caring for our zoo while the country works through this crisis?"

At first, nobody raised their hands as they looked at one another. It resembled a classroom of ninth graders who didn't know the answers to their teacher's question. Most attendees slunk down into their chairs, hoping to hide from Tommy's gaze. Eventually seven reluctantly raised their hands.

Tommy was incensed, and disappointed. "Seven? Really? You oughta be ashamed!" He swung back around and collapsed into his chair, shaking his head in disgust.

Dr. Boston took control of the room. "This is what I was afraid of. We simply cannot care for our animals with a handful of reluctant volunteers. To leave them in captivity with the hopes that the power grid will come on quickly is irresponsible. I cannot imagine these beautiful creatures dying of starvation or dehydration."

"We can't let them go," said a woman in the rear of the auditorium. "The predators would sweep through the city at will, killing people right and left."

Another chimed in, "Plus, studies have shown that animals in captivity can't survive when released back into the wild, much less Chicago. Look what happened to our primates."

"Yeah!" shouted another one, and suddenly, Kristi felt all eyes upon her.

After an internal investigation, many blamed her for teaching Knight too much and irresponsibly allowing him to become a part of her daily activities. The final report deduced that it was Knight who had taught the chimps how to escape. In fact, many believed she was hiding Knight at her home after he disappeared that day, and several drove by on occasion in an effort to confirm their suspicions.

Dr. Boston surveyed her subordinates, and a wave of sadness came over her. Her demeanor changed completely as she said the words.

"Then it leaves us no choice but to consider euthanasia."

CHAPTER 31

ALF Outpost
Bolingbrook, Illinois

Jerry Watson was dressed in all black clothing with a mask covering his face when he greeted his guests at an abandoned warehouse in Bolingbrook, Illinois, that evening. Many of the attendees of the hastily called gathering knew who he was but understood his need for anonymity nonetheless.

Watson, a former Bolingbrook firefighter, had been the poster boy for PETA, literally. A dozen years ago, he was selected by the People for the Ethical Treatment of Animals organization as their Hottest Vegan Firefighter in the world.

He'd suffered from various physical ailments and changed his lifestyle to eliminate any foods that weren't vegan. PETA, whose motto reads, in part, that *animals are not ours to eat*, praised Watson for his adoption of the vegan lifestyle and rewarded his good looks with the Hottest Vegan Firefighter honor.

The notoriety changed his life. He quit his job as a firefighter and devoted his life to animal rights. His wife, a zoologist on staff at Brookfield Zoo, supported his decision, as her salary was sufficient to pay their bills.

As Watson became more involved in the organization, he gradually became more fanatical in his beliefs. After a couple of years, PETA disassociated themselves from him because of his extremist activities in the name of animal rights. He fell into the welcoming arms of the Animal Liberation Front.

PETA had once tacitly supported ALF until their measures became so extreme that the FBI declared them to be a domestic terrorist group. PETA supported animal rights, whereas ALF focused on their version of animal liberation.

Those who became involved with ALF had a deep-rooted ideology that animals were equivalent to human beings and therefore deserving of legal rights. They had an intense perception of injustice and felt compelled to act in order to correct the exploitation or killing of animals. Such actions were most often extreme and criminal in nature.

Watson accepted the call to action by his new friends at ALF and immediately became self-radicalized. He searched online for manuals, which served as how-to guides for committing criminal acts on behalf of helpless animals. Treatises like the *Black Cat Sabotage Handbook* and *Arson Around with Auntie ALF* served to educate him on how to conduct terrorist, anarchist activities for his chosen cause.

They were known to kidnap animals from private collections and zoos when the opportunity presented itself. If they couldn't liberate a captive animal, they would direct their hostilities at the facility or organization that housed them. They'd firebombed zoo administrator's homes. Hijacked trucks transporting exotic animals on the interstate. They'd even held a Minnesota family hostage until the mink-pelt farm where the husband and wife worked agreed to release between thirty and forty thousand farm-raised minks. The action of the ALF extremists turned out to be disastrous.

Most of the minks died, as most animals that have been raised in captivity do. The released minks that were recovered were haphazardly thrown into cages, which disrupted their social groupings, eventually causing them to kill one another. Overlooked in the tragic ending was the fact that the minks were held on the pelt farm to eventually be killed for their pelts anyway.

ALF considered their operation a success, and it emboldened them to take on even greater challenges. Tonight would be their *ultime victoire*. Their greatest accomplishment.

Watson addressed the group. "We all know zoos to be nothing more than pitiful prisons! Those who operate these horrible places claim to be taking care of the animals and allowing their paying guests to enjoy them in their so-called natural environment.

"That's bullshit and we all know it! They don't live in their habitats. They live in cages. They're no different from a collection of art or baseball cards. They're possessions to be exploited by man!

"They're not living, they're merely existing. And what's worse is they're teaching the rest of mankind it's okay to lock up these beautiful creatures where they are cramped, deprived, and controlled for the rest of their lives.

"Everyone, I've called you here tonight because we have an opportunity to right these wrongs. Based upon what we've learned, we can save all of the beautiful animals at the Brookfield Zoo from being murdered and barbarically slaughtered!"

The crowd of forty activists began to shout at Watson.

"No!"

"What's happening?"

"Now what are they doing?"

"How can we help?"

Watson raised his hands to calm them down. "Freedom is a precious concept, and animals suffer both physically and mentally as a result of their captivity. But that pales in comparison to what Dr. Boston and her criminal cohorts at the Brookfield Zoo have planned.

"Let me remind all of you what happened to Marius, the young giraffe slaughtered at the Copenhagen Zoo. Killing healthy animals in zoos isn't a myth, it's business as usual, as we learned from what happened to Marius.

"Marius was sentenced to death because he couldn't breed. Yes, you heard me correctly. Marius was an otherwise healthy young giraffe who was incapable of breeding. So the barbarians in Copenhagen shamelessly and unapologetically, and in full view of the public, killed Marius, dissected his body for the world to see, and then unceremoniously fed his remains to the zoo's lions."

Watson paused to wipe a tear that had rolled down his cheek behind his bandana mask. This story tore him up inside every time he told it, and tonight it was used as a tool to rally support among his ALF soldiers.

"But the murderers at Copenhagen Zoo weren't done. Two adult lions and their cubs were killed shortly thereafter simply to make room for a mighty male lion that had been captured in Africa.

"Out with the old, in with the new! Why? Because it's all about making money. Yes, the almighty dollar drives these greedy bastards to do what they do. And it's about to happen again!"

"No!"

"They deserve our help!"

"Animals never harm anyone. Why are they locked up in prison?"

"We have to do something!"

Watson was on a roll. "We will. We absolutely will!"

He paused to allow the crowd to calm down.

"We have it on very good authority that sometime tomorrow, assuming President Houston announces that the power will be cut off, the zoo will order the zoothanasia of all the animals!"

Zoothanasia, as the term was used in the animal activist community, was nothing more than murder. It was not ethical or remotely humane. It was unnecessary and derided as a cost-effective alternative to returning the animals to where they belonged—at home, in their natural habitat.

The group was whipped into a crazed state of despair mixed with anger.

"Oh no!"

"We can't let that happen!"

"I'll kill anyone who tries!" shouted one booming voice from the rear of the room.

Under his disguise, Watson managed a huge grin. That was what he wanted to hear.

CHAPTER 32

Northwest Ontario
Canada

The guys slept fitfully as the wolves howled for much of the night. As the sun rose, Levi was the first to wander out of the close confines of the tail section to soak in its rays. It felt unusually warm on his skin, but it was welcome nonetheless. Moisture began dropping off the tall red pines, which in turn caused the snow on the forest floor to melt. If they were to travel on foot today, it would be through some wet, muddy conditions. However, a snowstorm like they'd experienced during and after the plane crash would've been worse.

Karl was the next to emerge. He had remained in good spirits despite the dire circumstances. "What time's breakfast being served? Pancakes with Canadian maple syrup, right?"

"Sure, comin' right up," said Levi with a chuckle as he stretched to work the kinks out of his neck and shoulders.

"Grumpy's still asleep," added Karl as he created yellow snow next to a birch tree.

"Good, let him rest."

Karl finished and zipped up his jeans. "I'm trying to give him a break because he got banged up so bad, but you also know how Eddie is. He doesn't listen to what we tell him, and then he complains about the situation he's put himself in. It's like he never wants to take responsibility for his own screwups."

Levi smirked and nodded. He was glad Eddie was asleep because he wanted to address the day's game plan with Karl alone.

"Can I see the compass?" he asked.

Karl handed it to him. Levi held it level in his hand in an effort to steady the needle to determine true north. He moved slightly so that the direction-of-travel arrow reached *N*. It was pointed directly toward the rising sun.

Puzzled, he shook the brass compass and wandered away from the tail section of the plane into the clearing under the presumption that something was interfering with the functionality of the compass.

"What is it?" asked Karl.

Levi tried again. His hands were shaking slightly, so he gripped his right wrist with his left hand as he leveled the compass. Once again, the needle found its way "north"—pointed directly at the sun rising through the pine trees.

"This thing has to be broken," replied Levi. "It's showing due north in that direction."

"So?"

"Well, the sun still rises in the east, right? I mean, since we all got Garmins, compasses became old school. But north is north, and the sun rises in the east. According to this thing, the sun is rising in the north."

Karl approached him. "Let me try."

After a minute of following the same process that Levi had employed, Karl tossed the compass in the snow. "Piece of junk. The old guy probably carried it around for good luck or something. Look what that got him."

Levi walked over to the snowdrift and retrieved the compass. He wiped it off on his shirt and shoved it into his pocket. "Well, I guess it doesn't really matter. The north pole can move to wherever it wants, but the sun's still gonna rise in the same place. It's not like the Earth decided to turn sideways or upside down or something."

"True," said Karl with a sigh. He faced the sun to warm his face. "I think it's a waste of time to sit around here waiting for help. We're gonna have to hoof it out of this godforsaken, cold-ass swamp."

Levi walked toward the sun and then spun around to survey their surroundings. "We need to find your gear and Eddie's too. It's warming up, so we should be able to travel."

"It was warm in Thunder Bay when we arrived there yesterday, and we were in a blizzard a few hours later. Weird."

"Yeah, but we can deal. Let's get Eddie up and dressed in something other than his goin'-to-McDonald's outfit. I know his left arm is busted up, but he needs to carry a rifle, too. Heck, if for no other reason than to let us shoot it instead of having to reload."

"You're expectin' trouble, aren't you?" asked Karl. He pulled the sleeve down on his fleece hoodie to wipe the moisture off his hunting rifle.

"You never know. That moose was crazy last night. It was beatin' its head against a doggone airplane. I shot at it, which should have scared it off, yet it kept on comin'."

"They don't normally attack, do they?"

"Not that I know of unless they're threatened. Somehow, he knew we were in the plane and decided to charge it. Either way, we're in their territory now. We've got to be ready."

Eddie emerged from the plane. "Ready for what?"

"Ready to hit the road," replied Levi.

"You found a road?" he asked.

"No, dumbass. That's a figure of—jeez, forget it. Listen, hang tight. Levi and I are gonna search for our packs and your guns. Then we'll talk about what to do."

"Sounds good. Say, Levi, now can I drink the snow? You know, since the sun's out and its warmer."

"Sure, Eddie. Just make sure it isn't yellow!"

Karl and Levi exchanged high fives and began slogging through the melting snow toward the rest of the wreckage. Eddie rolled his eyes and found a tree to add his morning contribution to the yellow snow. In his still slow-to-awake state of mind, he didn't notice that he wasn't alone.

CHAPTER 33

Northwest Ontario
Canada

The trio had walked for hours toward the south, using the sun as
their guide rather than the compass, which the three guys considered
to be defective. After much debate, they agreed they couldn't
definitively state whether the pilot had missed Smoky Falls to the
west or the north. In the blizzard-like conditions, and with no visible
landmarks during the ordeal, they had to simply operate on a hunch
as to where the closest settlement was. In the end, logic dictated to
head south back toward the United States and the more populated
areas of Quebec. North toward Hudson Bay would require them to
trudge through increasingly damp and potentially colder conditions.

"I gotta say, I appreciate the firm ground," said Karl as he shook
the last of the mud off his boots. After half an hour of searching, the
guys had located their backpacks and Eddie's weapons. They changed
into dry clothes and provided Eddie a rifle to sling over his shoulder.
Karl and Levi divided up his belongings and stuffed them into their
backpacks.

"How much farther, do you think?" asked Eddie for the third
time since they left the wreckage.

"Anybody's guess," replied Levi, who was showing far more
patience than Karl. Levi finally pulled his friend aside and asked him
to ignore Eddie and his complaining. His broken arm was beginning
to swell, and he was probably hurting more than he let on. He didn't
need to feel worse by Karl snapping at him. "We'll keep working
ourselves south until we can find some ground that's high and dry.
We'll set up camp and get a fire going. At the very least, the Canadian

Forest Service may come around and see what's up."

"Why can't we just stop now?" asked Eddie.

Karl rolled his eyes. "Just keep movin'. All this talkin' will just wear you out. I know it's draining my energy."

"Screw you, Karl. I'm hurtin' back here."

"Come on, guys," begged Levi. "Just another couple—"

Levi cut off his own sentence as the howls of wolves suddenly surrounded them. They echoed off the trees, raising the sound of their voices to a crescendo.

"What the hell?" shouted Eddie. "Shit, one's comin'!" He began to run ahead of Karl and Levi, deeper into the woods, until he got tangled up in the underbrush.

"Eddie! Stop! Don't run. You've gotta stay still."

Levi recalled a conversation he'd had with his grandpa when he first learned to hunt. He was warned to never run from wolves if he ever encountered them. If you run, you're dead meat, he'd said. The best thing to do was stay still. Stand your ground. At least you'll have a chance.

The late afternoon sun cast an eerie, pale yellow light through the stands of pines. Levi wiped sweat from his face and readied his rifle. His heart beat against the inside of his chest as adrenaline coursed through his veins.

Karl shouted, "Come back, Eddie! We need to stick together!"

Levi and Karl stood back-to-back, rifles raised, scanning the dense forest of pines and evergreens through their scopes. They stood in a slight clearing, which provided them thirty feet of clear sight should the wolves attack them. That wasn't a lot of time to react, but both of the guys were good shots.

Eddie raced across the clearing and arrived back next to the guys. "We should hide somewhere."

Levi calmly responded, "They'll hunt us with their sense of smell. We have to stand our ground and scare them away. It's the only way."

"You ready, Levi?" asked Karl as he dropped his backpack and gun case to the ground.

Levi did the same. "Yeah, buddy. The pack leader will come at us first. It's always the big, aggressive critters who are fearless."

Eddie raised his rifle in a third direction. He rested it on the makeshift splint created by Levi to immobilize his arm. He might miss, but he could frighten them off with a few well-placed shots.

The chorus howl began in earnest. The wolves were everywhere, or at least the echo effect of the forest made their numbers seem enormous.

"Get ready." Levi spoke in a hushed tone in an attempt to calm his nerves.

The first wolf broke cover, moseying along the edge of the tree line, stalking its prey.

"He's huge!" exclaimed Eddie. "Aren't you gonna shoot him?"

"No, not yet," said Levi. "Let him make his assessment. Stay cool and don't show your fear."

"I've got my eye on him," said Eddie.

Levi corrected him. "Fine, but don't stare him down. He'll see that as a challenge. You gotta remember, they're afraid of us, too. Animals are fearful of us and try their best to avoid crossing our paths."

Another wolf emerged on the opposite side of the clearing. One by one, paw by carefully placed paw, several more emerged until the guys were being circled as if they were in the midst of Custer's Last Stand.

Levi encouraged his friends. "Stay cool, guys. We can handle—"

BOOM!

The sound of Eddie's rifle reverberated through the air. He'd fired upon one of the wolves and missed wildly. This only served to agitate the animals, which were now poised to attack.

"Dammit, Eddie!" shouted Karl, who began firing on the animals. His first shot missed, but the second took down one of the second wave of wolves that entered the clearing.

Levi spun around to weigh his options. There was an incline that led to a rock outcropping to their south. If he could blaze a path for them by shooting at the wolves in their way, they might just be able to scale the rocks and get the high ground.

"Follow me!" he shouted as he moved methodically toward the rocks. "Karl, take the rear and back 'em off."

Levi took off at a steady, brisk walk with Eddie right on his heels. Karl was able to walk backwards and keep pace, periodically firing as the wolves feigned an attack.

"Levi, there are dozens of 'em!" shouted Karl.

Levi picked up the pace without running. Every fiber of his being told him to race for the protection of the rock outcropping, but he felt they still had a chance to back the wolves off without getting killed.

As the rocks came into view, Eddie panicked. He shoved his way past Levi and broke into a sprint. Disregarding the pain in his broken arm, he crashed through small trees and underbrush, hell-bent on getting to safety.

"Shit!" shouted Levi. "Come on!"

Eddie had a twenty-yard head start as he tore through the forest. He was hustling up an incline when a gray flash of fur leapt through the trees and tackled him.

"Edddieee!" shouted Levi as he fired his gun in the air to distract the attacking wolf. But it didn't make a difference. The wolf was ravenous, tearing at Eddie's flesh despite Levi's gunfire. Finally, on the third shot, Levi found his mark, tearing a hole in the side of the beast.

"They're comin'!"

Levi ran to Eddie's side and slid to his knees on the pine-needle floor. He didn't have to check for a pulse. Eddie's neck was gone.

Karl ran past and grabbed Levi under the armpit to lift him up. For the first time, Levi looked down the hill behind him.

The wolves were a swarm of ghostly gray apparitions winding their way between the trees. They made no noise. There was no howling or barking. Only the silent, methodical stalking of their prey.

Karl and Levi had one last chance. They tore up the path toward the rock outcropping. It wasn't much, but it was a way for them to avoid certain death.

CHAPTER 34

Northwest Ontario
Canada

A blackish-gray wolf suddenly appeared in the path between them and the rocks. He stood there defiantly, lowering his head as he prepared to lunge toward them. His eyes were as yellow as the setting sun, a monster of a beast that weighed nearly a hundred pounds.

Karl stopped abruptly in his tracks. "Levi, we'll never make it."

Levi walked into the back of his friend. "They don't respect weakness. We gotta take the fight to them."

"Let's reload," said Karl calmly.

The two guys reached into their jeans pockets and shoved several more rounds of .308 ammo into their guns. They stood back-to-back and took aim. Within seconds, they were surrounded once again.

The wolves began to mingle in the clearing, merging together and then spreading apart. Unlike before, now they were snarling, teeth snapping, and growling. Several began a series of staccato bursts of threatening barks.

Levi had killed one of theirs and they'd smelled the blood of Eddie. Somehow, Levi sensed *an eye for an eye, one of yours for one of mine*, wasn't going to satisfy these animals.

As if orchestrated by an unseen conductor, the wolves formed a circle around them. They'd lunge as if to attack, only to immediately retreat. The air filled with the chorus of howls and barks.

"What the hell are they waiting for?" asked Karl.

Levi could feel his friend shaking against his back. "Try to calm down, buddy. They smell your fear."

Karl's voice was trembling. "This sucks, man."

"Yes, it does. But this doesn't have to be our day to die."

Karl squeezed the trigger on his gun, and a shot went off in the direction of the rock outcropping. His aim was random, hoping to hit one of the wolves in the crowd that stood between him and perceived safety.

Levi felt the kick of Karl's rifle against his back. He glanced over his shoulder and saw a burst of blood sail into the air, followed by a whimpering howl.

Karl pulled the trigger again. Another howl, and more blood spray.

A wave of intense agitation began to move through the pack of wolves as they picked up the pace of their circling motion. A fresh swell of howls and crazed barking filled the air.

Levi had no choice. He took aim and fired on the largest wolf in his line of sight. He hoped to take out the leader of the pack. The beautiful white gray animal exploded in a mess of blood and flesh.

Karl fired again and hit.

Levi did the same.

But more appeared from the woods.

They killed seven more, but Karl had run out of ammunition. He fumbled in his pockets in an attempt to reload, but his nervous fingers wouldn't function. Then he panicked.

Leaving Levi alone, he raced toward the rocks, grabbing the barrel of his rifle and turning it into a club. The wolves raced after Karl, ignoring Levi and passing around him through the clearing.

The death of Karl Tate took just a fraction of a moment, a sliver of time so short that a blink of an eye wouldn't quite equate to it.

The wolves broke rank and descended upon Karl like a nest of angry yellow jackets. Their bodies became a whirlwind of fur, throaty howls, gnashing teeth, and ripping jaws—all piling upon their prey, and each other. He considered firing into the swarm of wolves in an effort to save his friend but knew it was useless.

Levi stood mesmerized by the scene. After a few minutes, the clamor died down. The swarming pack broke apart and roamed around the area where Karl's body used to lie. They sniffed the ground, playfully tumbled and growled at one another, and then gradually strolled off into the woods.

Levi carefully backed away from the feeding frenzy and found a large northern white pine. He glanced back to ensure the wolves hadn't turned their attention back to him. For some reason, he'd been spared. By the time he got to the tree, the wolves, now covered in Karl's blood and, well, all of what was once *Karl*, had disappeared into the forest. There was nothing left of his friend's body to speak of. Blood was smeared across the pine-needle floor, and bones were scattered about here and there. The feeding frenzy had lasted less than three minutes.

He stared up at the massive pine tree. The branches were evenly spaced and appeared sturdy enough to support his weight. He shouldered his rifle and began to climb until he could barely see the ground below him.

Roughly thirty feet off the ground, he found two branches together and created a seat where he could lean back against the trunk. Cradling his rifle, he closed his eyes, and mourned the loss of his lifelong friends.

CHAPTER 35

Brookfield Zoo
Chicago, Illinois

Neither Kristi nor Tommy said a word as they exited the auditorium, leaving the building before any of their coworkers. Dr. Boston's late-called meeting resulted in an uproar of arguing, name-calling, and general disagreement over what should be done in light of the potential unplugging of the nation's electricity supply.

Many took the occasion to critique the president's decision, while others simply shrugged and opined that one way or the other, the grid was going down. Therefore, nothing could be done. They were the votes in favor of euthanasia although none of them would actually be tasked with performing the act of killing the animals.

That would be left up to staff members like Kristi and Tommy.

As they walked alone into the zoo, darkness had overtaken Chicago, and an unusual quiet surrounded them. Ordinarily, the steady roar of vehicular traffic, law enforcement sirens, and aircraft overhead filled the air. Tonight, the world around them seemed to be grinding to a halt, an eerie change that didn't go unnoticed by the twenty-three hundred animals at Brookfield Zoo.

They were clearly agitated, either by the movement of the magnetic field or because their sixth sense warned them their execution was imminent. Unlike a prisoner facing lethal execution, who can vocalize his feelings, the animals' sad eyes spoke volumes as their fate was decided for them. Every creature had an innate ability to know when their time on Earth was done. It was a moment that Kristi could not bring herself to accept. Yet, as a doctor of veterinary medicine, she must.

"Let's take the long way." Kristi spoke in a low voice, clearly distraught over the unfolding events. Tommy gently placed his hand at the small of her back and gestured toward the hoofed-animals habitat. As they walked through the zoo, they paused at each of the habitats and made an assessment.

"Tommy, what are we supposed to do? I can't kill these beautiful animals. They're like my kids, for Pete's sake. Heck, I've helped birth some of them. Others I nursed back to health after being brought to us abused."

Tommy tried to be upbeat, emotionally supporting Kristi as much as he could. "We'll try to feed them. Seriously, I don't care if any of those assholes help us or not. This zoo isn't so big that you and I can't take care of them all. Besides, without power, what else are we gonna do? The Cubs won't be playing and the White Sox suck this year."

This drew a chuckle and a smile from Kristi, followed by a playful shove. "I didn't know you were a Cubs fan."

"There are a lot of things you don't know about me because, frankly, we've been a little busy since I walked through your door and immediately managed to get fired."

Kristi laughed again. She was feeling better. Comfortable around a man. Something alien to her over the last five or six years. "You know I was just kidding. You weren't fired. Just, well, humbled."

Tommy laughed as they approached the kangaroos. "In the animal kingdom, they call that establishing a hierarchy. I think we both know who will be the boss in this family."

Tommy had said the words before he realized he'd let his romantic feelings out in the open. His statement didn't go unnoticed by Kristi, but she didn't outwardly acknowledge it. She'd been developing feelings for Tommy even though they'd only known each other for a week. She knew there was something more between them when she saw how close to death he was in the big cats' habitat. The potential for loss went beyond a coworker dying. Tommy was someone she deeply cared for despite knowing very little about him on a personal level.

They stopped as a camel strolled aimlessly through the hoofed animals' habitat, alongside a zebra. The zebra turned toward a group of three others, which were curled up under a tree, while the camel continued, keeping pace with Kristi and Tommy as they walked along.

"Let's take these guys, for example," began Kristi. "Here we have zebras and camels. Across the way, there are kangaroos. In Habitat Africa, the giraffes have been the pride and joy of Brookfield. Who's gonna volunteer to kill them?"

Tommy shook his head and shrugged. "Nobody."

"What happens if we let them go? They'll never stand a chance."

Tommy spoke from the heart. "They never do. Releasing captive animals back into the wild is not automatically in their best interest, even under optimal conditions when they are returned to their natural habitats. Frankly, and I'm saying this as a zoologist who works in a zoo, the damage was done when they were brought from the wild in the first place. Now, I get it. We rescue most of ours and that's admirable. But ideally, we would've had a program in place to return them back to where they belong, in a protected game preserve, so they can be reintegrated back into the wild."

Kristi nodded in agreement. She stopped to pick up a paper cup and dropped it into a trash receptacle. "And we certainly aren't equipped to load up a giraffe and take him away from the city. What am I supposed to do, haul all these guys to Riverfront Farms? My father would lose his mind at the thought of these giraffes picking his precious apple trees clean."

Tommy laughed at the visual, and then he turned serious. "Sadly, I don't think that's a realistic option anyway. If the power is cut tomorrow like they say, gas pumps will be shut off, traffic signals will stop working, and most likely millions of people will be leaving the city because it will be way too dangerous to stay."

Tommy's words hung in the air as Kristi wiped a tear from her cheek. She began walking toward the buffalo pen, considering what to do. She felt selfish assuming that Tommy would stay with her to feed and care for the animals. She thought he should have the opportunity to say no.

"You're right, Tommy. The city is no place to be without electricity. Cops will be overwhelmed. It'll be lawless. I think you should consider going home and finding a safe—"

Tommy stopped and grabbed her by the arm. He pulled her around and looked into her face. "I'm not going anywhere without you. End of story."

"But—"

"Nope, Dr. Boone. Not another word. It's you and me. Got it?"

Kristi let out a hearty laugh. She pulled away from his grip and stepped backward. "No sirree, Bob. You're not gonna reestablish our hierarchy with some kind of *me caveman, you cavewoman* routine. Not gonna happen."

"Wait. That's not what I was—"

"Yes, it was, mister. I know that *take-charge* tone."

"But I was just trying to let you know that—"

Kristi laughed even harder, leaving a puzzled Tommy standing alone in front of the ICEE World booth that normally served up delectable frozen drinks. She decided to let him off the hook. "I'm just kidding. Enough groveling. Come on, I wanna show you something."

Tommy jogged to catch up to her. Once alongside, he studied her face in the low light to get a read on her emotions. She allowed him a smile and then picked up the pace as she half-jogged up the stairs to The Living Coast. She pulled out her security badge and swiped it over the wall-mounted scanner. The doors clicked and she opened one to allow Tommy to enter first.

Once inside, the sound of moving water was almost deafening, giving the visitor the immediate feeling of being underwater. The carpet was a spongy blue material that squished under their feet as Kristi led the way through the building. Deep, gurgling sounds mimicked echoes heard by a deep-sea diver.

Throughout the exhibit, large tanks immersed visitors in ocean life, including sharks that swam through artificial reefs surrounded by perfectly maintained cold water. Jellyfish drifted sideways along shifting currents created by the zoo to emulate the natural motion of the sea. Green sea turtles calmly paddled along the surface of the tanks in the man-made ecosystem resembling the west coast of South America.

"With everything going on, I haven't been in The Living Coast yet," said Tommy.

"It's an incredible accomplishment," began Kristi. "Its design is based on the Humboldt current ecosystem, one of the richest marine environments in the world, which happens to be adjacent to the driest, most barren desert in the world—the Atacama Desert in Chile. The zoo's intent was to teach visitors about how sea and land animals are connected."

"This is truly amazing," said Tommy as he took in the wonders of the exhibit like a young boy.

"This way," she said as she made her way down a series of ramps to the open ocean area. A six-by-ten-foot window of pulsating, bell-shaped moon jellies swam in all directions in pursuit of brine shrimp, a big staple of ocean sea life. "We're headed to Rocky Shores, a forty-four-foot-high geodesic dome that shines natural light inside the exhibit. Then we're going up. Are you in the mood for a climb?"

Tommy furrowed his brow. "Lead the way, Ranger Kristi, safari guide. I'm game for anything that takes my mind off this screwed-up mess."

Kristi laughed. "Same here." She swiped her badge on a security scanner again and passed through a steel door into a concrete and block stairwell. Rising up the middle was a steel spiral staircase. "Ninety steps. Can you handle it?"

"We'll find out. How do you know there are ninety?"

"I've counted nearly every time. The view at the top is worth it, you'll see."

Five minutes later, after a lot of huffing and puffing, the two arrived on the skywalk that surrounded the glass geodesic dome of The Living Coast. Kristi motioned for Tommy to walk out into the night air first in order to take it all in.

"Wow! The view is incredible. This has to be the highest point in the zoo."

"It is, which is why I've been here so many times. When I need to clear my head, or just get a grasp on what it is I do at Brookfield, I come up here, look around, and chill."

She joined his side and pointed out a few points of interest so he could get his bearings straight. The sounds of the animals reached their ears, giving them the sense they were sitting on top of a cliff in Africa, looking down upon a savannah teeming with exotic animals.

Tommy chuckled. "It's a jungle oasis in the midst of a concrete jungle."

"It is. And I don't understand why the very people who have devoted their lives to making Brookfield Zoo what it is are so quick to abandon ship and kill the animals in the process. It's just wrong, Tommy, and I can't bear the thought of it."

Tears began to stream down Kristi's face, and he immediately wrapped his arms around her. "We'll do it together. Whatever it takes."

Kristi sniffled and wiped the tears off her cheeks. "And if we fail? Run out of food? Then what?"

Tommy was firm in his convictions. "If we save just one of these magnificent, innocent animals, then it's worth the effort. I refuse to give up, and there's no way I'm gonna leave you to deal with this alone."

Kristi turned in his arms and looked up into his eyes. The sadness was replaced with hope, and newfound love. She closed her eyes as Tommy bent down to kiss her.

Just as their lips were about to touch, a loud, high-pitched sound of metal grinding on metal could be heard.

"What the hell?" asked Tommy, snapping his head up in search of the intrusion.

They broke their embrace and walked in opposite directions along the catwalk, looking for the source of the noise.

Then the sounds of gunshots filled the air.

Kristi shouted and pointed toward the opposite side of the zoo. "Oh, my god! They're killing the animals! Let's go!"

CHAPTER 36

Riverfront Farms
Southeast Indiana

Squire and Sarah had settled on to the sofa in an attempt to relax. They worked together to organize their home and prepared for the return of their children, who were scattered in parts unknown. The inability to communicate via cell phone was frustrating and was causing panic to boil over, as the news reporting indicated.

They were watching the NBC affiliate in Indianapolis to determine how these events were impacting their own state. The weatherman came on to describe an extraordinary event unfolding in the state. He explained.

"Good evening to our viewers, and thank you for joining me this evening. In yet another abnormal event recorded this year, I want you to take a look at our Live Doppler 13 Radar. Now, if you look outside, you'll see nothing but clear skies in all directions. Yet our radar indicates a massive image, a blob really, slowly making its way toward Central Indiana from Ohio.

"To the untrained eye, this might appear to be normal rain showers; however, it is anything but. While we are not biological experts, we've determined through input from our viewers across the state that this is a huge swarm of dragonflies possibly mixed in with other insects and birds.

"For some inexplicable reason, the dragonflies began to swarm in this massive grouping in an area just west of Cleveland, Ohio, and began to make its way toward our state. The size of the gathering seemed to double in the last hour as, according to viewers, the dragonflies began to mix with flocks of birds that were beginning their end-of-season migration south.

"Only, they are flying in a westerly path. We have reached out to the National Weather Service in Cleveland as well as an entomologist from Purdue, and we'll have that report in the next hour."

Squire paused the weather broadcast and stared at the radar showing the dark shadow moving toward Indianapolis.

"Locusts," muttered Sarah.

"No, he said dragonflies," Squire reminded her.

"I know, but the similarities are there."

"Actually, dragonflies are good for crops. They eat all kinds—"

"I'm not being literal, Squire. I'm just saying there can be a comparison drawn to locusts as a symbol of God's wrath."

Squire took a deep breath and switched to the cable news networks. He came across CNN first.

The news anchor was on a split screen with the White House in the background. Squire turned up the volume as a reporter stood on the North Lawn. "Let's now go to our White House correspondent for more on the leak that came out of a classified briefing held earlier."

"Thank you. As has been reported, and is now confirmed by two high-ranking administration officials who spoke on the condition of anonymity but who are close to the president, plans are being implemented to systematically shut down the nation's power supply.

"The goal of the administration is to avoid a catastrophic failure of the power grid and the critical infrastructure that relies upon electricity in the event of a massive geomagnetic storm. Administration officials see this as a preemptive measure that would enable the government to protect the grid for later use after the storms pass."

The CNN host turned to an in-studio guest for comment. "What do you make of this?"

A female scientist sat up in her chair and responded, "Naturally, I applaud the administration for thinking outside the box. That said, they're in for a rude awakening as they attempt to implement this plan. You see, the nation's power grid, except for Texas, is tied together."

"How so?" asked the host.

"The best way to look at the nation's electric supply is by region," replied the guest. "The U.S. is divided into two major interconnected power grids. The Western Interconnection spans the entire West Coast from Canada to Mexico, and then east over towards the Midwest. The Eastern Interconnection includes all of the East Coast and extends to the base of the Rocky Mountains. Both of the major power grids exclude Alaska, Hawaii and Texas."

"I can understand how Alaska and Hawaii are separated geographically, but why Texas?" asked the CNN host.

"Partly because of their historical desire for self-sufficiency and partly because of their independent streak epitomized by their motto, Don't Mess with Texas, the state maintained its separation from the rest of the country during the early days of building the grid. During World War II, Texas was home to several factories vital to the war effort. Their utility planners were anxious to keep the assembly lines running and were concerned about the reliability of the power supply from other states. Texas continues to be the nation's number one gas producer and one of the top coal producers."

The host interrupted. "Texas created its own island of energy. They didn't need the rest of the nation."

"Basically, yes," replied the scientist. "It has served them well. As a result, the Texas grid is exempt from the majority of regulations imposed by the Federal Energy Regulatory Commission because they do not sell electricity across state lines."

"How does this all tie together?"

The scientist took a deep breath and explained, "Using what happened in Europe as an example, depending on where the geostorm hits the hardest, parts of America may be in the dark and parts may not. It all depends on the strength of the storm and the cascading effect of the infrastructure failure.

"If the rumors coming out of the White House are true, then the president intends to avoid this cascading failure, but he's not seeing the pitfalls of this approach."

"And they are?" asked the host.

"For one, does the president plan on restarting the power grid after the storm passes? You don't turn on and off the nation's power supply by flipping a light switch. Or does he plan on leaving it off until the poles settle in place? Do you realize how long that may take?"

"How long?"

She frowned and shook her head. "A thousand years or more."

Squire laughed. He muted the television and set the remote on the coffee table. "Well, I don't plan on living that long, but I sure as hell don't plan on cutting my life short because of this crap."

Sarah stood and hugged her husband. "We won't go down without a fight." She paused to kiss him and then looked him in the eye. "I love you, Squire Boone. Always have, always will."

"Good thing. You promised to love, obey, and cherish."

She slugged him on the chest. "Two out of three ain't bad, you old cuss. You know, I wouldn't mind pickin' up a few more things from Walmart. Do you mind if I holler at Carly and—?"

Squire interrupted her. "How 'bout me? Can't I go?"

"You hate Walmart."

"That I do. But I love my missus, and I'm willing to make the ultimate sacrifice and head over to Walmart so that we can do it together."

"You are an unselfish, brave man, Mr. Boone."

Squire laughed as he slipped on his boots. "Don't tell anyone. Besides, these ropers are fallin' apart and I need some new ones. And I wouldn't mind pickin' up some more jeans. These are startin' to fall off me."

Sarah studied her husband's appearance. When you live with someone, seeing them day in and day out might cause you to miss noticeable changes in their weight, hair, etcetera. He had lost a lot of weight, and she inwardly chastised herself for not noticing.

"Am I not feeding you enough?" she asked.

Squire deflected. "I've been out in the orchards more, and with

159

the heat I sweat a lot. I've tried to take in lots of water, but I guess I'm burning more calories, right?"

Sarah seemed skeptical at her husband's answer. "I tell you what, I'll start fixin' some things that will put some more meat on those bones. If something goes bad wrong, like Chapman seems to believe, we'll be losing plenty of weight as it is. I'm just glad I saved all of my inspiration jeans from years ago. Wranglers never go out of style."

Squire reached for the front door handle, and he glanced back toward the television, which was showing more scenes of looting and civil unrest. He pointed toward the monitor. "That crap ain't happenin' up in Corydon, do you think?"

Sarah shrugged and then raised her eyebrows. "You know what? We're both licensed to carry. Let's grab our paddle holsters and handguns. It might not be a bad idea."

"What are your friends at Walmart gonna say about that?" asked Squire sarcastically. "Remember, they asked shoppers not to open carry in their stores years ago."

Sarah opened the gun safe in the hallway and handed him his Beretta .45 caliber with its holster. She carried a Springfield Armory XD subcompact, also chambered in .45.

"Here's what I'll tell that Walmart manager if he says anything," she began. She gestured toward the television as she slid the holster in her waistband. "Askin' ain't tellin', and if he questions my judgment, he can march his fanny back to those eighty-inch TVs mounted on the back wall and watch the news. Heck, he'll be carryin' too within five minutes of seeing that stuff."

CHAPTER 37

Walmart
Corydon, Indiana

The married couple of forty years hopped in Sarah's truck and made the twenty-five minute drive to Walmart without incident. Traffic was practically nonexistent on most nights in this rural part of Indiana, but it seemed especially so because so many residents had their eyes glued to their televisions. When they pulled into the Walmart parking lot, the numerous cars told a different story.

"I guess all our neighbors had the same idea," observed Squire as he slowly drove through, looking for a parking space.

"No, not our neighbors," said Sarah. "Look at the license plates. I see a lot of Ohio and Kentucky plates. Illinois, too. There are some from Missouri, West Virginia ..." Her voice trailed off.

"There are more out-of-towners than there are locals. They must be off I-64."

Interstate 64 ran east-west, beginning in St. Louis and terminating at the Virginia coast. Sarah pointed to the other side of the strip center, where the parking was less crowded.

"I see the spots," acknowledged Squire. "I guess folks aren't eatin' Japanese at Yamato's tonight."

"I don't mind the walk," said Sarah. "As long as we can find a shopping buggy. I've never seen it like this."

The two braved the crowds, and what they found was nothing short of remarkable. The swarm of dragonflies that had appeared on the NWS weather radar Sarah said resembled locusts had nothing on the mass of humanity that apparently descended upon the Corydon Walmart Supercenter. It was madness inside as people pushed and shoved to put anything that was edible into their carts.

"Tell me you don't have food on the list," begged Squire.

"No food, thank goodness. I need to focus on cleaning supplies and personal hygiene, plus some clothes for you and the grandkids. I wanna buy things for them that they can grow into, you know? Just in case."

"Listen, I'm not gonna question anything you suggest. After what we've seen on the news, and now this, I wish we'd started thinkin' like this years ago. We could've avoided this madness."

As if on cue, two women began screaming at each other in the baby formula aisle. Their men got involved, and soon a fistfight broke out. Squire steered their shopping cart clear of the melee and helped Sarah load up cleaning supplies in a nearby aisle.

"Okay, that's good. Let's hit the pharmacy area and pick up some first aid supplies as well as some over-the-counter medications."

"What about more ammo?" he asked.

"Yeah, I forgot."

They went the long way to the pharmacy, picking up some jeans and clothing for the entire family before making their way through the sporting goods section. They bought the last of the rifle ammunition before the gun counter was closed. Their entire inventory had been wiped out with the Boone's purchase.

Sarah chuckled. "This is why I told Allen about what Chapman said. I hope he listened and kept plenty for himself."

They spun around as a loud crash could be heard from the back of the store as two kids attempted to pull down bicycles off the top rack of the display. The bike fell and the two teens quickly started to make their way out of the store through the automotive section. Sales personnel were screaming at them, but they just kept on going without hesitating.

"You know what, Sarah, let's pick up the pace. This whole situation makes me uncomfortable."

"Okay, I agree. This might've been a bad idea."

"No, good idea, unexpected complications. That's all."

After loading all the medical supplies they could use, they checked out through the garden center, which was located nearest their truck. They made their way into the dark parking lot and pushed the cart down the sidewalk in front of a shuttered Papa John's and other closed businesses.

Sarah spoke softly. "This may sound crazy, but this might be the last time we go to a Walmart for a long time."

"It all depends on whether this grand plan of the president's works out. Thanks to you, I feel like we're better prepared than others. Now, we just need to get our kids home."

Sarah suddenly stopped the cart and stared ahead of them. She was wearing a button-down shirt over a white tee. She slowly slipped her hand down to grip her pistol. "Squire, heads up."

He immediately picked up on her concerned tone of voice. After what they'd experienced inside, he immediately raised his awareness of his surroundings. There was a group of men ahead, lurking in the shadows of the GameStop that had closed for the evening.

"I see them. Let me push the cart. I wanna get out in the middle of the parking lot aisle."

Squire picked up the pace and pushed between two parked cars until they were out in the open. Sarah was close behind, eyeing the suspicious men.

Her voice became excited. "Squire, they're moving through the cars, too. I think they're gonna block our way."

"You push the cart and be ready to draw on 'em," he said as he pulled his own weapon and used a two-handed grip to point at the men as they appeared in front of their path to the truck.

Without warning, two of them darted into the parking lot driveway to face Squire and Sarah.

"Don't move, asshole!" Squire shouted.

"Whoa! Chill out, *jefe!*"

"Where's the other guy?" Squire yelled back.

The response startled him. "What's in the buggy, old man?"

Squire spun around and saw the man emerge from the shadows between two pickup trucks. He also noticed that Sarah was gone.

His eyes darted in all directions; he was immediately concerned that they'd done something to her. He shouted, with a hint of fear in his voice, "Back off or I'll shoot!"

The men started laughing. "You ain't shootin' nobody, *jefe!*"

"He may not, but I sure will!" shouted Sarah, who'd circled behind the man who'd tried to ambush Squire from the side. "Hands up or you're a dead man!"

The man slowly raised his hands and revealed a knife.

Sarah continued to take charge. "Drop the knife, too!"

The man dropped the knife and she pushed him forward with her left hand, causing him to stumble into the driveway and land on his knees. She kicked the knife under the pickup and kept her weapon trained on the mugger. Meanwhile, Squire turned his attention to the man, allowing the other two to bolt into the night.

"Come on, we didn't mean nothin'."

"Shut up!" yelled Sarah.

The man tried to protest, but his words were drowned out by the sounds of a siren. Soon, the blue lights of a Harrison County sheriff's car illuminated the parking lot, creating a strobe-light effect.

The doors of the Ford Explorer flung open, and one of the deputies used the patrol car's public address system to give orders to Sarah and Squire.

"Drop your weapons and raise your hands over your head!"

Squire shouted back, "It's not what you think! These men tried to rob us!"

"Drop your weapons! I'm not gonna ask twice!"

The other deputy stepped out of the patrol car and racked a round into his shotgun. The sound was unmistakable, and Squire immediately glanced at Sarah. She acknowledged that she'd heard it.

She addressed the deputies. "My name is Sarah Boone, and this here is my husband, Squire. We're going to holster our guns and raise our hands over our heads. We both have permits for these guns and were using them in self-defense."

"Slowly!" screamed the deputy.

They complied, and within seconds after they'd completed the task, the deputies were on top of them with their weapons drawn.

Soon thereafter, they were surrounded by Harrison County deputies and the sheriff, one Randall Clark, the older brother of Bully Billy the Banker.

CHAPTER 38

The White House
Washington, DC

Information leaks coming out of the White House had been a part of every administration's headaches dating back to the Nixon years. Sometimes, they were used by a president's aides as a way to shape the political narrative on a particular issue. In some cases, they were used by career staffers who vehemently disagreed with their new boss's policies. Regardless, the *New York Times* article, followed by more in-depth reporting in the *Washington Post*, had created a media feeding frenzy that resulted in a rise in social unrest around the country.

It also panicked Wall Street. Markets liked stability, and the thought of cutting off the nation's energy supply was unfathomable. The grounding of all aircraft had been met with significant consternation from the entire world, but the thought of willfully cutting the power to a hundred thirty million homes and six million businesses was mind-blowing to most.

The White House switchboard had to be taken off-line. A three-block perimeter around the White House was cordoned off, and the National Guard was hastily dispatched to keep the peace. Congressmen went into hiding and government buildings closed to the public as the nation's ire was brought down upon anyone associated with the federal government.

Despite the enormous political pressure brought down upon President Houston, he remained steadfast in his convictions. He instructed his press secretary to contact all the major media outlets

166

and cable news networks to hastily arrange a televised address to the nation.

Since the media leak to the *Times*, a significant amount of disinformation had been disseminated by opponents to the president's black start plan. He needed to make his case to the nation, explaining how this preventative measure was designed to prevent the country from being thrown back into the nineteenth century.

Short-term pain, long-term gain.

Only, neither he, nor anyone else within the government, could accurately define the length of time the power would be down.

What, exactly, does short-term look like? he'd asked his advisors, and the lack of response spoke volumes. There were shrugs. The looks of the proverbial deer in the headlights. Noncommittal utterances. In other words, he surmised, he was the guy who got paid the big bucks, and therefore, as President Harry S. Truman once said, *the buck stops here.*

Fine, thought President Houston as he allowed the makeup artist to provide some powder to his forehead to hide the perspiration that had plagued him for the past twenty-four hours. He'd already determined he would not be responsible for the collapse of America when the nation's energy infrastructure could be protected for a hopefully brief period of time.

Wasn't the loss of modern inconveniences for several weeks better than losing them for many years, as predicted by FERC? He thought so, and in just a few minutes, he planned on making his case to the American people.

There was another concern that weighed heavily on his mind—the collapse of the banking system. Once the word was out, the nation's wealthiest investors made an unprecedented run on cash as economic fears rose.

Market pundits immediately took to the airwaves after the *New York Times'* story broke. Public equity markets crashed in after-hours trading. The New York Stock Exchange had already announced that it would remain closed until further notice as a result of the president's anticipated announcement. That didn't stop traders from inundating the foreign exchanges with sell orders.

Major banks, which remained open until 6:00 p.m. that afternoon, found themselves calling the police to forcibly remove depositors from their lobbies. ATMs ran dry, tellers' cash trays were emptied, and bank vaults looked like the liquor cabinet after a teenage party while the parents were away—bone dry and empty.

The price of precious metals had skyrocketed tenfold as wealthy investors sought out alternative investments. Cash was converted to all forms of gold and silver, both in the form of certificates and physical coins.

Retailers began to feel the pinch as well. Consumers were so hungry for cash, they made small purchases like a bar of candy and requested a hundred dollars cash back on their debit cards. If the store restricted the amount of cash back, the consumers took what they could get. In a matter of hours Fiserv, the largest credit card processor in the U.S., suffered a major collapse of its servers. This set off internet rumors that the banks were insolvent, and soon retailers were demanding cash payments for their goods.

The president had been briefed on these events throughout the day and had voiced both dismay and amazement at how quickly the economic collapse was upon them.

President Grant Houston's Call to Action, as his brief address came to be known around the world, would be delivered in just minutes, but it would be replayed on a continuous loop over broadcast networks and radio stations for so long as the power remained on. Then it would be transmitted across ham radio airwaves and emergency band radios, with the additional request that listeners stay tuned for updates as to when the power might be restored.

As he prepared to address the nation, programming was interrupted on every television network and radio station. The Call to Action was blasted through loudspeakers attached to military and law enforcement vehicles, and dropped in print form by helicopters called into service by the National Guard.

On a gigantic screen located in New York's Times Square, an image of the Blue Goose, the nickname given to the presidential podium, appeared, drawing the attention of anyone who happened to be on the street. Remarkably, the usually packed streets of the city were devoid of traffic, as everyone had abandoned the island of Manhattan and headed for the suburbs in search of gasoline.

The president appeared somewhat disheveled, the stress of the day having clearly taken its toll. The White House producer checked the teleprompters and began the final countdown to the most important speech of President Houston's life. It would be an address that would last less than seven minutes, about the time it took to smoke a cigarette. But the ramifications of which could last for many years, if not lifetimes.

CHAPTER 39

Brookfield Zoo
Chicago, Illinois

Kristi raced down the sidewalk, with Tommy close on her heels. They didn't hear any more gunfire, but the metal grinding sound continued. She fumbled with her keys to unlock her office door, and once inside, she grasped Knight's empty cage and flung it out of the way. Underneath it sat an elevated platform made of plywood. She dropped to one knee and stuck the index fingers of both hands into two holes that had been drilled in the center of the board, and lifted.

"Whoa!" exclaimed Tommy. "Are those legal?"

Within the hidden compartment, Kristi had a shotgun, two handguns and a few boxes of ammunition. Kristi ignored his question and grabbed a nine-millimeter pistol and quickly inserted a magazine. She pulled the slide to load a round.

"Can you shoot? Or, more importantly, will you?"

Tommy hesitated. "Um, yes, but it's been a while. And, yes, if I have to."

Kristi spun the weapon around so she was holding the barrel and handed it to Tommy. He took it and became familiar with the location of the safety. He held it so it was pointed safely away from Kristi as she retrieved two more guns.

She mumbled as she readied her weapons, "I can't believe the cell service is still down and the damned landlines are constantly in circuit overload. We need to call the cops."

"I don't hear any sirens," added Tommy. "Surely somebody in the neighborhoods will get through to them."

Kristi removed her lab coat and tucked her sidearm into a paddle holster inserted into her waistband. She grabbed a box of shotgun shells and loaded them into her Remington 870. She racked a round and headed for the door when the sound of more gunfire could be heard.

"Stay behind me," she said as she bolted onto the sidewalk.

"Kristi, maybe it's something else. I don't think any of our people would shoot the animals."

The metal grinding noise was getting louder and was now coming from all parts of the zoo. The two of them jogged toward the middle of the zoo toward the Roosevelt Fountain. Kristi thought the first set of gunshots had emanated from the East Gate.

As they approached the fountain, the metal grinding grew louder, and Tommy came to a conclusion. "That's the sound of an angle grinder. They're cutting into the fences."

"Hey!" shouted Kristi as she saw two people dressed in black pants and sweatshirts run through the trees of the West Mall separating the pachyderms from Tropic World, where the primates were located.

Bam! Bam!

More gunshots. Louder this time.

"This way!" She raced around the fountain, past the entrance to the big cats' habitat and toward the north gate of the zoo. What she discovered there shocked her and immediately heightened her awareness.

Tommy pushed past her and knelt down next to the security guard lying in a pool of blood on the concrete sidewalk. He'd been shot in the back twice. Near the snack stand, a zoo maintenance worker had also been shot and killed, left slumped over a trash can he'd been emptying.

Kristi walked around with her shotgun pointing in all directions. Tommy called 9-1-1 once again, getting through this time. He got a recording instructing him to leave a voicemail, and he promptly unleashed a profane-laden tirade demanding police respond to the zoo. After he disconnected the call, he stood behind Kristi, pointing his gun in the opposite direction. The two now spoke in hushed tones.

"What do you think is happening?" asked Tommy.

Before Kristi could answer, the sound of a stampede coming their way caused them to seek cover. The loud clapping of hoofs on the sidewalk grew in intensity until several antelope and zebras came streaking past them toward the north gate.

"Shit!" she exclaimed. "Somebody's letting the animals out." She began to run in the same direction she and Tommy had walked just an hour earlier, when they heard gunshots coming from the south side of the zoo.

Tommy abruptly stopped. "They're not shooting animals. They're shooting people. People like us. Employees."

"We've gotta help them!" Kristi started to run, but Tommy grabbed her arm, swinging her around toward him.

"No! We gotta wait for the cops to handle it."

"They're killing innocent people and maybe the animals, too. They can't just let them loose. That's insane!"

"Kristi, I've never shot anyone. I don't even know if I can hold my hand steady."

She walked up to him and stood barely six inches from his face. "All I need you to do is have my back and follow my lead. My brothers and I have practiced this stuff back on the farm. Trust me. Okay?"

Tommy gulped and nodded. "I'm with ya. One hundred percent."

The sounds of the saws starting up again gave them a new sense of urgency. Without another word, they raced back across the zoo, dodging startled animals that suddenly found themselves free and unsure what to do.

At the Roosevelt Fountain, she paused and listened. Tommy whispered in her ear, "They're moving west, along the perimeter."

"Crap! The bears and wolves. Tommy …" Her voice trailed off.

"I know," he said through gritted teeth. This time he took the lead, throwing caution to the wind as he ran as fast as he could along the West Mall. As the grinding noise got louder, the two knew they were about to encounter the people responsible for the mayhem.

A flock of birds suddenly flew over their heads, startling them both and causing them to drop to a knee. This likely saved their lives as several gunshots rang out, sending bullets flying over their heads and ricocheting off the trees.

"Dammit!" shouted Kristi in anger. She resisted the urge to wildly fire back until she had a target in sight. Most likely, she surmised, the murderous intruders didn't expect the zoo personnel to have firearms. At every gate was a prominently displayed sign that the zoo was a gun-free zone. That was why she'd kept her weapons hidden from her coworkers. She wanted them for protection and didn't appreciate anyone else deciding whether they were necessary or not. In this moment, she was glad she had them.

"Hrrrwrrrwrrr!"

A low, guttural, menacing growl was heard just ahead of them. They remained low to the ground, as they were familiar with the surly tempered, grumpy voice of a bear. To their left the creature lumbered through the trees, pawing at the ground periodically and sniffing at the air.

"Stay perfectly still," advised Kristi.

"No problem."

The bear sniffed again and glanced in their direction. Fortunately, the black bear had been raised in the zoo since birth and was familiar with the scent of humans. This helped avoid a hostile interaction with Kristi and Tommy, but would not serve the bear well after it made its way through the East Gate thirty minutes later.

Tommy and Kristi remained in a low crouch as they ran along the tree-lined walkway toward the Great Bear Wilderness. The saws had stopped and they heard shouting up ahead. They also had to be aware that they'd been spotted by someone who'd fired wildly in their direction. It was obvious that the people responsible for letting out the animals were willing to kill anyone who stood in their way.

Chapter 40

Brookfield Zoo
Chicago, Illinois

Shouts of jubilation and triumph suddenly could be heard from the area of Swan Lake located at the far western end of the zoo. A nature trail wound its way around the lake, touching the perimeter security fence of Brookfield at Salt Creek.

"Woo-hoo! We did it!"

"That's all of them!" shouted another before adding, "Every single prison cage has been torn down."

"Well done, people! Well done! Now, listen up."

Kristi and Tommy inched along the low side of Habitat Africa to get a better look at the revelers. Under the sidewalk light at the entrance to the nature trail stood two to three dozen people dressed in all black clothing with bandanas over the faces. They were gathered around a group of four men, who'd removed their face guards. Kristi and Tommy crouched along a fence at the back of the bear habitat to listen.

The leader continued. "We got a call from our scouts who are monitoring the gates. We need to wrap things up, but first, let me tell you the animals have done their job and are finding their way out of this hellhole!"

"Yeah!"

"Good on them!" exclaimed a man with an English accent.

"Mission accomplished, right, everybody?" another man proudly asked.

The leader continued. "It is mission accomplished, although we need to get out of here as planned. Is everybody accounted for?"

The leader paused as his gang of anarchists accounted for their partners. They'd established a buddy system to keep track of each other.

While there was a pause, Tommy leaned in to Kristi. "Whadya wanna do?"

"They're murderers," she replied. "We can't let them go."

"I agree, but there are thirty of them and just the two of us." Tommy paused before continuing. "Wait. Do you hear sirens?"

Kristi whispered back, "Barely, but yes."

The leader continued. "Okay, we've got to get out of here, so remember the plan. Take the nature trail around the lake and make your way through the woods to the neighborhood just west of here. We'll have cars waiting to take us back to Bolingbrook."

Kristi suddenly stood and motioned for Tommy to join her. "I've got an idea, but we have to move fast."

Without hesitating, she moved steadily through the trees toward the north entrance to the nature trail. She knew the trail well, walking it with Knight whenever she had time. It was always an opportunity for her to allow Knight some playtime in the trees without being under the watchful eye of her coworkers.

The two entered the trail and began to run toward the back side of the zoo.

Tommy kept up but was unsure of the plan. "Now what?"

"This trail is narrow and is surrounded by the lake on the inside and the creek on the outer perimeter. Our only chance to keep them from escaping is to pin them down and drive them back into the zoo before they reach the west side and the work sheds. If the cops are coming, at least there will be a chance of arresting these killers."

They reached the point where the trail neared a service road that led to the maintenance buildings and the surrounding neighborhoods.

"So what are we supposed to do? Shout *stop, go back*? Kristi, there are thirty of them and they're armed."

"And they'll be surprised and scared. Nobody wants to die. They'll tuck and run, I guarantee it. Especially when they hear this." She lifted the Remington shotgun in front of her.

"I hear them running this way," said Tommy.

"Me too. From both sides, actually. Can you hold your ground?"

Tommy shuddered. "I'll hold them off by firing over their heads. If they shoot back, well—"

"They'll run the other way. This exit isn't worth dying for."

Kristi hoped she was right.

The two split apart, and Tommy took the north side of the trail that encircled Swan Lake, and Kristi took the south side, which was closer to where they were just gathered. As soon as she saw the first wave of people round the bend, she fired birdshot into the tree limbs hanging over the trail, sending hundreds of lead pellets into the foliage. The loud boom caused by the shotgun caused all of the oncoming anarchists to shriek in fear. The close proximity of Kristi's first round of shot scared them even more as pellets and foliage alike rained down upon their heads.

Seconds later, she heard Tommy fire two rounds toward his oncoming group. Likewise, they shouted in fear, and she heard the words she'd hoped for.

"Quick! Turn around!"

"Go back! Somebody's ahead."

"It's more than one! I heard two shots!"

"Shut up and run!"

Tommy fired again.

And again.

"Shit!" she cursed under her breath. She didn't want him to deal with this alone, especially with his lack of training. She'd played with Chapman as a kid, and they grew up practicing with all types of weapons. As Levi got older, the two would teach him the things they'd learned during family gatherings. It was a Boone rite of passage that had been handed down for centuries.

She walked backwards toward Tommy's position. She was considering joining him when movement caught her eye. Someone, or something, was lurking in the woods along the trail. She hesitated to shoot because the person could be unarmed, but that was not the real reason. Anyone associating with armed thugs knew the risks and they could die.

She didn't want to shoot one of the innocent animals that had been released from their habitats. That was something she couldn't live with.

Kristi inched into the trees on the opposite side of the nature trail and took cover behind an oak tree whose trunk had split during its early growth period to create a V-shaped gap. She settled in behind this tree and pointed her shotgun through it.

Then she waited.

Their feet were heavy on the mulch-covered woods. The shouting had died down from both sides of the trail, and a tense quiet came over the zoo.

Kristi was protected, yet she felt exposed. Whoever was stalking her had no compunction about killing and was intent upon murdering anyone who worked at the zoo. It was if they wanted to exact some kind of revenge or punishment on Brookfield Zoo and its staff.

She gripped the shotgun a little harder. *This is not my day to die.*

"Kristi! Where are you?" Tommy whispered loudly.

Oh no!

"Tommy! Go—"

Three shots rang out in rapid succession from across the trail in Tommy's direction.

"Shit!" a male voice, not Tommy's. It came from where Kristi caught a glimpse of a muzzle flash.

She unloaded two rounds in that direction. It was the second round of birdshot that found its target.

A man screamed in agony as he took the lead pellets in his chest and shoulders. Kristi didn't hesitate. She looked down the trail to make sure no one was coming up on her, and she raced across to the other side. She crouched down and carefully walked through the trees, like a deer, as her grandfather had taught her, barely making a sound.

The sound of the man groaning could be heard twenty feet away.

He was making so much noise from the pain that he didn't hear her approach.

When Kristi came upon him, he was lying on his side, doubled over in pain. Keeping the shotgun pointed at his body, Kristi walked around and grabbed his AR-15 rifle. She ran her arm and head through the sling to secure it on her back.

Her eyes darted in all directions, looking for any of the attacker's friends. She couldn't hear any movement, so she turned her attention back to the gunman.

"Who are you?"

"Screw you!"

"Tough talk, tough guy." Kristi kicked the man in the ribs, causing blood to splatter on her pants.

"Arrrggghhh!" He doubled over and tried to crawl away but didn't have the strength.

"Let's try again. Who are you?"

"Kiss my ass!" The man lifted himself up to his knees and tried to crawl away.

Kristi smiled and shook her head. "Whatever. Here, let me help you."

Kristi pulled her right leg back and kicked the man in the butt, causing him to lose his balance and surge forward toward Swan Lake. The momentum carried him toward an embankment, where he began to roll down the hill into the swampy, algae-covered water.

She quickly returned to the trail and whispered for Tommy. "Hey, where are you?"

"I got one," he replied in a whisper.

Kristi raised her shotgun and ran toward Tommy's voice. She entered the trail and stood waiting for him. Seconds later, Tommy walked out of the dark cover of the woods, holding the hand of a chimpanzee.

CHAPTER 41

Walmart Parking Lot
Corydon, Indiana

Sheriff Randall Clark, the oldest of the Clark siblings, was never interested in following in his father's footsteps in the banking business. His younger brother Billy showed an aptitude for that at an early age when he would dupe other kids out of their allowance or lunch money. Sheriff Clark didn't even care about arresting people like his brother when they pushed the envelope of criminal activity. He simply wanted to control them.

Power can be vested in someone in many ways. Those with political influence, wealth, and status tend to exert their will over others more than those who don't have these social benefits. As a young man, Sheriff Clark learned people in a position of authority can also control others, thereby feeding his need to elevate his importance in society.

He was not political by nature, although his job as sheriff required him to run for office. The wealth and stature of the Clark family in this small county ensured his election. He didn't need to play games with the Harrison County Council or its three commissioners, who made up the executive body. They were all bought and paid for through years of dealing with the Clarks' bank.

He was autonomous and operated the sheriff's department largely unchecked except for the occasional inquiry from the Indiana Office of Inspector General or being required to respond to an inmate complaint made to the Indiana State Police. These matters were usually disposed of by a toothy grin and a slap on the back or a bulging, plain white envelope.

The motto of the Clark family of Harrison County, Indiana, was *there ain't nothin' that time and money can't solve*. Sheriff Clark lived by that, and he was a patient man.

If the actor who portrayed Roscoe P. Coltrane was the pride and joy of Harrison County, as evidence by his life-size poster standing at the local feed and seed, Sheriff Clark was a tall, potbellied version of Boss Hogg.

When he exited his Ford Raptor pickup, a newly constituted version of the 2014 model that sported over four hundred horses under the hood, the superduty truck rocked back and forth, adjusting itself to the weight shift. Sheriff Clark had a habit of hitching up his pants in a never-ending battle to keep them around his waist. Within the first few steps, as they were prone to do, they dropped down below his considerable belly.

"Well, what do we have here?" he bellowed before sarcastically answering his own question. "If it ain't Bonnie and Clyde."

Squire and Sarah remained stoic as the sheriff got close enough for them to smell the onion on his breath from a burger he probably ate at Bill's on the Hill, a local steak and chop house overlooking the Old Capitol Golf Club, the known hangout of the Clark family. Even after the restaurant closed to regular patrons, the sheriff, his prosecutor sister, and Bully Billy could gather with friends for free food and drink. They didn't even have to run a tab. The accommodation was simply a perk earned by financing the renovations to Old Capitol's clubhouse and allowing a late payment or two.

This was how business was done in Harrison County, and everyone understood that, willfully playing the game that began during the Great Depression and carried forward over a hundred years. Everyone, that is, but the Boone family.

Sheriff Clark circled the Boones like a rancher might walk around a horse at an auction. If Squire didn't know better, he could've sworn that the man was sniffing them, trying to ferret out any sign of weakness. Squire wasn't going to make the anticipated harassment easy on him.

"Evenin'."

"Boone. Mrs. Boone."

Sarah didn't respond.

Sheriff Clark nodded at his deputy and pointed toward Squire's weapon. The deputy holstered his own gun and quickly moved to take Squire's and Sarah's.

Sheriff Clark continued his stroll around the Boones, stopping to dig through their Walmart grocery bags. He found the two hundred rounds of bullets and hoisted them out of the cart. He held them high in the air and walked in front of Squire. "You folks pay for these separately?"

"We did."

"Got a receipt?"

Squire gulped. He couldn't remember if he put it in the bag or crumpled it up and dropped it in the bottom of the shopping cart. "It's either in the bags or the bottom of the cart, Randall. I'm sure if you'll—"

"Boone! This is an official matter and a bona fide investigation of a possible crime. You'll address me as sheriff when you answer my questions."

Squire bristled. "Come on, Randall, I've known you since you were a roly-poly kid on the church playground. We were attacked by these men and were defending ourselves. There's no need for—"

"He pulled his gun on us!" yelled the assailant.

"What men?" asked Sheriff Clark. "I only see this one fella here, and he's unarmed."

"Yeah! I ain't got no gun. These two drew on me and knocked me down. See, look at my skinned-up hands."

"Randall, he's lyin'!" countered Squire. "He had two friends who ran off. They were lurking around in the dark and planned on robbin' us."

"With what, Boone? His good looks? This boy's a hundred forty pounds soakin' wet. He doesn't have a gun, and he sure has a different story. Plus, I don't see anybody else around here, do you, boys?" The sheriff turned to his deputies, who all shrugged or shook their heads.

"See! I'm innocent. I wanna file a complaint against these two!"

Sarah tried to stay out of the fray, but grew frustrated. She tried to take the high road with Sheriff Clark. "He had a knife, I swear. So did his pals. When I pulled my gun, I made him drop the knife. Then I kicked it under the truck over there."

"She's lyin'!" the man screamed. "Ain't nobody dumb enough to take a knife to a gunfight. They drew on us!"

Squire immediately picked up on the man's mistake. "See, Randall? He said us."

"I meant me!"

The sheriff was over it. "Enough! Everybody shut the hell up!"

"But—" began Squire before Sarah reached over her head for his hand and squeezed it.

"Shhh, Squire."

Sheriff Clark pounced on the exchange. "That's good advice, Mrs. Boone." Then he turned to his deputies. "Okay, take them over to the jail and separate them all in different holding cells. Don't allow any of them to talk to one another."

"Randall, this is ridiculous! Why would we pull our guns on some punk kid unless we had a reason?"

"I don't know, Squire Boone, but your attitude toward law enforcement sure makes me wonder if you are mentally stable," replied Sheriff Clark. He puffed out his chest and tried for the thirty-ninth time that day to pull his pants above his belly button, only to achieve the same result.

"Come on, that's a load of crap and you know it!" Squire was incredulous.

Sheriff Clark walked closer to Squire and hissed into his ear, "You may think it's a load of crap, but Indiana's red flag laws state otherwise. You give me some time to talk to our astute circuit court judge of this fine community, and we'll see if we can't fill your pants with crap."

CHAPTER 42

Gallia County Jail
Gallipolis, Ohio

Jenna and her sister, Carolyn, waited outside the Gallia County Jail for their boyfriends to walk out the jail's door. The two women didn't look any different from any other friends or family members awaiting their loved ones to be released from jail. The only difference was that the two men—Troy Martin and his co-defendant, Lawrence Clemente—were being held without bond for assault with a deadly weapon and armed robbery charges.

This was the third felony offense for each of the men, and both were now facing the probability of twenty years in an Ohio prison if convicted. The men, lifelong partners in crime since high school, were in their mid-forties and too young to cut their lives short by a jail sentence that would end when they were old men.

In their opinion, anyway. So from the moment they arrived at the new Gallia County Correctional Facility near Gallipolis, Ohio, they plotted their escape. They'd been held in a detention center in Cincinnati, where they were arrested while on the run following the liquor store robbery. As their trial approached, they were transferred from more secure facilities to the older jail in Gallipolis in order to make their initial court appearances. They were later transferred to the rural facility as they awaited their trial.

The guys prided themselves on their ability to *sweet-talk the ladies*, as they liked to call it. During their two-month-long stay in the small county jail, they'd befriended two female guards, who frequented their cell for friendly chats while bringing extra trays of food for the guys.

As a result of the fast-developing friendship with the two female guards, Martin and Clemente enjoyed extra recreation time and longer, unmonitored visits with their families.

But not with their girlfriends. From day one, Martin and Clemente had a plan. Their girls would stay away from the jail and therefore remain off the list of visitors who were allowed in the facility. This would allow them plausible deniability if, and when, the men attempted their escape.

The girlfriends were not in the dark, however. Clemente provided his brother all the details of their planned escape, who in turn advised the two women. Martin and Clemente had studied the guards' schedules, their break habits, and their mannerisms. It was their job to escape, and they devoted every waking moment to studying the operations of the jail, even going to the extent to sleep in shifts so they didn't miss any activity.

The day had come. It was a Sunday and the jail's administrative staff was off-duty. The guards were not at full strength, and the only matters to attend to involved allowing the inmates out of their cells to attend a church service.

Make no mistake, these two career criminals couldn't care less about God, the Bible, or Christianity. They attended the Sunday morning service to look for a way out of their predicament.

Every other Sunday, the two female guards oversaw the worship services only. Other guards delivered the inmates to the small meeting room that was used as a chapel on Sundays. The female guards, armed with pepper spray, were responsible for keeping the inmates in line and sounding the alarm in the event of trouble.

Martin and Clemente knew this because they watched, listened, and learned.

The meeting room was located at the corner of a building near the rear recreation yard. The outdoor space was surrounded by a chain-link fence with razor wire strung across the top to prevent anyone from climbing over it. There was a concrete-filled drainage ditch surrounding the rear perimeter, used to control flooding of the Ohio River and its tributaries. It was seen as a physical barrier preventing the use of any vehicle to aid in an escape if an inmate tried to scale the razor wire.

The drainage culvert was no match, however, for Martin's Ford F-150, which was jacked up like a monster truck on a Friday night at the fairgrounds. And his sweetheart, Jenna, could drive it like a champ.

Church began and moved along smoothly. The guys sat in the back row, nearest to the steel exit door leading to the recreation yard, which remained locked at all times. As the preacher gave his sermon, Martin and Clemente studied the female guards, who took up a position to their left along a wall. One checked her Facebook notifications and the other lazily picked at a hangnail. Their lackadaisical approach to monitoring violent criminals was something the two men had picked up on within days of their arrival at the jail.

Martin reached into his pocket and pulled out his shank, a plastic toothbrush he'd ground down to a sharp point. Clemente had two of the homemade knives tucked into his socks. He casually crossed his legs to retrieve one, and then crossed the other over his knee to slide the other into his sleeve.

On Clemente's signal, the men acted with catlike reflexes, jumping out of their seats, catching everyone in the room by surprise. Before the guards could react, the men buried the shanks in the women's throats, expertly severing the carotid artery, just as they'd practiced on each other for days.

Martin grabbed the guard's keys as she bled out on the floor. Clemente threatened the preacher if he moved an inch. And in less than a minute, the rear security door was flung open and the two convicts formerly on trial for aggravated felonies ran out of the Gallia County Jail as murderers with nothing to lose.

Jenna fired up the big four-by-four pickup that was jacked up high enough that a child could walk under it. She drove down one side of the drainage ditch and up the other, mashing the gas pedal to send the grille guard of the front bumper crashing through the chain-link fence.

The escaped convicts jumped into the pickup bed, slapped the top of the cab's roof, and Jenna took off toward the bridge that would immediately carry them into West Virginia, hootin' and hollerin' as if they were on the old Dukes of Hazzard show.

CHAPTER 43

Harrison County Sheriff's Department
Corydon, Indiana

Squire, Sarah, and the man who planned on attacking them were all taken into the Harrison County Jail and placed in separate holding cells where they couldn't communicate with one another. As promised, Sheriff Clark summoned the county's circuit court judge out of bed and insisted she immediately come to his office to discuss the situation.

His baby sister, the youngest of the three Clark children, was Joella Clark Kincaid, one of two circuit judges in Harrison County. She'd begun practicing law in Corydon following her graduation from the Maurer School of Law at Indiana University.

Thirteen years prior, she longed for a judgeship but doubted her ability to defeat the sitting circuit court judge, Johnson Carlson. Judge Carlson had been a mainstay in Corydon for decades and was considered an honorable man.

However, he was accused by a new staff secretary of inappropriate touching and unsolicited sexual innuendo in the workplace, and despite his protestations, he was forced to resign. The secretary, inserted onto the judge's staff and paid for by the Clark family, had been a former stripper in Fort Wayne who took advantage of the #MeToo movement to ruin Judge Carlson's career. After his resignation, she quickly disappeared into obscurity, ten thousand dollars richer for her trouble.

A special election was held, and the county was ripe for a change in gender on the bench. With the financial support of her family, together with an intriguing vote-suppression scheme orchestrated by her brother Randall, attorney Joella Clark Kincaid became Judge Kincaid, whose primary responsibility was hearing criminal cases.

Judge Carlson, like many other politicians in Indiana, fully embraced the *red flag* laws adopted by the Indiana legislature. Indiana was one of the first states to adopt the measure, designed to allow law enforcement to seize guns from people who were deemed a danger to themselves or others.

In theory, the red flag laws were designed to balance two competing concerns. This method of gun control allowed law enforcement the ability to limit a potentially dangerous person's access to firearms while establishing a method to protect that person's Second, Fourth, and Fifth Amendment rights.

In practice, without a warrant or a judge's signature, police could confiscate firearms from a person alleged to be dangerous. After the warrantless seizure, the officer submitted a written statement to the local judge describing why the person was considered dangerous. Within fourteen days thereafter, the gun owner was given the opportunity to prove they weren't dangerous and therefore should have their weapons returned.

The laws arose after a series of mass shootings in the United States in the first two decades of the twenty-first century. The highly emotional issue created a public outcry for lawmakers to act, and the red flag laws were seen as a reasonable means to protect the public from unstable people.

However, it was only a matter of time for the well-intended law to have unintended consequences. Some gun rights advocates compared what happened next to *swatting*, which found its origins around 2008. Similar to the prank calls made to emergency services in the 1970s claiming a bomb threat, callers used increasingly sophisticated techniques to direct law enforcement SWAT teams to a location alleging an active shooter or armed hostage situation.

The goal of the caller was to trick emergency authorities into responding with a heavily armed SWAT team to a fabricated emergency that might, with a little luck from the caller's perspective, result in the unintended shooting of the unsuspecting target.

This concept was further expanded around 2014 by an action known as *doxing*, which was the obtaining and broadcasting, usually via the internet and social media, of the personal details or documents of an individual with the intention of inciting others to harass or endanger them. Doxing was most often used to attack people whom a group disagreed with politically.

This progression of personal harassment—bomb threats, to swatting, to doxing—led to a new tactic utilized by those who demanded extreme gun control and weapons confiscation. It became known in the United States as *flagging*.

Sophisticated measures had been undertaken by the people behind the flagging of Second Amendment rights supporters. Using caller ID spoofing, TTY devices for the deaf, virtual private networks on the internet, and phone phreaking techniques designed to avoid law enforcement traces, the caller would notify law enforcement that an individual was a danger to himself or others. Through trial and error, and by studying law enforcement reaction to these allegations, a script was created that virtually ensured law enforcement would conduct a warrantless search of the target's home, office, or vehicle in search of weapons to confiscate.

Most times, the confiscations resulted in the gun owner spending many thousands of dollars in attorney fees and lost wages to obtain his weapons back. On some occasions, there were deadly consequences.

Recently, a flagging scenario had unfolded in the Berry Hill neighborhood of Nashville, Tennessee. A vocal proponent on social media of Second Amendment rights had drawn the ire of a local group, who undertook a sophisticated flagging operation. They gathered evidence in the form of social media posts, photographs of the target purchasing ammunition at a local gun shop, and capped off the dossier with a seven-second video of the man berating an umpire at his kid's Little League game.

After being provided this evidence, the Nashville Metro Police Department conducted a warrantless search of the family's home. They arrived at five in the morning and pounded on the front door, demanding entry.

The family's chocolate Labrador, startled by the incessant knocking, ran to the door and began barking loudly. The man's wife, and mother of their three children, walked to the top of the stairs and insisted the dog stop barking. At one point, she called to her husband to help her quieten the dog.

In the fracas, the only word the police officers could discern was *help*. That was all they needed. They busted in the front door, and when the chocolate Lab barked louder to warn the family of the intruder, the officers felt threatened and killed it. The man of the house, frightened that someone was breaking in, emerged from the master bedroom with a shotgun he owned for protection.

"Gun!" one of the officers yelled, and the man was immediately killed in a barrage of bullets. The bullets fired by the fully automatic weapons used by the officers sailed past the man's body and struck his wife, who was cowered against the wall, killing her instantly. Another penetrated the walls of the family's youngest child and lodged in her spine, rendering her a paraplegic.

When it was over, the family's two unharmed children emerged from their bedrooms screaming in fear, scarred for life, and orphaned.

It was an example of a lawmaker's good intentions having devastating unintended consequences.

The ramifications of this incident, and others like it, forced law enforcement to be more careful in acting upon red flag complaints. Harrison County required the sheriff to consult with either the state's attorney assigned to the county, or a circuit judge. Sheriff Clark, naturally, always consulted with his sister the judge.

She was fussy when she learned that the suspects associated with this particular red flag case were Squire and Sarah Boone. Judge Kincaid, while very loyal to the Clark family, was the youngest and the most forthright among them.

"Come on, Randy. The Boones? In what universe do you expect me to find that those two old people are a danger to themselves or others?"

"Jo, they held a young man at gunpoint for no reason. They claimed he had a knife and two partners, but there wasn't anybody else around, and a knife ain't a gun."

"Did the kid have a knife?"

"Well, Jo," he began sarcastically, "this is an active crime investigation."

"What crime did they commit?" she asked.

"Well, potentially assault with a deadly weapon. Making terroristic threats. Um, and, maybe purchasing two hundred rounds of ammunition during a single purchase in violation of federal law."

Judge Kincaid rolled her eyes. "Are you sure you don't wanna add parking on a yellow line to this list of heinous acts? Gimme a break, Randy."

A knock on the door interrupted their back-and-forth. One of the deputies on the scene stuck his head through the door, holding a zip-locked evidence bag containing a hunting knife. "Sheriff, we found this at the scene underneath a pickup truck."

Sheriff Clark sighed and shook his head. "Dammit. Bring it here."

The deputy handed it to him, and he quickly shoved it into his desk drawer.

"There's one more thing," began the deputy.

"What!" he bellowed.

"Um, I checked the alleged assailant's prints and compared them to the prints I pulled off the knife. They matched."

"What the hell? Did I ask you to do that? Are you trying out for the dang FBI?"

"Well, no, but I just thought it was necessary to see who was—"

"Go!" Sheriff Clark yelled. He waved his arms, shooing the young man out of his office.

As he was leaving, the deputy added, "But, also, after running his prints, I ran them through NCIS and got a hit. He's wanted in Louisville for strong armed robbery. He was with his two brothers when they mugged a church bus on their way—"

"Shut up, already!"

The deputy left and pulled the door closed behind him.

His sister, now wearing her Judge Kincaid hat, glared at the sheriff and shook her head. "Randy, let them go and apologize or you might be facing a big, fat civil rights lawsuit for this."

"I didn't arrest them, Jo. And I didn't file a formal red flag report. That's why I called you down here."

She stood from her chair and leaned over her brother's desk. "I know exactly what you did. You wanted to stick it to the Boones, and you needed me down here to give you my blessing as a circuit court judge."

"You're family, Jo."

"Yes, I am. But neither one of us can do the Clark family any good in the future if there are investigators from Indianapolis swarming our little town. Listen to me. We've got it good here. Why go stirrin' up trouble?"

Sheriff Clark slumped in his chair and clasped his hands together over his belly. "Well, I 's'pose you're right. The shit's about to hit the fan for them anyway. Billy's gonna foreclose the day after their note comes due, and we'll run 'em out of Harrison County that way."

Judge Kincaid smiled. "There ya go. That's doin' business the legal way."

"I'm not gonna apologize, Jo."

"That's fine, just let them go and get your department ready."

"For what?"

"Have you not seen the news tonight?" she replied. "The president's gonna cut the power off nationwide for a few days 'cause of some solar storm. You might wanna get your act together and quit harassing people like Squire Boone."

CHAPTER 44

Highspire Service Plaza
Pennsylvania Turnpike
Near Harrisburg, Pennsylvania

It had been an hour since Chapman turned their newly acquired BMW R1200GS-sidecar combo into the Highspire Service Plaza on the Pennsylvania Turnpike. The motorcycle, which was capable of going just over two hundred miles on its five-gallon tank of gas, was not completely full when they took delivery from the dealership in Teterboro.

After wasting thirty minutes driving around the fairly large city in search of fuel for the additional five-gallon gas can the dealer gave them, Chapman and Isabella opted to hit the open road. They made their way to the Pennsylvania Turnpike, which would take them westbound toward Harrisburg. At that point, Chapman planned to drop down into West Virginia for a route that would avoid the major cities of Pittsburgh, Columbus, and Cincinnati.

The chaos they'd experienced in Teterboro searching for fuel warned them away from any metropolitan areas. Rumors had been running rampant about what had happened to the power grid in Europe. Political pundits began to raise the specter of a coordinated terrorist attack against the West, while others believed that it was an effort by the Russians to gain a geopolitical advantage in the region. With flights grounded, gasoline was scarce near major airports.

Regardless, panic had set in as Americans began to think this type of calamity could come to their shores. People rushed to gas stations and grocery stores, stocking up on essentials like fuel, food, and supplies.

They weren't completely out of gas when Chapman began to weigh his options. The Pennsylvania Department of Transportation had erected emergency warning signs along the turnpike, advising motorists that the service plazas had limited fuel and would only allow ten gallons per vehicle.

The fuel gauge had just hit yellow when they pulled into the Highspire Service Plaza on the outskirts of Harrisburg in Central Pennsylvania. While they waited their turn to purchase ten gallons, Chapman and Isabella chatted with their fellow motorists.

They heard evidence of society collapsing around the nation, especially in the larger cities. It confirmed Chapman's decision to take a more southerly route, opting for back roads instead of the nation's interstate system whenever feasible. If the delay during this fuel stop was any indication, their chances of finding gasoline might be better on the less-traveled roads.

Isabella had been a real trooper throughout the first leg of their journey to Riverfront Farms. Her leg was somewhat better, but the three-hour motorcycle ride was certainly not what she was used to in Paris. Chapman could tell the newness of the adventure was wearing off for her and the drudgery was setting in.

"Chapman, look at those two couples," she whispered to him, nodding in the direction of a lifted pickup truck with Ohio license plates. "They look, as you Americans say, sketchy."

Chapman studied the two couples. The women were hanging all over the guys they were with, making no attempt to hide their overt public displays of affection.

The line of vehicles inched forward, so Chapman, who'd turned off the motorcycle to conserve fuel, pushed it forward a car length. The recently remodeled service plaza had added an access ramp so that both the westbound and eastbound lanes of the turnpike could access the fuel pumps and restaurants. Four lanes had been established, using orange cones to separate the motorists, and wound around the building and encroached upon the parking spaces set aside for the eighteen-wheel rigs, not that there were any. America's over-the-road supply chain was slowly coming to a screeching halt.

Barely a hundred yards away, primarily automobile traffic sailed along in both directions of the turnpike, with some travelers reaching speeds of a hundred miles per hour to get to their destinations. The Pennsylvania State Police and their local counterparts were occupied with crowd control in the local towns and responding to emergency calls on the interstates. Breaking speed limit laws was the least of their concerns. Chapman averaged seventy miles an hour, which was probably a little too fast considering his inexperience and the fact the sidecar was attached. Based upon what they'd experienced in New Jersey, however, he couldn't get to the farm fast enough.

They finally made their way to the pump. There were a total of eight pumps, two attendants and a like number of armed members dispatched from Troop H of the State Police's Harrisburg Headquarters.

At first, Chapman was refused the opportunity to fill the five-gallon gas can that he carried in the sidecar with his luggage. The attendant hadn't encountered a situation where a total of ten gallons was requested but only half to be used in the actual vehicle. After some discussion between them, which included grumblings from the drivers behind Chapman, who were waiting impatiently in line, the attendant agreed to allow ten gallons to be pumped.

Anxious to get back on the road, Chapman was securing the gas can in the sidecar when suddenly the ground began to shake. He glanced over at Isabella, whose eyes were wide, darting in all directions.

The tremor continued, increasing in intensity. The canopy built over the gas pumps swayed sharply back and forth even after the initial tremor stopped. People were surprised, many screamed in fear, and some pulled out of line just as the tremor stopped.

Then it happened again, just seconds later, except much more violently. People began to scream and left the safety of their cars to look around. Chapman hurried through the repacking of the sidecar, trying to keep his balance during the tremor as if he were riding a surfboard. His legs almost buckled as he held onto the sidecar for stability.

That was when the Earth ripped open along the Lancaster Fault and sent speeding traffic careening off the interstate to avoid being swallowed by the fissure that had split the Pennsylvania Turnpike in half.

CHAPTER 45

Highspire Service Plaza
Pennsylvania Turnpike
Near Harrisburg, Pennsylvania

Lancaster County, Pennsylvania, had no active fault lines and was by no means a hotbed of seismic activity, yet it was the most seismic region in Pennsylvania. So much so that USGS geologists referred to the area as the Lancaster Seismic Zone.

There weren't many quakes in the region, and in no way did they compare to other active seismic zones in the U.S. Deep within the bedrock of Central Pennsylvania near the Susquehanna River, the makeup of the substrate was changing. Earthquakes originated in the deep Earth, far below the relatively shallow limestone deposits.

About three miles underneath the limestone, in the so-called crystalline basement, was very old metamorphic rock that was highly fractured. Over many thousands of years, tectonic forces caused by the gradual migration of North America toward the Pacific Ocean created stress on those rock fractures.

As the poles shifted and the magnetic field began to reverse, the planet changed as well. These fractures began to slip to relieve the stress, and therefore the Earth began to quake. The strongest earthquake ever recorded in Pennsylvania occurred in 1998, and it had a magnitude of five-point-two.

Until now.

Chapman didn't hesitate to push the motorcycle away from the gas pump canopy as he heard the steel supports begin to squeak. The motorists behind him in line for fuel were conflicted. *Would these tremors pass? Should we give up our place in line—a line we've waited in for nearly two hours?*

The steel roof supports began to bend, and Chapman saw the potential for collapse. "Everyone get away from the pumps. The roof is collapsing!"

Some of the travelers heeded his warning and began to drive away. The sudden response caused a massive traffic jam, and soon the vehicles pointing in all directions looked like a scrum of drunk rugby players.

The quake continued, widening the gap in the interstate. Vehicles swerved to avoid the fissure, and two crashed into one another, sending a KIA careening across the median into the path of an oncoming Sunoco fuel truck.

The big-rig driver swerved to avoid the crash, catching his right-side wheels on the grass shoulder separating the highway from the service plaza. He couldn't maintain control.

The tanker tilted and crashed onto its side. Then it began to slide directly for the fuel pumps.

"Run, Isabella!" Chapman shouted, grabbing her by the hand.

The two raced for the back side of the service plaza as the sound of metal crashing into metal could be heard amidst the hysterical screams of fearful travelers.

The eighteen-wheeler made contact with the gas pumps with dramatic results. The gasoline-filled tanker ruptured, spilling fuel around the pumps. Sparks ignited the flammable liquid, and a massive explosion rocked the service plaza. The blast killed everyone within twenty feet of the gas pumps instantaneously and caught many others on fire.

The concussive effect of the blast broke the plate-glass windows out of the service center and knocked Chapman and Isabella to the ground. Chapman shielded her from the fireball that rose into the sky, which singed the hairs on his arms. The sounds of people screaming in agony filled the air.

Chapman pulled her behind a dumpster and asked if she was okay. She'd landed hard on her elbows and was bleeding from the scrapes, but other than that, she was fine. And concerned.

"We have to help them," she suggested despite the obvious danger.

Chapman stood and walked a few paces to look around the side of the building, which had protected them from the blast.

He returned, wiping off his sweat-drenched face. "I'll do it. You stay here."

"I'm coming, too. Do you hear them?" The screams of despair had reached a crescendo.

"Okay, let's do it."

Isabella, who was still favoring her leg somewhat, walk-hobbled around the building at a fairly brisk pace. That was when the two of them first saw the extent of the devastation. Bodies and body parts were strewn about, some fully engulfed in flames. Vehicles were on fire. Those who'd managed to avoid the fire were knocked to the ground by the blast, lying in the parking lot dazed and confused.

Chapman raced ahead and began to pull people away from the intense heat caused by the gasoline burning. The temperatures were so high that the asphalt was liquefying where it met the concrete pad around the gas pumps. Periodically, vehicle tires exploded as the flames melted the rubber and encountered a healthy blast of compressed air.

Isabella helped women and children who'd survived the blast. She pulled them onto the grass and tried to calm them down. Chapman became more and more daring, braving the heat generated by the fire and rescuing people who'd been knocked unconscious.

After ten minutes, they were able to pull away every living person who had a chance to live. Others who were trapped in cars had succumbed to inhaling the noxious fumes or burned as the fire overtook their vehicle.

Exhausted, Chapman collapsed on the grass next to Isabella, who was holding a young girl as the child sobbed about the death of her mother. The mom, who was two cars behind where their motorcycle was in line, had hesitated to leave after Chapman shouted his warning. She'd pushed her little girls to safety but remained with her car until the tanker slid into the vehicle behind her. She never had a chance.

He wiped soot off his face and turned his shirt inside out to find a clean spot to wipe his eyes. His vision was slightly blurred, but it was recovering now that the smoke was starting to dissipate.

Isabella suddenly stood up and began walking slowly toward a group of injured people who lay prone on the grass.

"Chapman," she said softly at first to get his attention. Then she started running toward the injured survivors and screamed his name. "Chaaapppman!"

CHAPTER 46

Highspire Service Plaza
Pennsylvania Turnpike
Near Harrisburg, Pennsylvania

Chapman scrambled to his feet and had to run in his attempt to catch up to her. Isabella was on a mission, and she began screaming at someone as she approached the group.

"What are you doing? Leave them alone!"

Chapman could see what had garnered her attention. The two couples from Ohio she'd pointed out earlier were stealing from the defenseless victims. As the injured writhed in pain on the ground, the two men and two women were rifling through their pockets or their bags that they'd managed to save from the fire.

One of the men was attempting to wrestle a woman's wedding set off her finger, and when they wouldn't come over her knuckle, he quickly produced a switchblade from his pocket, flipped open the blade, and cut off her ring finger before shoving the rings into his leather jacket.

"My god! Stop, puhleeze," shouted one of the victims.

The four attackers were relentless, like a pack of wolves eating their prey. They were so intent on robbing these injured people that they didn't see Chapman race past Isabella toward the man who'd cut off the woman's finger.

Chapman lowered his head and lunged at the man's back, striking him in the kidneys with the crown of his skull and knocking him to the ground in pain.

The man had lost his breath, and Chapman didn't hesitate to take advantage of his brief incapacity. He began to throw punch after punch into the man's stomach and throat until he was gasping for air.

"Look out!" warned Isabella.

The man's friend stepped over bodies to come after Chapman. He threw himself across the last two moaning victims and landed on top of Chapman. They rolled down a slight incline until they reached the asphalt.

The two women turned their attention to Isabella, who had reinjured her leg.

"Oh, look at little Frenchie. She's busted a wing. I think we should put her out of her misery."

Isabella spied the switchblade on the ground near the man who was gasping for air in an effort to stay alive. His knife had been knocked out of his hands and stuck in the ground. Isabella quickly hopped over to the groaning attacker and picked up his knife.

"Come on! I am not afraid of you, *putain!*"

The two women, who'd succeeded in helping their boyfriends break out of the Gallia County Jail earlier that day, didn't know Isabella had very rudely and impolitely referred to them as whores, but somehow they sensed what she called them was demeaning. They turned their insult into anger and came after her.

Isabella set her jaw and got a firm grip on the knife. She was patient, letting the women make the first move. With anger boiling inside her as hot as the flames soaring into the sky just a hundred feet away, she intended to stab them as many times as necessary, without hesitation.

The heavier set of the two women stumbled and fell, leaving her friend alone as she took on Isabella. While Chapman tumbled across the pavement, wrestling with the other man, Isabella steeled her nerves and deftly stepped out of the way as the first woman swung wildly at her head and missed. The momentum of the attempted punch pulled her off balance, so Isabella quickly thrust the knife in the woman's side just beneath the rib cage. The woman twisted as she screamed in pain, but Isabella kept a firm grip on the knife, wrenching it clear of her attacker with a little extra turn of the wrist.

Seeing Isabella's success in sticking her friend with the

switchblade, the other woman backed off and began to run back toward their pickup truck, which was within a couple of car lengths of the flames.

"Come on Jenna, Troy. Let's get out of here. I hear sirens."

The fourth member of their criminal enterprise, Lawrence, had died from asphyxiation, not that his girlfriend cared. For her, it was all about self-preservation at that point.

Isabella turned on Jenna and threatened to stick her with the knife again. That was all it took for her to chase after her friend, crying from the pain and the blood streaming down her side.

Chapman was now beating the second man without mercy. He was crazed as he alternated beating the back of his head against the hot asphalt and punching him in the chest.

Isabella ran to his side and tried to stop the onslaught. "Chapman! Chapman! It is over. He is not conscious. Stop. Look. He is knocked out."

Chapman stopped the pummeling and took a deep breath. He pushed the man's battered chest hard one last time and triumphantly stood over the lifeless body. He turned to her and she immediately hugged him.

"Are you okay?" he asked.

"Yes, and you, *mon amour*?"

Chapman nodded and then broke their embrace. The two of them turned in a circle, taking in a three-hundred-sixty-degree view of the disaster caused by the earthquake. A gust of hot wind blew across the service plaza, stoking the flames, causing them to dance higher into the air. Beyond the fire, and through the black smoke, he saw their motorcycle sitting alone just beyond the smoldering asphalt.

He reached for Isabella's hand, who tossed the switchblade into the fire. Despite not having any blood on her hand, she felt compelled to wipe it off on her jeans. Mentally, she needed to cleanse her body of what had just happened, thanking God she didn't kill anyone.

That would come later.

CHAPTER 47

The White House
Washington, DC

President Grant Houston began his Call to Action in a solemn manner befitting his mood. It was hard to be upbeat when he was about to ask the nation to willfully abandon all modern conveniences and help one another through these trying times.

"My fellow Americans, I find myself addressing the nation from the Oval Office for the first time and under the most dire of circumstances. As a nation, we are about to face one of the most difficult tasks in our history.

"I have instructed the Department of Energy, under the guidance of the Federal Energy Regulatory Commission, and in cooperation with local electricity service providers around the nation, to begin systematically shutting down America's power grid, one substation at a time. This will be a massive undertaking, the first of its kind on a nationwide scale, that will take the better part of twenty-four hours, but one that is absolutely necessary to preserve life as we've come to know it.

"For many years, there has been a heated debate in this country, and around the world, over the matter of climate change. During my brief time in office, I have pressed for legislation to curb man-made causes of the warming of our planet.

"However, in the last few days, I have learned, along with many in the scientific community, that there may be an alternative explanation for the warming of our planet, as well as the abnormal weather patterns we've been experiencing.

"Our planet is very much like an enormous rotating magnet. Deep within its core, molten iron rotates to generate a magnetic field that protects us and our electronics from the harmful effects of the Sun. The sun gives us life, but it can also cause us substantial harm. That's why I'm speaking to you tonight.

"Earth is undergoing some extraordinary changes, the most significant of which involves the moving of its magnetic north and south poles. Now, many might think that this phenomenon is nothing more than looking at a compass in a different way. That's the furthest thing from the truth. Many aspects of our life, from the use of GPS to animal behavior, relies upon the location of these magnetic poles.

"But there's more. During the time the shift occurs, our magnetic field weakens. The solar matter that is ordinarily deflected by our protective field can now get through to the Earth's surface. It can be damaging to our skin, and it can cause our sensitive electronics to cease to function. In addition, the powerful particles emitted from the Sun can destroy our critical infrastructure, namely, the electrical grid.

"There is an option. It's an option that requires patience and sacrifice, understanding and harmony among us all. It's an option that I successfully used in California as my state was besieged by wildfires in years past.

"It's known as the black start plan, and here's what it entails. In order to protect the power grid from being devastated by the enormous pulse of energy generated by the potential geomagnetic storm that threatens our planet, we can unplug, so to speak. What that means is that we can eliminate these geostorms from causing catastrophic failures of our electrical supply.

"However, in order to do that, and in the interest of public safety, we must necessarily take it down with the goal to restore the grid as soon as practicable. Once the threat of a geostorm and its massive pulse of energy from the Sun has passed, an assessment will be made, and we can consider reestablishing power to our homes and businesses in order to get on with our lives.

"Now, what does that mean in the short term? I'm calling my

address a *Call to Action*. I'm asking the American people to come together as one this evening. I know that great hardship will come upon all of you in the short term, but it will ensure the viability of our nation if we can endure it together, in harmony, arm in arm with our neighbors.

"I ask you to share your resources with one another. There's no need to hoard food or gasoline, as this temporary inconvenience will soon pass. Please, respect one another and the rule of law. As a nation, we can come together, set aside our differences, and agree not to take advantage of the weakest among us."

President Houston's words fell upon deaf ears.

CHAPTER 48

Northwest Ontario, Canada

Levi was emotionally and physically exhausted. Once he got settled into a semi-comfortable position draped over two branches midway up the pine tree, he barely went through the usual stages of sleep and passed out into a deep REM sleep.

Characterized by rapid eye movement and, at times, vivid dreams, REM was very different from stages one through four of the sleep process. Muscles became atonic, meaning without movement. Breathing was more erratic than the other stages, and the body's heart rate increased dramatically.

During REM, as dreams consumed the mind and were oftentimes loosely based upon recent events in the person's life, external stimuli such as sounds and movements were sometimes disregarded by the brain despite the fact they were real. Even upon awakening, during those initial moments, the brain tried to reconcile the dream together with the external stimuli in an effort to determine if the events were, in fact, real.

In Levi's dream, he was holding onto a tree limb for dear life, grasping at the wet limbs to avoid falling as a large bear shook the tree in an attempt to dislodge him. As he slept, Levi's body convulsed, trying to shake itself awake to face the threat, but physical exhaustion kept him in REM sleep.

That was until a fat glob of wet snow fell off the upper branches of the lofty pine and hit him square in the face. This rude awakening served two purposes. It confirmed to Levi's brain that he was in danger of falling from the rapidly shaking pine tree. Only, it wasn't a bear that caused the swaying.

It was an earthquake.

Levi panicked, dropping his rifle thirty feet to the snow-covered ground below, and he almost slipped from his perch. He slung his right arm over a branch and hung like a coat hanger on a rod until he was able to reach up with his left hand to get a firm grip. He eased his right hand to grab the branch, and soon he looked like a spread-eagled X swinging from the tree.

Levi glanced down and then expanded his perimeter surveillance to determine if there were any hungry critters waiting below. Satisfied that the wolves were gone and there wasn't a bear trying to shake him loose, he held on until the tremor stopped.

Finally, the Earth rested and Levi was able to exhale and assess his situation. In his panicked state, he hadn't noticed how the wilderness erupted in a clamor of animals howling, chirping, and growling as their lives were disrupted by the unusual seismic activity. Now their roar was deafening.

His arms began to tire, so he inched his way along the branch over to the trunk of the tree and shimmied to the ground, using branches and knots to position his feet. Less than a minute later, Levi was back on terra firma, gun in hand, his mind racing as he recalled the events of the night before. He glanced up the slight incline toward the rock outcropping that was initially seen as a safe haven from the attacking wolves but ended up presiding over Karl's mutilation.

He hesitated at first. Then he summoned the will to approach his friend's remains to pay his respects. As Levi approached, he began to see bits and pieces of Karl's blood-soaked clothing, which were now frozen solid. There was very little left of his body, and the gruesome sight began to turn Levi's stomach. However, it was not until he found the remains of Karl's head that Levi emptied his stomach, retching over and over again until he convulsed.

It took him several minutes to get over the gruesome scene, and despite his well-intentioned plan to give Karl some type of proper burial, he couldn't muster up the intestinal fortitude to do it. Besides, he rationalized, he wouldn't be able to dig a grave deep enough to prevent the smaller mammals of the forest from digging up what was left of his friend.

Remarkably, Levi didn't cry as he said goodbye to his buddy. Perhaps he was still in shock, or something had changed within him. It was almost as if he were a soldier at war, where death was expected and thus accepted. Levi knelt in a patch of snow without regard to the blood that was mixed with it. He said a brief prayer and began to stand, when something metallic caught his eye near Karl's head. Levi bravely walked toward it, focusing on the shiny object and disregarding the gore.

It was Karl's gold St. Christopher medal. It had been given to him by his mother, who was a devout Catholic. The medal, in honor of St. Christopher, the patron saint of travelers, depicted a man with a child over his shoulder and a staff in his hand. Levi carefully wiped the blood off the oval medallion and chain and respectfully slipped it into his pocket.

"I'll give this to your mom, buddy. I'll miss you and I'm sorry."

Levi turned back down the hill to find Eddie, or what was left of his body. He carried some guilt with him as he went. All the guys wanted to make this trip, but they always looked to Levi to be their tour guide. He hunted more than the others and was more capable of dealing with the harsh conditions of the wilderness. He felt responsible for their safety, but he couldn't protect them from everything.

And he couldn't make them listen to his instructions. Eddie hadn't packed appropriate clothing, as Levi had suggested, which complicated their survival following the plane crash. Karl bolted and ran when Levi told him to remain still. The inability to remain calm in the face of the threat cost both men their lives, and for some unexplained reason, Levi was spared as the wolves raced past him to kill Karl.

Now he was alone and he had to find a way to survive.

He came upon the spot in the clearing where Eddie had been slaughtered. His body was being picked over by birds, which Levi promptly shooed away. In recent years, he wasn't as close to Eddie as he was to Karl, but he paid his respects just the same. Like Karl's body, there was nothing left of Eddie to bury. After another few words to God to deliver his friend's soul to Heaven, Levi gathered his thoughts.

First, he set about to gather their backpacks and weapons. He couldn't carry everything, so he went through all of their belongings and determined what would be the most useful. Karl's sleeping bag was a must, as was his extra ammunition. Socks, long johns, and gloves were also useful.

Once Levi was outfitted for the trek out of the forest, he studied the sky. Then he retrieved the compass from his pocket and recalled that the needle pointed in the wrong direction. One thing about a compass, he thought to himself, its operation was all relative. Much like a scale that might be off ten pounds, as long as it was consistent, a person could gauge whether they were losing or gaining weight. The compass worked in much the same way.

Rather than pointing north, it was now pointing east toward the rising sun. "That means if east is the new north, then on the compass, south is the new east, or somethin' like that."

Levi laughed at himself for talking out loud. Then he shrugged and answered himself. "So let's head east, young man, even though that's south, which is where I wanna go."

Levi shook his head and grinned. He momentarily paused and then added, "I think I'm losin' my shit."

CHAPTER 49

Kristi Boone's Residence
South Scoville Avenue
Oak Park, Illinois

The anarchists from the Animal Liberation Front scattered like cockroaches when the lights were turned on. They scrambled over fences and through drainage culverts in an attempt to avoid the police descending upon Brookfield Zoo. When the dust settled, five zoo security personnel had been killed, two anarchists were discovered trampled in the pachyderm habitat, and Kristi's assailant was treated for fifty rounds of birdshot embedded in his body.

It was nearly dawn when they gathered their personal effects from their respective offices and loaded them into Tommy's car. Kristi, as was customary, rode with Uber to and from her home in nearby Oak Park. She rarely had a use for a car, as nearly every waking moment was spent at Brookfield.

As the two drove off, she looked back at the zoo, wondering if she'd ever return. Then she smiled as she admired the adorable young chimpanzee Tommy had found in the woods near the melee at Swan Lake. She was sleeping like a baby in the back seat, buckled up for safety, of course.

"Take a right on Harvard," she said to Tommy, who was also quiet after the ordeal.

The two of them were assessing what had happened and what it meant for their futures and the lives of the animals they cared for. He drove slowly through the older neighborhood. At this hour there was no traffic.

"There's the Montessori School you mentioned. Your street is Scoville, right?"

"Yes, in fact, next block, take a right. I'm the fourth house on the right."

Tommy chuckled. He reached over and squeezed her hand. "It's gonna be all right, right?"

"That's a whole lotta right," said Kristi with a laugh.

"Yup, nothing wrong with being right!"

They both started laughing, and the young chimp began to stir in the back seat. Kristi turned around to give her a look and raised her index finger to her lips. "Shhh. You'll wake the baby."

This caused them to truly laugh out loud, finally able to release the tension of the ordeal they'd just been through. Tommy slowed as he pulled in front of her modest craftsman-style home.

He turned off the motor and turned to Kristi. "I can come in to help."

She gave him a sweet smile and thanked him, but declined his assistance. She needed to be alone while she gathered a few personal effects.

Kristi exited the SUV and bounded up the stairs to unlock the door. She entered the foyer and immediately noticed that something was wrong. At first, she was confused as her eyes adjusted to the darkness. For a brief moment, she thought she'd entered the wrong house.

Kristi backed up a few steps and reached behind her to flip on the light switch. That was when she discovered her home had been ransacked. She immediately became afraid. She raced out of the house and ran back to the side of the truck. Tommy had lowered the windows to allow some fresh air in, as the chimpanzee smelled like, well, a zoo animal.

"What's wrong?" he asked.

"Somebody broke into my house. Tommy, it's been trashed."

"I'll call the cops," he offered.

"Cell service is down, remember."

"Shit, yeah. Um, do you have a landline?"

"In the kitchen, but I don't——"

Tommy finished her sentence emphatically. "Nor will you go in alone. Hang on." He closed the windows to leave a slight crack, and then he exited the truck, allowing the chimp to slumber in the back seat.

Tommy raced around the truck and grabbed Kristi by the hand. They ran up the stairs but cautiously entered the house.

"Hello?" asked Tommy loudly. "If you're still in here, you need to get out. I've called the police and I have a gun!" he lied. The police had confiscated their weapons as evidence. Kristi didn't put up a fight. She had more at home.

"Help me turn on the lights."

He slipped his arm around the wall in the formal living room to the left and flipped on the ceiling fan, light kit combination. Kristi darted into the dining room and pushed the dimmer button on the chandelier before turning it up to full brightness. Every piece of china and décor on her dining table had been swept onto the floor or thrown against the china hutch, smashing out the glass.

The sound of glass shattering came from the kitchen, followed by the clinking of jagged shards tumbling piecemeal to the floor. Kristi started in that direction, but Tommy grabbed her arm.

"It's too dangerous," he whispered.

"They're trashing my house," she complained.

"Well, me first." Tommy pushed past her as the sounds of cupboard doors slamming and canned goods being dumped out filled the downstairs of the house.

The kitchen was dark, but Tommy was unafraid. He rushed in there, screaming, "Get out of here or I'll shoot!"

The crashing sounds stopped, but heavy breathing could be heard in the silence of their surroundings.

Kristi entered the kitchen and found the light switches. The fluorescent overhead bulbs started up with a hissing sound before illuminating the room. Sitting perfectly still on the kitchen counter was a familiar face.

Knight, or what used to be Knight. In just a short time, he was changed, both mentally and physically. He had developed muscles. They were tight, robust, and solid looking. His face reflected this change. It was ravenous, lean, and hungry, and partially covered by long rangy hair that dangled over his forehead.

She whispered to Tommy, "He remembered how to get here. Somehow, he remembered."

"Kristi, please be careful," Tommy warned.

"Knight? It's me, Kristi. Do you remember me?" As Kristi spoke, she used sign language.

Knight was unresponsive.

Kristi moved a little closer, causing him to immediately tense and slide onto his rear legs into a lunging position. There was no recognition of her in his eyes.

"Be careful," warned Tommy again. He stepped slowly to Kristi's left, putting himself in a position to intercept any attack by Knight.

Knight's nose was running, and his eyes were bloodshot. His nose sniffled continuously as he tried to assess whether Kristi and Tommy were threats. Every decision Knight made was based upon his genetics, utilizing his senses of sight, smell, and hearing to determine if he was being threatened.

"Knight, good morning. Are you hungry?" Kristi was speaking while signing at the same time. She reverted back to the earliest commands and conversations she'd taught him as a young chimp. She hoped to reach deep into his mind in an effort to spark some recollection of her.

Knight was processing her actions. They weren't threatening, but they were not recognizable. Still, he appeared intrigued.

Kristi suddenly stopped as Knight began to rock back and forth as his confused mind processed visions of Kristi opening the door of his cage, carefully cradling him in her arms, and speaking in soft, hushed tones in an effort to soothe him. He was starting to remember. It was kindness, and it came from this human.

"Oo-oo-oo-oo."

"Yes, Knight. Hello. Good morning. Use sign language." Kristi was desperately trying to get through to him. She felt that he was coming around, because his facial expression went from guarded to relaxed. As she got closer, Knight no longer recoiled.

Kristi smiled, crouched somewhat, and held her hand out to him as if she were a queen asking one of her subjects to kiss the ring. For primates, it was a submissive gesture, her way of reminding Knight that she was not a threat.

Knight extended his index finger and cautiously reached out toward Kristi's hand. She stretched her arm, convinced that if they could make physical contact, he'd remember how close they were, and that she was not a threat to him.

She could see the change in his eyes. A softness. The glare turned into a look of familiarity. They were so close and then …

The still of the early morning hours was shattered by the sound of two vehicles crashing into each other on the nearby Eisenhower Expressway just beyond Rehm Park a block away.

The loud noise frightened Knight. He recoiled and immediately jumped to his feet.

Waving his arms high over his head, Knight shrieked, "Heeaagh!"

It was a violent squall. Noisy. High-pitched. Grinding on the senses.

"Heeaagh! Heeaagh! Heeaagh!"

Instinctively, Kristi moved forward to comfort Knight. "It's okay. I'm here. Stay, please."

Knight would have none of it. He launched himself across the kitchen until he hung from a Tiffany-shade chandelier over the kitchen table. He swung for a moment and then launched himself across the room toward the back door. He began to violently pound on it.

"Heeaagh! Heeaagh! Heeaagh!"

Kristi and Tommy approached him from different angles, both speaking in calm tones and holding their arms out to appear comforting.

It was too late. They'd lost him.

Knight bounded forward and knuckle-ran between them across the shards of glass in the dining room. He never hesitated as he leapt through the same broken window he'd created at the side of the house when he'd found his way there earlier.

Without so much as a hoot or a holler, Knight, or what was left of him, was gone forever.

CHAPTER 50

Point Pleasant, West Virginia

By the time Chapman and Isabella reached the Ohio River at Point Pleasant, West Virginia, they were riding on fumes and decided they'd better stop before they crossed into Gallipolis, Ohio.

They bore little resemblance to the young couple who'd had drinks the first night Chapman arrived in Paris. He now had a full understanding of why Harley riders walked into a gas station like they had a severe case of diaper rash.

Isabella, who rode the entire trip on the back of the BMW with her arms wrapped around Chapman's waist, occasionally caught a glimpse of herself in the side mirrors. She didn't like what was looking back at her.

Certainly, the two had every right to appear disheveled, to put it mildly. Neither had the clothing customarily used by experienced bikers to protect themselves from the wind, sun and road grime while they rode in the open air. Leather was easier to wipe off than blue jeans and cotton shirts. The wind was brutal on their hair, especially with no bandanas or helmets, both of which were lost during the chaos at the service plaza. And the sun, which continued to beat down on the Midwest, was especially brutal as the magnetic field weakened.

Chapman slowed to exit before the bridge and pulled into the sleepy little town known for its role in *The Mothman Prophecies* movie starring Richard Gere. The movie was about a big-city journalist whose wife continuously experienced supernatural mothlike visions before she was suddenly killed in a car accident. Obsessed with finding out what they meant, he left the city and traveled to Point Pleasant, West Virginia, and its sister city across the Ohio River, Gallipolis, Ohio.

The first few gas stations near the highway were out of gas, so Chapman slowly drove farther into the small town until he located a rundown, old Chevron station near city hall. It only took him a minute or two to fill the tank of the motorcycle and his spare five-gallon tank. It took even less than that for the proprietor to extort a C-note for payment.

Ten dollars a gallon was ridiculous, but it represented the law of supply and demand at the moment. Chapman's choice to avoid the busy interstate system had proven to be a good one, as traffic was minimal, and the exposed ride took a little less of a toll on their bodies.

They were both anxious to strip out of the smoke-covered clothing they'd worn since the incident at the service plaza. Isabella went into the restroom first and tried to clean up her face and hair. She changed her clothes and left her soot-stained jeans and shirt in the trash bin.

Somewhat refreshed, she watched their belongings while Chapman tried to become more presentable. They still had two hundred fifty miles to travel, and their efforts at sprucing up would be undone within an hour, but they tried just the same.

While he was inside the restroom, she wandered about to stretch her legs. Something in the small pedestrian median down the street caught her eye. She turned to check on the bike and sidecar, and then wandered down the street until she was face-to-face with the Mothman.

"Isabella!" shouted Chapman, who was surprised to emerge from the restroom and not find her near the motorcycle.

"Over here!" she shouted back.

She stood in front of the statue, reading the plaque titled *Legend of the Mothman*. She shielded her eyes to block out the sun as she studied the hideous creature. Chapman joined her side and frowned.

"That is one ugly, um, moth-thing."

"I do not understand," she began. "Why would this town celebrate this monster? In France, we pay homage to heroes and beauty. Not this."

Chapman took her by the hand and they stood together, taking in a good look at the Mothman one more time. He explained to her that this creature was depicted in a movie nearly thirty years ago that was based on this town.

"You see, small towns in America struggle to create an identity for themselves. They want to be known as being important or famous for something. In Pennsylvania, where we left a few hours ago, there's the town of Hershey known for being the place where the famous chocolate was made. And there's Punxsutawney, which has the famous groundhog."

"Groundhog? What is that?"

"It's a woodchuck."

"Why would they celebrate a woodchuck or groundhog?"

"Because every year on February 2, the town gathers around to see if Punxsutawney Phil the groundhog sees its shadow. This is how they predict if the town will have six more weeks of winter or an early spring."

Isabella furrowed her brow and studied Chapman's face. She playfully thumped his chest. "I warned you not to lie to me, *Monsieur Boone.*"

Chapman started laughing while he rubbed the spot where she'd slugged him. "No, I'm serious. It's American folklore that if Punxsutawney Phil emerges from his hole on that day and sees his shadow, there will be six more weeks of winter."

"That's stupid," she said and slugged him again. "I will ask your mother if this is true, and if she says no, you will need to hide from me this winter."

Isabella glanced up at the Mothman and gave it a disapproving look. As she crossed the street, a hot gust of wind blew between the buildings, and a printed flyer swirled toward her, catching on her leg. She immediately grabbed the paper and flipped it over to see what it said.

Chapman lingered for a moment and finished reading the plaque until Isabella called out his name.

"Chapman! It is them. Come see!"

"Who, them?"

"The sketchy hooligans from the fire. Look." She handed him the flyer and read parts of it aloud.

"Damn," he muttered. "They were escaped convicts. Their

girlfriends were accomplices."

Isabella pointed to the paper. "Killers, too. Chapman, we battled killers and won."

"Or lived to tell about it," he mumbled under his breath. He looked toward the sky, and the sun immediately began to warm his face. He'd been wearing a long-sleeve tee shirt since they left Teterboro and noticed how it protected his arms from the sun's intensity. He held his hands out to inspect them.

"What are you doing?" asked Isabella.

"Look at my hands," he replied, turning them over and over again to inspect the damage they'd sustained. "I washed them in the restroom, but they're still very dirty looking. Almost sunburned."

He turned to Isabella and gently pulled her blouse away from her neck and shoulders.

"Do not get frisky with me in public, Chapman Boone," she threatened.

"No, I'm looking at your skin. The sun is burning us. We need to put on more clothes."

"It's so hot."

"I know, but the magnetic field is weaker, and the sun-protection factor has diminished."

Isabella sighed and wrapped her arm through his. "How much longer to your farm?"

"About five to six hours or so. If we drive at a steady pace with no more stops, we can get there around dark."

She nodded as they reached the motorcycle, and then added, "Soon, we may have to live in the dark."

CHAPTER 51

Northwest Ontario, Canada

Levi walked due east, according to the compass, which was more south-southeast by the position of the sun. The terrain was increasingly rocky the farther he traveled from Hudson Bay and the lowlands that surrounded it.

Twice he came across small streams that flowed toward the east and back toward the north where he came from. Ordinarily, as every kid learns in *Boy Scouts 101*, when you get lost, travel downstream and you'll make your way out of the woods. In this case, all streams led to Hudson Bay, and Levi had no desire to go back in that direction.

He chose the easiest terrain he could find as he steadily moved in a southerly direction toward more populated areas. Without a map and a functioning GPS device, he simply assumed he'd come across a town or a hunting cabin at some point.

He kept his water bottles full of snow and tucked them under his armpit so he would have a constant supply of water. When he came across a stream, he'd gulp the fresh water down and refill the padded squeeze bottles to stay hydrated.

Levi had walked for hours, and the sun was quickly setting in the west when he crossed another wide, but shallow stream. As he emerged on the other side, he found himself trudging through several sumps full of standing water and muddy soil. The bog had been formed in an area surrounded by rock outcroppings that jutted out like the upper deck of a football stadium.

His feet sank in the muck, at times forcing him to use his arms to pull his leg out of the mud. He'd just emerged from the mess when he came across a wolf caught in a trap. The beautiful grayish-white creature was bloodied around her hindquarters where the powerful steel trap had clamped down on her leg.

As Levi approached, the confused and frightened animal backed away, straining at the trap chain that was wrapped around a pine tree and padlocked in place.

Levi raised his rifle and pointed it toward the wolf. Thoughts of Karl and Eddie's mangled bodies raced through his mind, and for a brief moment, he considered exacting his revenge on the defenseless wolf, which was most likely not involved in the slaughter.

Instead, Levi, in the dimming daylight, scanned the perimeter to make sure none of the wolf's friends were lurking about. Satisfied he was safe, he held his rifle barrel down and slowly approached the trapped animal.

"Hey, girl," he said in a calm voice as the wolf snarled at him. He pointed at her belly. "Your teats sure are swollen. Where are your pups?"

Levi crouched down without getting too close to the wolf, who'd pulled away from him as far as she could. A frightened, cornered animal, even if restrained, could lash out and possibly kill him.

He studied her leg. The powerful jaws of the trap had clamped down near her hips. It had punctured the meaty part of her leg and would most likely cause her to bleed out within days.

He grimaced and stood, turning in a circle as if seeking answers to what he should do next. She'd only recently been trapped, which meant her pups might be nearby. Finally, he turned back to the wolf and said, "Let's have a look for your babies. From the looks of your belly, they're probably hungry."

Levi headed for the arena-shaped outcroppings in search of the wolf pups. There wasn't any snow on the ground as he traveled south, but the soil was muddy, and he hoped he could come across the mother's tracks. He found where the mother wolf had pawed at the soil on a barely discernible trail leading downhill to the bog. He followed the trail through the pine saplings up toward the rocky slope.

As he drew closer, he heard a squeaking sound. Levi raised his rifle and cautiously approached a part of the rocky face that stuck out to create a ledge. That was when he noticed the wolf puppy paw prints in the wet soil. They'd ventured out of the den from time to time in search of their mother, only to retreat to safety when they couldn't see her.

Levi knew wolf pups to be shy and cautious, and he certainly wasn't small enough to crawl under the ledge and retrieve them. Instead, he decided to lure them outside. He began to imitate their high-pitched squeaks. He dropped to his knees and elbows, as if he were a large dog lying on the floor, and tried to emulate their voices again.

It took a few minutes of coaxing, but first one, and then three more snow-white wolf puppies emerged from the den and slowly approached Levi.

"Wow, you guys are fresh out of the hopper," muttered Levi as they shyly crawled toward him. He removed his gloves and wiggled his fingers. The four pups began suckling on his fingers, allowing their fear to be displaced by their hunger.

Levi removed his jacket and spread it open on the ground. He picked up the pups and set them in the middle before swaddling them up. He carefully descended the slope to where the mother was trapped.

The wolf spotted Levi's approach and immediately picked up the scent of her young. She stood erect, ignoring the pain that must've coursed through her body. She gathered the energy to let out a high-pitched mournful whine, begging Levi not to harm her babies and give them over to her.

Staying a safe distance away from the wolf, Levi dropped to his knees and unfolded his jacket. The pups squealed in delight and raced toward their mother. She immediately dropped to her side and allowed them to latch on to her for a long overdue meal.

"Now what?" Levi asked aloud. He tried again to get a look at her leg, but with every approach, the threatening growl rumbled out of her throat.

Levi backed off with his arms raised. "Hey, I get it. No need to thank me, by the way." He was being sarcastic, yet he still wanted to help. Despite the mother wolf's belligerence, she needed nourishment to live as long as she could to feed her pups. Levi decided to search for food.

It was getting darker now, and he had to hurry. He'd spotted several deer during his hike through the woods, but he wasn't interested in hunting. He still had some Clif bars stored in his backpack that would provide him nourishment for several days. Now, he planned on hunting to provide for the mother wolf and her family.

He worked his way around the low side of the rock outcropping and along the solid banks of the stream. When he'd crossed a stream earlier, he'd come across the unmistakable signs of feral hogs who'd been rooting in the mud. Levi's grandfather referred to them as *rototillers* because the way they rooted for food and wallowed on the ground would leave a farm unrecognizable. But it was that very activity that made them easier to hunt than fleet, light-footed deer.

A wild pig would make a fine dinner for the wolf, and himself. Levi focused on the banks of the stream, having now walked nearly a mile away from where he'd left the wolf and her pups. Then he spotted what he was looking for.

A single hog was lying on its side at the foot of a tree. It was either sleeping or it was exhausted from making a mess. The ground all around it was torn up. The creature lay with its belly and head exposed to Levi, making the shot an easy one for an experienced hunter like himself.

He dropped to one knee and slowly raised his rifle, eyeing his target through his scope. A shot through the bottom of the feral hog's throat would have nothing but soft tissue to travel through as it reached the animal's brain. Just as Levi was prepared to squeeze the trigger, he furrowed his brow. Something wasn't right.

CHAPTER 52

Northwest Ontario, Canada

Levi immediately stood and walked toward the animal, continuously looking through his scope to be prepared to fire. Then he lowered his rifle. The hog wasn't breathing because it was already dead.

He shouldered his weapon and drew his knife out of the sheath strapped around his thigh. Once he was only a few feet from the dead hog, he figured out what had happened. The animal's back had been broken by a boulder that was equal its size. Apparently, during the earthquake tremors Levi had experienced, several rocks had dislodged from the ledge uphill from where the hog was rooting by the stream. Three or four rocks were lying just below the dead hog, whose back was bloodied.

Levi reached down to feel the animal's blood, which was cool to the touch. The temperatures were just above freezing, so it wouldn't take long for the dead body to cool.

Butchering the hog in the wilderness would be quite an undertaking, and Levi's plan was to feed the wolf for at least this evening and possibly the next morning before he continued his journey south toward the States. He lifted a hindquarter of the hog and cut through its coarse fur and tough skin. Then he used the serrated blade of his hunting knife to cut the animal's leg off at the hip.

He walked quickly along the bank, retracing his steps to find his way back to the mother wolf. As he approached, she growl-barked at him, sending a clear message for Levi to keep his distance.

Levi tossed the back leg of the hog at the wolf's mouth. He spoke softly. "Okay, momma, here's supper. However, I'd really appreciate it if you'd stop threatening me. C'mon now. I'm gonna keep helping you until it's time to leave."

She was ravenous, tearing apart the leg and consuming large chunks of hog meat. Levi shook his head and rolled his eyes as he realized he would be making a few more trips to the *Dead Hog Market*.

First, he needed shelter and fire. He looked around and found a cluster of three trees that were uphill from the wolf and near the base of the rock outcropping. Over time, snow had collected on the boughs of the tree, leaving a natural pit at the base. He quickly swept away any rocks and twigs from the ground to provide himself a clean work space.

Then he gathered all the pine needles he could find to create a nice, twelve-inch-thick mattress, which acted as insulation between him and the wet ground. This would work well with Karl's sleeping bag, which he'd wrap around his body.

Finally, he gathered up fallen tree limbs ranging from three to four inches in diameter and five feet long. He used them to build a triangular shaped lean-to, which he then covered with leaves and pine needles for insulation.

Lastly, he gathered rocks from the outcropping to create a circle in which to build a fire. With his shelter prepared along with the fire warming the area around him and the family of wolves, Levi hustled back and forth to the dead hog for food. While he fed the wolf chunks of raw meat, he cooked his portion over the open fire, being sure to overcook it in order to avoid the many diseases feral hogs carry.

Soon, it was pitch dark outside except for the light coming from the dancing flames of the fire. Levi's belly was full, the mother wolf ate every piece of pig meat he tossed her way, and the pups drained her of nutritious milk.

"One big happy family," Levi commented as the mother wolf fought sleep. "You need to rest, momma. I've got your back. No worries." His soothing voice must have convinced her. She was soon in a deep sleep.

Levi crawled into the lean-to and surrounded himself with the sleeping bag. He lay awake for a while, thinking about what had happened to him since the plane crash, and silently chastising himself for not focusing on how much he missed Carly and his kids.

Lying on his back, he clasped his hands behind his head and tried to look at the stars through the roof of his shelter. It was peaceful in the woods, but in Canada, it was far different from back home in Indiana. At that moment, he couldn't hear a single thing except the occasional hoot of an owl and a wolf calling out to his pals. There were no airplanes overhead. No cars roaring down a distant highway. No machine of any sort to interrupt the beauty of night.

But then the silence began to disturb him. It was too quiet. Too serene. The lack of activity was not normal.

Levi broke out in a cold sweat. He fought the feeling of anxiety that was beginning to overwhelm him. He felt trapped, but not like the wolf. It was surreal. Like he was in a coffin, unable to escape.

He began to panic, and he maniacally fought his way out of the sleeping bag like he'd been sleeping in a pit of vipers.

He emerged from the shelter and jumped to his feet. He spun around, looking at the sky, until he was dizzy. Levi screamed, "Dammit!"

Or at least he thought he did. The wolf family barely stirred through all the commotion.

Levi ran his fingers through his hair and covered his ears and then quickly uncovered them. There was no noise to block out. None of the things his mind was used to hearing was present now. Yet he knew it was there. He shook his fist to clear the disturbance, and that worked for a moment.

And then it came back.

Relentlessly.

Levi's mind tried to process what was happening, and then he spoke softly to the wolf.

"You know, the quiet out here can get real loud."

CHAPTER 53

Tommy Bannon's Residence
North Michigan Avenue
Chicago, Illinois

Kristi couldn't stop crying. She barely recalled walking through her wrecked home, gathering up personal mementos that hadn't been broken, and a couple of duffle bags of clothes. Tommy did all he could to comfort her, but losing Knight this way had a profound effect on her emotions. For Kristi, it was tantamount to losing a child.

As daylight approached, Chicago woke up as well. Tommy was astonished at the amount of traffic headed into the downtown business district. Kristi was curled up in the passenger seat with the female chimp, sobbing.

"You know." She spoke finally. She'd recovered somewhat, and her voice was remarkably calm. "I thought I knew all of the primates because I spent so much time in Tropic World. I just can't seem to recall ever interacting with this one."

Tommy glanced over to take another look at the smallish female. "How old do you think she is? One? Two?"

"Closer to one," Kristi replied and then looked lovingly at the youngster. "Knight was about her age when I began teaching him to sign."

Tommy didn't continue the conversation immediately. After witnessing the primates' behavior over the last week, including Knight's, there was an elephant in the room that needed to be addressed. Watching Kristi bond with this young chimp prohibited him from addressing what to do with her.

"Okay, we're almost there." He changed the subject. "I don't get it. Don't these people realize the power could be cut off at any moment? Are they trying to get a little more work done at the office before the president pulls the plug?"

Kristi looked out the window for the first time, turning her attention away from the chimp she'd cradled the entire trip from her house. "Yeah, this is weird. Maybe they changed their mind about cutting the power. I'm not sure that's such a good idea anyway."

Tommy shrugged. "It kinda makes sense, if their predictions are true about what these geostorms can do to electronics. But, I mean, logically, how long will it last? Who gets to decide when to issue the all-clear signal?"

Kristi leaned forward to admire the massive skyscrapers that lined Michigan Avenue. "The same guy who decided to flip the switch, I guess."

"Check it out, Starbucks is open."

"Is that the new one? You know, the Reserve?"

"No, that's on the other side of the Lincoln Park Zoo."

She paused for a moment and then turned to Tommy. "Are you rich or something? I mean, either you've decided to give me the nickel tour of the Magnificent Mile, or you're lost."

The Magnificent Mile in Chicago's Central Business District was one of the most famous retail stretches in the world. Every high-end retailer and restaurant had a presence there. The hotels and office buildings had an incredible view of Lake Shore Drive and Lake Michigan.

Tommy laughed. "Not rich, but maybe richer by comparison to other zoologists you know. I was fortunate enough to be born into a well-to-do family. My grandfather was the founding partner of Goldberg, Bannon, and May."

"The lawyers? The ones with the billboards all over town?"

"The same," replied Tommy. "When my grandfather died, he had a complicated estate that used some kind of IRS generation-skipping loophole to avoid estate taxes. I got a decent trust fund that pays a little each month as well as a condo in the city."

"Not bad. What did your father do? Was he a lawyer also?"

"Yeah, international law. That's why he and Mom were in London when the terrorist attack occurred."

"I'm sorry, Tommy. I shouldn't have brought it up." Kristi adjusted the chimp in her lap as she turned toward Tommy.

Tommy grimaced. "That's okay. I was really angry at everything and everybody for a few years, but time has passed and I'm better now. The trust still has some real estate holdings here that are managed by a trustee who works for the firm. He also handles my finances, not that there's much to it. My place is paid for, the trust pays the associations fees, taxes, utilities, etcetera. I get a monthly check to spend. Which is a good thing because I probably lost my job at the zoo."

Tommy looked out the driver's side window and rested his chin on his fist. Kristi studied him for a moment, and then she also looked away. Their lives had been turned upside down, and now they were suddenly thrust into a relationship of sorts, something neither of them had addressed. Except the near-kiss that was preempted by chaos, of course.

"Here we are," announced Tommy as he approached a high-rise mixed-use building. He crept up to a card reader and swiped a keycard, instantly opening a steel gate. He drove toward a bank of elevators and parked in one of several spaces marked *Loading Zone*.

Kristi exited first and hoisted the chimp onto her hip as she took in her surroundings. The entire garage area was impeccable. Polished brass adornments and elevator doors glistened under the chandelier lighting in the open hallway. Vehicles ranging from Bentleys to Porsches were parked all around them. Yet, with all the wealth around him, Tommy drove a Chevy Suburban.

He walked around the truck and found Kristi standing quietly by her door. She appeared vulnerable and unsure. The moment had suddenly become awkward, as the two really hadn't discussed what was going to happen next.

He immediately picked up on her feelings and tried to address the ticklish situation. "You know what I think?"

"What?" she asked, her voice hopeful that he had a solution to the somewhat embarrassing moment. Kristi didn't know if he was gonna ask her to move in with him, or tell her to wait in the garage with the chimp.

"Let's go upstairs, grab this little one some fruit to eat, and figure out a plan."

Kristi looked down and nodded. Her eyes began to well up with tears. "Okay," she said shyly.

Tommy gently cupped his hand under her chin so that she'd look him in the eyes. "We haven't had a moment's rest in days. I'm exhausted, and I'm sure you are too. Let's unwind and talk it through. How's that sound?"

"And have an adult beverage?"

Tommy laughed. "Sure, why not? We've been up all night, and it's five o'clock somewhere."

The chimp began to squirm in her arms, so she set her on the ground. She took their new companion by the hand and smiled at Tommy. "Lead the way."

Thirty minutes later, the chimp was chowing down on apples and bananas. Kristi and Tommy had thrown back a few glasses of bourbon. He'd changed clothes into shorts and a University of Wisconsin sweatshirt with a badger embroidered on the front. He'd retrieved Kristi's duffle bags, and she rummaged through them to find some fresh clothes, but ultimately ended up wearing one of Tommy's tee shirts.

"Come check out the view," said Tommy as he opened the sliding glass door that led to the balcony of his tenth-floor unit. The condominium building towered over the low-rise structures below it, affording an incredible view of the south end of Lake Michigan and Lake Shore Drive.

Kristi joined his side and wrapped her arm through his. "Tommy, um, I think I ..." She stopped mid-sentence.

He laughed and gave her a shy smile. "I think we have a little unfinished business before you keep talking." He bent over and kissed her. Gently at first, and then more passionately.

She responded and turned to hug him. The tension that had been between them since they'd met was now being released as they let their inhibitions down. But just as their kiss was interrupted on the rooftop at the zoo, so it was again.

A flock of birds came chattering by them, catching their eye.

"Wait, are those?" Tommy began to ask.

"They are, indeed."

A flock of two dozen green-winged macaws sailed past them at eye level. They made a complete circle, dove downward, and then raced toward Lake Michigan.

"That's unbelievable," said Tommy as he accepted another kiss from Kristi, filled with excitement.

"They're free," she said. "I don't like how it happened, but they're getting to live their lives as God intended."

"Wait, where are they going?" asked Tommy. The flock of macaws suddenly raced toward a target by the south shore of the lake. Then he exclaimed, "No way!"

Both of them leaned over the rail slightly as if it would give them a better look at the unusual sight. Two of the elephants from the zoo lumbered along Lakefront Trail, the pedestrian path built between the water's edge and Lake Shore Drive.

"They're taking their jungle back," said Kristi with a laugh as she wrapped her arm a little tighter around Tommy's.

Before Tommy could add his thought, the unmistakable sound of the power draining from the city could be heard. Air conditioners stopped running. Refrigerators shut down. Lights popped and flickered as they went dark.

As if the opportunity to ruin the moment wasn't already upon them, in the sudden quiet of the normally bustling city of Chicago, gunshots could be heard echoing off the walls of the concrete jungle.

Tommy sighed. "If the animals plan on taking their jungle back, they're gonna have a fight on their hands."

CHAPTER 54

Northwest Ontario, Canada

Levi wasn't in his right state of mind that evening. When his surge of adrenaline finally subsided, he opted to sleep under the stars, as he put it, and ripped apart the lean-to shelter he'd so meticulously built. Rather than using the sleeping bag for protection from the nighttime cold, he slept on top of it, curled up in a fetal position. He'd convinced himself that it would make sense to be *one with nature*.

At dawn the next morning, he was awakened by the curious wolf pups, who were sniffing his face and hands. Levi lay perfectly still, not wanting to frighten them and actually enjoying the feel of their fur on his skin.

He slowly opened his eyes and glanced at the mother wolf, who had become increasingly annoyed that her youngsters would be so bold as to sniff a human. Levi began to consider how weak she'd become despite the nourishment and that soon she would die.

The wolf let out a squeaky yelp, and her pups scampered back to curl up under her belly. Levi sat up, moving slowly so as not to appear threatening. "I wish I could get you to trust me. Then I could loosen those clamps."

He stood up, stretched his sore back, and then modestly relieved himself behind a tree several feet away from the campsite. The mother wolf's head snapped up as a slight breeze carried the odor of his urine to her nostrils. She sneered slightly, a natural reaction to the human scent.

"Hey, sorry about that," said Levi with a laugh. "I'll pee downwind next time. How 'bout some breakfast?"

Levi added some dried leaves and pine needles to the still-smoldering coals and brought the fire back to life. Then he hustled back to the Dead Hog Market to gather breakfast for himself and his new friend.

Over the next few hours, he divided his time between talking softly with the wolf, playing with her pups, and feeding her more hog meat. Little by little, he was trying to gain her trust. Each time he interacted with her, he'd edge a little closer, being careful, however, not to get within her reach limited by the chain.

By early afternoon, the group was growing more comfortable around each other. Levi sat cross-legged in full view of the wolf, periodically feeding her hog meat and trickling creek water down into a swale near where she lay. She would lap it up, and her pups would roll around in it. It became a playful routine of nourishing, comforting, and convincing her he wasn't a threat.

All of them fell asleep as the warm midday sun peeked through an opening in the trees.

After a short rest, Levi was awakened by the pups sloppily nursing. He thought for a moment, and then something compelled him to take a chance.

He sat cross-legged, as he had all morning, but he slowly inched forward, the closest he'd been to the wolf yet. He tossed her a few more pieces of meat, which she ate heartily. She'd begun to regain her appetite and her strength.

A potentially good news, bad news story based upon what was about to happen next.

Two of the pups broke loose from her teats and moseyed toward Levi. The mother lifted her head and glared at him. The puppies slowly walked into his lap and curled up to sleep.

That was when it happened.

It was fast. Imperceptible. But Levi noticed it nonetheless.

The mother wolf wagged her tail.

A breakthrough.

Levi smiled from ear to ear, careful not to show his teeth to her. He petted the pups for a while, speaking in hushed tones and even singing a lullaby.

"Hush, little baby, don't say a word. Papa's gonna buy you a mockingbird. And if that mockingbird don't sing, Papa's gonna buy you a diamond ring."

Those were the only words he could recall, but he repeated them because they appeared to have a relaxing effect on the wolf. He gently lifted the pups out of his lap, and they staggered sleepily toward their mother before flopping on the ground against her belly.

Levi inched closer and the wolf didn't move. She noticed. She just didn't care.

He scooched on his butt even closer, well within the length of a chain. This was almost the moment of truth. Either she was going to let him touch her, or he was going to die trying.

He studied the mechanics of the trap. It was made like most, with two springs flanking a set of sharp-toothed jaws. He looked at how it had clamped on her leg. The wounds were deep, but not so much so that she'd lose the leg. She might be gimpy, but she could still be somewhat mobile.

Under the watchful eye of the wolf, who continued to lie on her side, but turned her head to follow Levi's movements, he gently ran his fingers through her fur several times. The two had locked eyes, but the more he snuggled her, the more her steely eyes softened.

"Okay, please don't bite me. This won't take long."

Levi used plenty of force to press down on the two springs, and fortunately, the jaws flew open and didn't cause her further pain. This was the moment when he became the most vulnerable.

If he lost control of the trap and it snapped shut, she'd feel threatened. If she chose to attack him now, he'd only have his fists and his knife to defend himself. He held his breath and quickly pushed himself away from her with the heels of his feet.

She stood and tried to put weight on her injured leg, but it was unable to sustain her, so she landed hard on her left hip. She tried again. Whimpering, she stood favoring the injured leg. She loped about as her pups ran around her, emitting joyous yelps. They nipped playfully at their mother's neck and front legs as she tried to maintain her balance.

For some reason, Levi felt safe. He no longer tried to back away, nor did he pull his knife. He enjoyed the moment, hoping the mother wolf would gather her pups and vanish into the wilderness.

Instead, she lowered her head and slowly hobbled toward him. He remained completely still. She sniffed his hands and arms. The pups crawled in Levi's lap, and he softly petted them, as he'd done before. She raised her head and pushed her snout directly toward Levi's face. His eyes grew wide, but he remained still.

Then she licked him. Gently, over and over again.

Tears poured out of Levi's eyes, which only encouraged the mother wolf to lap up the salty moisture. This went on for a minute until Levi finally exhaled and the tears subsided.

With one final sniff of his perspiration and tears, she raised her head slightly as if to say goodbye, and wandered into the woods, with her pups running as fast as their little legs could to keep up.

Levi sat there for hours, never once getting up from that cross-legged position until darkness came. When the first chorus of wolf calls could be heard, he began to laugh. It was comforting, reassuring, and natural.

He tilted his head back and considered howling at the moon himself, and instead his mouth fell open as an incredible aurora grew in the sky, silently painting the horizon in hues of green, purple, and blue.

Levi never wanted to leave this spot as he took in the wonder of the sky and the serenity of the wilderness. He'd forgotten about plane crashes and wolf attacks. He'd put out of his mind his sadness over missing his family.

And he didn't even know that the town of Hearst, Ontario, population five thousand, was barely two miles down the other side of the ridge from where he sat.

In that moment, Levi Boone wouldn't have cared. He was home.

CHAPTER 55

Riverfront Farms
Southeast Indiana

It was late afternoon and Sarah sent Squire to fetch Carly and the grandkids for supper. That morning, the three adults had gotten together to discuss their game plan for when the power would be shut down. Squire had volunteered to focus on the news for so long as it was available to watch. Their DirecTV satellite feed had been experiencing difficulties as a result of the recent solar activity, not to mention the fact that many news networks were operating with skeleton crews as the nation hunkered down for the upcoming blackout.

Sarah and Carly developed a rigid meal plan that, if followed, would sustain their immediate family plus Chapman's unknown friend for almost six months before they'd have to dig into their canned vegetables and bulk dry goods.

Squire pulled some of the farmhands off their regular duties to gather firewood for the main house, as well as the tenant houses that dotted Riverfront Farms. January, the coldest month for Southeast Indiana, generally had daily high temperatures around forty-two degrees, with lows averaging in the mid-twenties. In recent years, there had been a warming trend, but Squire wanted to make sure there was plenty of seasoned firewood on hand to be used as a heating source and fuel for cooking.

He'd embraced the whole concept of preparing for a long-term power outage. He'd also learned a lesson from their interaction with Sheriff Clark and his deputies that night. The Clarks believed they were above the law. With the three siblings acting as sheriff, judge, and banker, they controlled most aspects of the county's government and finances. He'd been wrong to challenge the sheriff under the circumstances, and especially with Sarah involved. He'd learned from the experience, and it would serve him well later.

Besides, Squire surmised, he'd be getting the last laugh on the Clarks and their greedy banking ways. As far as Squire was concerned, once the power grid was taken down, all bets were off and all debts were cancelled. After all, how can a man be expected to pay his mortgage when there's no online bill payment methods or any way to deposit his check, right? With this little nugget of a last laugh tucked away in the back of his mind, Squire began to relish the prospect of living in a powerless world, like his namesake from the eighteenth century.

"Squire!" Sarah shouted from the kitchen. "Unless there's somethin' you need to watch, why don't you come in and fix your plate before it gets cold? I'd like us to sit together to eat since it might be a little different from here on out."

"Okay, on my way," replied Squire. He walked away from the television as a news report came on the screen from Chicago, where gang violence had overrun the city and the Brookfield Zoo incident made headlines. Squire stopped in his tracks and spun back toward the television. He glanced over his shoulder to make sure no one came out of the kitchen.

He barely turned up the volume and blocked the monitor from the others' view. They reported on the anarchists' activity at Brookfield and that several zoo personnel had been killed. Then a helicopter filmed Chicago from above. High-rise buildings were burning out of control, and an image of stampeding elephants was shown running along Lake Shore Drive. The chyron on the screen read *Chicago Descends into the Abyss*.

"Dammit. Kristi, where are you?"

Squire had tried a dozen times an hour to call all of his children. His futile attempts required him to keep the cell phone plugged into a power source at all times. Despite his vigilance, he'd had no luck, and now he'd confirmed Chicago's power grid was shut down.

"Squire!"

Sarah called for him again. This time, he changed the channel to a local Indianapolis station and then turned off the television.

The five of them joined hands while Squire said the blessing. They chatted about what it would be like without power. Sarah and Carly spoke at length about how their ordinary, daily tasks could be performed without electricity with a little change in lifestyle. The kids were embracing the change, although they grumbled considerably about the lack of video games. When Squire promised Jesse and Rachel that he'd take them fishing for walleye and bass along the banks of the Ohio River, they quickly forgot about video games.

Just as they finished dinner, Sarah stood and reached across the table to clear the empty plates when the lights suddenly grew bright, flickered, and then turned off. The grandkids shrieked and Carly immediately reacted to calm them down.

"Well, there it is," said Squire matter-of-factly. "Just as the sun went down, the lights went out. Back to the good old days, I guess."

Sarah was ready for this eventuality. She rummaged through her apron pockets and found a Bic lighter. She ignited it and a soft, orange glow filled the room. Carly slid two candlesticks in her direction and the room got brighter.

"That's not so bad, is it, kids?" asked Sarah as she mussed Jesse's hair.

"Yeah, who needs power, anyway, right, Grandpa?" asked Jesse.

He fist-bumped with Squire, who was doing his best to keep up a positive demeanor in light of what he'd just seen on the news.

"You're right, young man. We're Boones, and just like Squire and Daniel of the old days, we'll make it without power in these new days. Trust me, we've got it way better than they did. We don't have to hide from wild Indians all day and night."

Carly raised her hand. "Do y'all hear that?"

The noise grew louder. "Is that a tractor?" asked Sarah.

"No. A motorcycle. Sarah, grab your rifle. Carly, take the kids to the back bedroom and stay out of sight."

Everyone scrambled around and took their positions as Squire had instructed. He readied his shotgun and cracked the front door, ready to stick the barrel through it and fire if necessary.

The motorcycle arrived and the driver shut it off. Squire could make out two riders unloading themselves from the seat. They started toward the front door.

"Don't move!" he shouted.

"Dad? It's me. Chapman."

Sarah screamed from the kitchen and raced through the darkened house to the front door. "Chapman! Oh my. Thank you, Lord. Thank you!"

"Hey, Mom," said Chapman as she forced her way past Squire and crashed into her son with a hug of a lifetime.

Tears were flowing down her face. "Oh, son. My god, we've been so worried about you." Squire joined in the hug, unable to find the words to speak, but not trying to hide his emotions as he sobbed out of joy and relief.

Sarah looked past Chapman and saw Isabella standing shyly several paces behind him. "I'm so sorry, are you Chapman's, um, friend?"

"Girlfriend, Mom," Chapman replied for her. He broke the group hug and reached for Isabella's hand. She hesitated, but then took it, somewhat overwhelmed by meeting the love of her life's parents for the first time. "I'd like you to meet Isabella Dubois. We met in Paris."

Squire found his voice. "You're French?"

"*Oui, Monsieur Boone*," she replied quietly.

"Holy smokes! Did you hear that, Sarah?" he asked without caring to hear an answer. He was giddy. "Isabella, is it?"

She nodded.

"Um, can you say that again?"

"What, Dad?" asked Chapman.

"You know, the wee thing."

Isabella blushed, but played along. "*Oui, Monsieur Boone.*" Then she wrapped her arm through Chapman's and added, "*J'adore* Chapman." I love Chapman.

Sarah stepped in to protect Isabella. "Don't you pay this old coot any mind. Come on in, dear, and let's get you something to eat."

Sarah tried to lead her toward the door, but Isabella held back. "*Madame Boone*, I am so, um, grimy."

Sarah burst out laughing as she gave Isabella a hug. She whispered in her ear, "Please, call me Sarah, and don't you worry about any of that, honey. You're with family now. Let's get you inside and I'll draw you a hot bath. Well, maybe lukewarm. We just lost power, but you can have the rest of the hot water."

Suddenly, Carly and the kids emerged from inside. "Uncle Chapman!"

They raced across the porch and arrived at Chapman simultaneously, nearly knocking him off his feet. The three hugged for a long time, and they peppered him with a thousand questions.

"Hey, guys, why don't y'all let Chapman get in the door first, okay?" asked Carly as she waved to her brother-in-law. A tear rolled down her cheek, as she was happy to see Chapman, but truthfully she would've loved to see her husband at the front door instead.

"Carly!" shouted Squire, who could hardly contain his excitement. "Come meet Chapman's girlfriend. She's from Paris."

Carly joined the reunion, and the three women moseyed inside arm in arm. Isabella turned to smile at Chapman. It was dark and he couldn't see her face completely, but he sensed she was happy and relieved.

Sarah gave the guys their marching orders. "Jesse, gather up Isabella's things and put them in the guest bedroom at the top of the stairs. Rachel, I want you to go around and light up all the candles we set out earlier. Carly and I are going to draw Isabella a warm bath and let her relax."

"What about me and Chapman?" asked Squire.

"Stay out of trouble!" Sarah shouted back over her shoulder as the women disappeared into the house. Then she added, "Thank God you're home, Chapman."

Chapman gave his father another hug. "Dad, you have no idea what we're in for. Heck, what I've been through in the last week could make enough stories for a lifetime."

Squire wandered off and shoved his hands into his pockets. He stared up at the nearly full moon and began to sniffle as his emotions got the better of him. Chapman walked to his side and put his arm around his father's shoulders.

"Dad, I'm sorry to bring all of this up now. Let's celebrate and—" Chapman stopped midsentence. He turned and looked toward the house, and then he gathered the courage to ask, "Hey, where are Kristi and Levi?"

Squire, with tears streaming down his face, tried to find the words. "Son, we haven't heard from Levi since he left for Canada for huntin' days ago. All I know was that there was a freak blizzard around the time he was supposed to arrive at the camp. I've called and called, but I can't get through."

"What about Kristi?"

There's always a special bond between a father and his daughter. Squire's mind raced as he recalled the times he'd lovingly swept her hair behind her ears as a child, or when he'd picked her up and twirled her around, promising that he'd always be there for her. All of the times he was proud of her when she won ribbons at the county fair, or when she became a vet, or when she was on television being interviewed for all of her accomplishments at the zoo. He was simply overwhelmed to the point where he couldn't speak.

Chapman turned his father around to look him in the eye. "Dad, please, what's wrong? Where's Kristi?"

Squire wiped the tears off his face with his sleeve, and then he used his hands, rough from years of working on the farm, to massage his temples. "Son, I don't know. All I do know is that there was an attack at the zoo last night, and several employees were killed. I don't know their names. Chicago lost power earlier, and they said it's like a war zone."

Chapman shook his head and walked a few paces away as he stared into the darkness. "My god, Dad." He stopped, and with a puzzled look on his face, he pointed to the upstairs windows overlooking the porch. A realization came over him. "Does she—?"

Squire grimaced and the tears began to flow again. "No, son. She has no idea, and I don't know how in the world I'm gonna be able to tell her."

THANK YOU FOR READING
GEOSTORM: THE PULSE!

If you enjoyed it, I'd be grateful if you'd take a moment to write a short review (just a few words are needed) and post it on Amazon. Amazon uses complicated algorithms to determine what books are recommended to readers. Sales are, of course, a factor, but so are the quantities of reviews my books get. By taking a few seconds to leave a review, you help me out and also help new readers learn about my work.

And before you go …

SIGN UP for Bobby Akart's mailing list to receive special offers, bonus content, and you'll be the first to receive news about new releases in the Geostorm series:

Visit Bobby Akart's website for informative blog entries on preparedness, writing, and a behind-the-scenes look into his novels.

BobbyAkart.com

VISIT Amazon.com/BobbyAkart, a dedicated feature page created by Amazon for his work, to view more information on his thriller fiction novels and post-apocalyptic book series, as well as his nonfiction Prepping for Tomorrow series.

Made in United States
Orlando, FL
08 January 2022

13171426R00168